The Reincarnation of Peter Proud

The Reincarnation of Peter Proud

MAX EHRLICH

THE BOBBS-MERRILL COMPANY, INC.
INDIANAPOLIS · NEW YORK

For Margaret

PART ONE

The Body of B. Franklin
    Printer
Like the Cover of an Old Book,
  Its Contents Torn Out
  And
Stripped of its Lettering and Gilding,
  Lies Here
  Food for Worms.
But the Work shall not be Lost,
For it Will as He Believed
  Appear Once More
In a New and more Elegant Edition
  Revised and Corrected
    By the Author.

BENJAMIN FRANKLIN

Chapter 1

He walked out of the cottage and into the night.

He was stark naked.

The moon hung low over the mountain at the north end of the lake. Its phase was almost full. It seemed to bounce, lopsided, through the passing clouds. He grinned at it, swaying unsteadily. It double-imaged before his eyes. Now there were two moons instead of one. He concentrated hard and focused them together again.

The lake spread before him, dull gold. A chill breeze, honed with the snap of early autumn, rippled its surface. It sang a small, sad song as it rustled through the pine and oak and maple. It smelled of balsam and wood smoke and dying leaves. Too early, it promised winter. He shivered a little as he caught the first fine cut of the wind. But after that, he hardly felt it. In fact he found it exhilarating.

He laughed aloud exuberantly, thinking, Hey, hey, look at me, Big Chief Two Moons, with my war club flopping in the wind, and here I am in the forest primeval, by the shining waters, on the shores of Gitche Gumee.

He started down the short slope toward the dock. There was a gravel walk lined with whitewashed stones, but since he was in his bare feet, he avoided it. The grass was covered with balsam needles. Underneath, a cool carpet.

He padded onto the dock. He had never felt more marvelous in his life. He did a little war dance on the dock. He cupped his hands to his mouth and sent a wild war whoop echoing across the lake. Nobody out there to hear him. All the cottages were dark and shuttered. Everyone had gone home.

Nobody around but me. Chief Two Moons.

The last of the Mohicans.

He laughed aloud, again.

Crazy. He knew he was drunk. Yet his perception seemed sharper

3

than ever. He saw everything very clearly, as though it were all part of a familiar painting.

The shadow passing behind the curtain of the lighted window in the cottage, back there in the darkness of the trees. The outdoor fireplace, a grotesque shape in the moonlight, its iron grate rusted, blackened by the burned fat of a hundred barbecues. The picnic table, splotched with bird droppings and now almost covered with dead leaves. Every detail was so clear. A pair of swimming trunks hanging stiffly in the crotch of a tree. The Boston whaler, beached and lying on its back—through for the season. Its white hull was partly covered by a tarpaulin. The canoe on the other side of the dock. An old sneaker lying in two feet of water. The toe was caught in a waterlogged interlace of submerged branches. Like some dead fish it swayed gently, looking up at him, reproaching him. The glint of a beer can, a little farther out, shining up through the water like a baleful and sightless eye.

Across the lake itself, on the far shore, he saw the red neon sign rising above a grove of pines. It was still illuminated.

The sign spelled out the word: *Puritan.*

Well, he thought, *here goes nothing.*

He did not dive in. The water near the dock was too shallow. If he had to go, he didn't want it to happen that way. Not by breaking his neck. He sat on the edge of the dock and slid himself gently into the water. It was very cold. He caught his breath as the icy shock hit him in the groin. He could feel his genitals shrivel.

Then he began to swim with long, easy strokes. Straight out toward the center of the lake. Straight toward the neon sign on the far shore.

After the first shock, the cold no longer bothered him. His naked body seemed impervious, insulated. He felt strong and very powerful. He felt that he could go on and on like this forever.

He swam on and on. He had no idea how long it had been. But after a while his rhythm began to falter. Just a little, imperceptibly. But it was only his imagination, of course.

Gradually, the exhilaration he had felt at the beginning began to drain away. He knew he was becoming sober. Cold sober. It was the chill of the water and the exercise, of course. He should have had another drink back there, one for the road.

Not that he was worried. Not really. He was a hell of a good swimmer. He was sure he could make it. He had swum this lake many times before. And no sweat.

But never when the water had been so cold.

His arms seemed to become heavier and heavier. His shoulders began to ache. His body was losing its alcoholic wet suit. He could feel the numbing chill seep through to his bones. He was almost at the center of the lake now.

He turned on his back and floated for a while. He stared at the ugly scar just above his left hip. And at his genitals, shrunken by the cold. Tiny strands from the mat of black hair in his crotch broke free and waved to and fro gently with the swell of the water.

He felt tired, very tired. He tried not to panic.

Somewhere a fish jumped. From the direction of the mountain, far away, he heard the cry of a loon. From this point he had a panoramic view of the entire shoreline. The foliage was almost in full blaze. Autumn colors. Reds, russets, yellows. He could see a patch of smooth-faced stone on the mountain, a bald spot amid the thick growth of trees. Suddenly it disappeared as a cloud obliterated the moon. The shoreline was dark now. Except for the single distant light in the window of the cottage he had left.

He began to swim again. He estimated he was in the middle of the lake now. He could go forward, or he could turn and swim back. Six of one, half a dozen of the other. The distance was the same. He decided to keep going.

Stupid bastard.

He had forgotten. He was as naked as a crow. He pictured himself stepping out of the water on the far side. Asking people if he could use their telephone. They'd probably call the police.

God, he must have been loaded back there.

He turned and started to swim back. The moon, he knew, was gone for good. The cold was getting to him in a way he didn't like.

It seemed to him now that he'd been swimming forever. It seemed to him that the expanse of lake between him and the shore had grown wider instead of narrower. The light in the cottage window hadn't come closer. If anything, it had receded. It didn't make any sense. He should have closed the gap by now.

He was having trouble getting his arms out of the water. They ceased to be flesh and became stone. His legs kept sinking. He began to sob, fighting for each tortured breath.

Now he knew he could never make it.

He knew this was all there was, and there would never be any more, and this was the end of his young life, and what a lousy, stinking way to die. The distant light blurred; his breath was fire in his lungs, and he heard himself crying. He no longer felt the cold. His body was numb and impersonal, a machine, still moving through the water somehow, by instinct, by reflex, no longer by any force of will. Give up, he thought now. Give up, baby, you've had it; just stop and rest, and let yourself go, to sleep, to sleep . . .

Then he heard it. The sound of an outboard motor in the distance. It grew louder and louder and seemed to be headed toward him.

He started to tread water. He began to shout. "Over here, over here!" He yelled and screamed and prayed, afraid that whoever it was would miss him in the dark.

Then he saw her, steering the boat toward him. She cut the motor, and glided in close. *Ah, Christ,* he wept. *Good Marcia, sweet Marcia, beautiful Marcia. I love you, baby.*

A sliver of moon peeped out from behind the cloud. It suffused the lake in an eerie glow. She looked like a ghost dressed in a fur coat. Her face was ash white and set like wax. Expressionless. Coldly beautiful.

He found new strength. Now he felt warm, strong again. He waited, treading water, waiting for her to get to him.

"Look, Marcia," he said. "I didn't mean what I said back there."

Her face was rigid. "Get into the boat."

"I'm sorry. I mean it. I'm sorry."

"I know. You've been sorry so many times before."

"I was drunk. I didn't know what I was saying. I hate myself for what I did to you back there." He was really contrite. He thought he saw her face soften a little. Now he hit home. "I love you, Marcia. I always have."

"I know that, darling," she said. He knew he had finally gotten to her. "It's all right. We won't talk about it again. We'll never talk about it again."

She picked up an oar and maneuvered the boat, trying to present the stern to him so that he could pull himself up without tipping over the craft. He watched her, thinking how beautiful she looked here in the moonlight. And how strange. Her face was still expressionless. In this light it didn't look quite real. It was a delicately tinted golden mask. Blue, blue eyes, almost too blue to believe. The small straight nose in the perfect oval of the face. The black hair, dark and tumbled, a bird's wing of it curling down her cheek and along her white throat. There was a faint Oriental cast to her face. The artisan who had painted this mask had gone a little overboard with the mouth, as he had with the eyes. It was ripe red, crushed-strawberry red, the lips soft and full and moist. In this light it looked almost obscene, a sensuous gash in the papier-mâché.

He turned on his back and floated, waiting for her.

The boat drew alongside. He was about to turn over and reach for the stern when, surprisingly, she stood up. The mask became animated now. There was a sudden strange look on her face. It was evil, contorted. The red slash parted to reveal her bared teeth. She raised the oar high over her head, holding the handle with both hands. Her fur coat fell open as she did so. Underneath, she was stark naked. He saw the red bruise marks around her neck and shoulders. He saw the long, lithe white body; the high round breasts placed well apart, the nipples stiff with the cold; her small waist; the tight, flat belly; the long, milk-smooth thighs; the little tuft of fine black curling hair; and in this moment, in this frozen moment, he even noticed the small birthmark on her lower abdomen, just above the tuft of hair, the strange blue birthmark shaped like a tiny diamond.

She brought the oar down hard with all her strength. Straight down on his exposed crotch.

He screamed with pain. He turned on his stomach, still screaming. He looked up at her. She raised the oar over her head again. She sobbed as she swung it down. It caught him on the head, and the blow seemed to penetrate his skull. She hit him again, and again.

Dimly he heard himself crying, "*No, Marcia, no, no!*"

It seemed to come from very far away. His skull seemed to be exploding. He could barely see her now. Desperately he reached out to grab the boat. He managed to catch the side, just barely. She brought the oar up again and slammed its edge against his clutching fingers. He let go. Looked up at her face for one last moment. Saw, through the blur, her wild, staring eyes, the bared teeth, the hot blazing hatred.

Then her face was gone.

Suddenly it was dark and very cold. There was a roaring in his ears. He was turning around and around as he went down. Like an acrobat tumbling through the air in one of those slow-motion films. Around and around, arms flung wide, legs spread apart, down and down. He did not try to move. He could not move. It was a strange and slow and dreamy descent.

His head hit the bottom first. His face sank into the cold muck and weeds, almost up to the neck. His body arched over a moment later and lay inert in the ooze.

Then his lungs exploded.

Chapter 2

He opened his eyes. His body was drenched in sweat.

Always, whenever he had this particular dream, this nightmare he had come to call the Lake Dream, he awoke exhausted, as though he had never slept at all.

"My God, Pete!"

Nora was leaning on her elbows, staring down at him, her blue eyes wide, her face pale. She had thrown the bedclothes from her, and her breasts had fallen free from her nightgown.

"Oh." Then, mumbling, "What is it, Nora? What's wrong?"

"Wrong? You just scared hell out of me, that's all." She showed him her arm. "Look. Gooseflesh. I'm still shaking. There I was, asleep, when I heard this voice yelling out. Right next to me. I wake up and there you were. Talking in your sleep. Or rather, shouting. Only it wasn't *you*."

He knew it was bound to happen again, sooner or later. He turned his head and looked out of the window at the familiar scene: palm and lemon trees just beyond the terrace; across the pool and patio, garden apartments. Beyond them the line of high-rise office buildings on Wilshire Boulevard, gleaming white in the early sun. And beyond them the great spread of East Los Angeles, already beginning to blur in the smog.

"Pete, you're not listening to me."

"I heard you."

"I'm trying to tell you, it was awful. This crazy voice coming out of *your* mouth. It didn't belong to you at all."

"Oh?" He tried to be casual. "What did it sound like?"

"Not it. *He*."

"All right. He."

"Weird. Deeper than yours. Coarser. God, I'm still shaking."

It's like some horror story, he thought. *X speaks again.*

8

He saw that she was really frightened and tried to humor her out of it.

"Nora, have I ever told you I was a schizo?"

"What?"

She looked at him blankly and he grinned. "It's true. By day I am known as Doctor Peter Proud, brilliant young associate professor at the University of California, Los Angeles. Pursuing the history and culture of the North American Indian as my chosen field. Known for my gentleness, tolerance, and humanitarianism. Beloved by all my students and my fellow faculty. You might call that the Doctor Jekyll side of my personality. But at night . . ."

"Stop it, Pete," she said angrily.

"I'm sorry."

"Who's Marcia?"

"Marcia?"

"You were yelling her name in your sleep."

"I don't know any Marcia."

"You're sure?"

"Never knew anybody by that name."

"Never?"

"Never in my life. The lady is a stranger."

"Well, you must have heard it somewhere. You must have known a Marcia somewhere, but you've forgotten. Anyway, you were yelling something like, 'Don't, Marcia, don't!'" She shuddered. "Or to put it more exactly, *he* was doing the yelling." She swung her long legs over the edge of the bed. "I'm still shook up. Excuse me while I run for the nearest john."

She padded out of the room, and he heard the bathroom door slam behind her.

He turned to look at the clock. It was 6:15.

The Lake Dream. There were others just as insane, and he gave them other names. But this was the one that came most often. Of late, it had been coming to him about twice a week. And it never varied. It was always monotonously the same, down to the last detail.

Always, he died in the same way.

He was swimming in this lake, and this woman Marcia came along in the boat, and each time they said exactly the same things to each other. The picture never changed; each detail was frozen. Always, he turned on his back to float, and always she raised her paddle and smashed him in the balls and then on the head and then on the fingers,

9

and after that, he went down and down, turning around and around, in the same old way.

And Marcia. *The girl of my dreams,* he thought.

She was in many of the others, too. They were shorter dreams, fragments really, but they kept repeating themselves, like the Lake Dream. None of them had anything to do with any memories of his life or childhood. They were clearly of some other time and place. Six months ago they had begun to creep into his unconscious. They not only stayed; they became more frequent and more intense. And they seemed to drive away every other dream he might have had—the usual or normal kind, the kind you forgot the next day.

The strange part of it was he remembered each of them in every detail. He had recorded them in a notebook he kept, and as with the Lake Dream, nothing in them ever varied.

In the dreams he was always this same man, the man he thought of as X. And this strange and mysterious lady, Marcia, was usually with X. They seemed to live in a particular city or town. The town seemed very familiar to him in these dreams. He could see the main street with the arched railroad bridge spanning it. He could see a kind of municipal tower facing a central square. He could see the shops, the houses, the faces of the people on the streets. He knew he had never been in this particular town in all his life. He was sure of it. Yet he could see it all so clearly. Neighborhoods, even suburban streets.

Many of the dreams were winter scenes. Deep snow on the ground. Blizzards. But the fact was that he had rarely seen snow, except on the tops of the mountains surrounding the Los Angeles basin. Or when he had gone skiing at Aspen or Mammoth. He had been born in California and had lived there all of his life.

But even more weird was this "Puritan" thing. The word "Puritan" occurred not only in the Lake Dream, but also in the other fragments. He saw it on signs, on buildings, and in limbo. It seemed to suggest New England. But he had never been in New England in his life. He'd been east several times, in New York City and Washington, but never in New England.

Now, it seemed, he had a new problem. He was beginning to talk in his sleep. Not he, really. But the man he had come to think of as X.

A couple of weeks before, he had stayed overnight at the house his parents owned in Palm Springs. He had awakened to find them both in the room, dressed in night robes and staring at him. They had looked terrified. They had heard someone shouting in his room. Like Nora, they said it had sounded like someone else, a stranger. They had thought it was a burglar who had broken in and who had perhaps awakened him and had been shouting in the middle of a struggle. . . .

And even before that, in the hotel at Las Vegas. That night with Sybil Wilson. They had been shooting some film about the Apache at Twentieth Century-Fox, and they had decided they wanted everything really authentic—the tribal dress and customs and so forth. So they had hired him in the capacity of what they called a technical adviser. They had been shooting desert locations in southern Nevada, using Vegas as a base, and Sybil Wilson had been the script girl. One thing had led to another, and finally she had come to his room.

Early in the morning, he had awakened from the Lake Dream to find her staring at him white-faced and throwing on her clothes. She had run from the room terrified. When he called her later, she coldly informed him that she did not like men who talked in their sleep, especially in some weird kind of voice. In effect, she had implied that he was some kind of crazy.

He knew he was going through some strange psychic experience. He didn't know where these fantasies came from, or why they were happening to him. And naturally he was disturbed. He had gone to see a psychiatrist, a Dr. Ludwig Staub, very expensive and highly recommended. After a few sessions with Staub, he could sense that the psychiatrist was baffled.

"These dreams of yours," Staub had said, "do not seem to be dreams at all in the ordinary, classical sense. I would call them hallucinations. They are fixed and repetitive, and you have extraordinary recall. They do not seem to come from any subjective sensory stimuli we can trace. If it is of any comfort to you, they are not schizoid in character. The dreams of the schizophrenic are usually flat, vacant, unevocative. He might dream of a chair, or a teakettle, or a road leading somewhere—an object of some kind. These dreams have no action and no people. Your dreams—or, again, let us call them hallucinations—are much more elaborate than that. And you do not have any apparent symptoms of schizophrenia."

He had found *that* a relief. And Dr. Staub had gone on: "You do not seem to be greatly disturbed at this point—I mean emotionally. Naturally you are curious. These are psychic aberrations of some kind, screen memories, perhaps. It might be possible to dig them out, but it would take a long time. Other than this, Dr. Proud, I must tell you frankly that I cannot give you any real answers."

"But the dreams," Peter had insisted. "They all seem totally about someone else."

"You mean this man X you refer to?"

"Yes."

"X is yourself."

"But what about this town I keep seeing—?"

The psychiatrist had smiled. "Dr. Proud, are you implying that you are hallucinating about some past life? That this is some psychic manifestation of reincarnation?"

"I don't know. The thought has crossed my mind."

"I guessed as much," Staub had said. He had continued to smile. "But I doubt it. When you're dead, you're dead. Clearly it's possible to regress in one's sleep back to childhood, and even infancy. But only as far as one has actual living memory. I've had people, patients, who actually believe they are reincarnations of some pharaoh, or a Roman soldier in Caesar's legions, or some member of Abraham Lincoln's cabinet. They quote Edgar Cayce; they tell you all about Bridey Murphy. They want to believe that after they die they will be born again. It's usually harmless, and it gives them some kind of comfort. It's all part of the occult scene today. Many people can't face reality. Or they find it ugly. They find their lives empty and unrewarding, so they look for other answers—karma, voodoo, astrology, even witchcraft. All of these are nonsense, of course. But they all have the same mystique. If you believe it, it is so."

Nora came out of the bathroom and got back into bed with him.

"All right," she said. "Now you can tell me what it was all about."

"What *what* was all about?"

"That dream."

"It wouldn't make any sense to you."

"I don't expect it to. But tell me anyway."

Reluctantly he told her. She thought about it for a while. Then:

"That Indian stuff in the dream. The fact that you teach the subject. Probably some kind of simple association."

"It could be a little more than that."

"Yes?"

"I happen to be one-sixteenth Indian."

She stared at him. "Come on. You're putting me on."

"No, seriously. My great-great-great-grandfather, or whatever the sequence, was a Seneca. The Senecas are part of the Iroquois nation. The story goes that he was a chief, took this white woman a captive—my great-great-etcetera-grandmother—and made her his squaw. It's part of our family history, and I'm not quite sure I believe it. It could be a lot of romantic crap."

"You never told me."

"You never asked me." He grinned. "I hope you're not prejudiced."

"Me? Are you out of your mind?" She laughed. "How many other girls get a chance to sleep with an authentic early American like you? Part Indian, the rest old Wasp. It's in to be ethnic these days." Then her smile vanished. "The thing I can't get over is that *voice* I heard coming out of you."

"Mr. Hyde."

"Yes. You know what I kept thinking of?"

"What?"

"The 'little man.' Sir James Frazer wrote about it in *The Golden Bough*. It's a classic study of myth. I wrote a paper on it in my senior year. Frazer said primitive man believed that an animal lives and moves only because there's another animal living inside of him. Same with a man. A man lives and moves only because there is a 'little man' inside of him. Today we'd call it the soul. If the 'little man' is present, there is life. If he is absent, there is death. Sleep is the time the 'little man' is temporarily absent. In dreams, the 'little man' leaves the body and wanders around—visiting the places, seeing the persons, and performing the acts of which the dreamer dreams. In this case, *your* 'little man' had a date. With some lady named Marcia. A very murderous little date."

"Very interesting," he said.

"I knew you'd be fascinated." Then, abruptly: "Time to get dressed. Who showers first?"

"You," he said.

He lay there, thinking of Nora Haines.

She's a good kid—bright, lovely to look at. Great in bed, good to talk to. Apparently we like each other. The proof is here—between these no-wrinkle sheets.

Question: Premature, of course. But still. Could this last? Go the whole route?

Answer: Who knows? It's much too early to tell. But it could, it could. I'm a little tired of running around.

They had met a little over a month before. At the moment, she was a teaching assistant in a course on Introductory Sociology. She was a girl who knew what she wanted, she seemed to take to him right away, and she had no particular hangups when it came to sex. In fact, she took a healthy pleasure in it. A week after they'd met, they had gone to her small pad and she'd taken him to bed, and they had found they pleased each other very well.

It was just as simple and as good as that. Three weeks later she had moved in with him.

She came out of the bathroom glowing, one of his big Turkish towels wrapped around her, and began to get dressed.

"Nora," he said, "what's your hurry? Why get dressed now?"

"I've got things to do."

"It's still early."

He threw off the bedsheet and lay on his back, naked, sprawling. She studied his reflection in the mirror, then turned for a better look.

"I thought you were tired."

"Not *that* tired."

She smiled. "So I see. You know, darling, that girl in your dream— Marcia—she was a bitch. Trying to smash that beautiful thing. It's really a work of art. A monument. She just didn't appreciate you."

"True." He grinned. "But do *you?*"

"Oh, I do, I do."

"Enough to stay a little longer?"

"Sorry, but not today, Napoleon. I know it's early, but I have a class at nine, and I want to get to the office early and correct a few student papers and gradually put on my normally stern face, so that I can stand up before all those eager young faces looking properly professional and harried. I don't want to look like some contented Cheshire cat who's had a long night with some virile tom and has just lapped up a whole bowl of heavy cream besides. My students are very bright, very perceptive. They notice these things. Especially the girls. Now, for God's sake, darling, get up so we can have breakfast. I'm starved."

He rolled out of bed and went into the bathroom. He studied his face in the mirror. It looked haggard, as though he'd been up all night. Shadows under the eyes, the eyes themselves narrow slits.

Twenty-seven, and today I look forty.

Right now, he thought, he could simply fall into the bathtub and go back to sleep. He would have all he could do to get his ass through the day. He thought of Sam Goodman now. Goodman was a friend of his, and a tennis partner, but he was more than that. He was the professor in the psychology department who ran the experimental Sleep Laboratory at UCLA. He had told Sam about these wild hallucinations he'd been having, and the obvious fact that his sleep patterns had been disturbed by them. Sam had shown immediate interest. He had suggested that Pete come over to the Sleep Lab and go through the routine.

Maybe they could come up with some answers. There wasn't any room at the moment, but at the first opening Sam would let him know.

He picked up his electric shaver and began to buzz it over his stubbled chin. Then he stepped into the shower. In a way, he regretted telling Nora about the Lake Dream. He had not told her, of course, that it happened over and over, in the same way. Neither had he told her about all the others. The ones he had listed in his black notebook, each with a special name. He ticked them off, one by one, in his mind.

The City Dream. The Tower Dream. The Tennis Dream. The Window Dream. The House Dream. The Cliff Dream. The War Dream. The Tree Dream. The Baby Dream. The Prison Dream. The Cotton Mather Dream.

He stared into the mirror, and for an instant he saw a face that wasn't his. X.

Or was it? *My God,* he thought, *I must be going psycho.* He shivered.

Chapter 3

His first appointment was at ten with a couple of graduate students. They wanted to discuss possible subjects for their dissertations. After that, lunch, then one class and one seminar. And, finally, a late appointment at the dentist. A normal, unexciting day.

The Summit Plaza was a high-rise apartment house of fourteen stories, the top two of which were penthouses. Its name was emblazoned in gilt on a great red awning over the imposing entrance. It had a switchboard staffed around the clock, and there was always a uniformed attendant waiting to park your car in one of the lower garage levels. Peter had a large one-bedroom on the fifth floor, and he drove a Mercedes 450 SL. All of which, of course, was impossible on the salary of an assistant professor and made him an oddity among his colleagues. But Peter was fortunate in that he didn't have to teach to live.

He walked into the lobby. The girl at the switchboard, a pudgy, freckle-faced bleached blonde, smiled at him. When she was not taking calls and messages, she alternated between the soap operas on a portable television stand next to the switchboard and a book on astrology. Right now, Peter noted, it was astrology.

"Good morning, Dr. Proud."

"Morning, Edna."

They played their usual little game.

"What's my horoscope for today, love?"

"Let's see. You're a Libra. Right?"

"Right."

She knew his sign by heart, but she always asked anyway. She screwed up her face, concentrating.

"Let me think. This is December. The sun transits your solar fourth house. Uranus and Pluto continue their slow transit of your solar second house." She opened the book, found the page. " 'Uranus, ruler of your solar house of true love, makes it possible to seek and find romantic episodes that transform your life into colorful and lively events.'" She looked up at him and smiled. "I'll bet I know who."

He grinned. "I'll bet you do, too."

She went back to her book. Then her face clouded as she studied the page.

"Oh-oh. There's more."

"Yes?"

"'However,'" she read, "'there may be trouble for you ahead today. Unexpected events. Disturbances. Your planetary influences advise against your usual daily activities. It is better to stay home today, rest quietly, read, sleep, meditate.'"

"Oh, fine," he said.

She stared at him, concerned. "I really don't think you ought to go out today."

"Got to, Edna. I have appointments, classes, things like that."

"Can't you cancel them?"

"No. No way."

"Then be careful. Please. Watch out when you drive."

"Thanks, Edna. I'll do that. It's sweet of you to warn me."

He took the elevator down to the garage.

Crazy. She really believes that stuff.

His car was already on the ramp. He waved at the attendant and drove off.

Moving up Sunset, he tried to figure out what it all meant.

Why was he getting these weird hallucinations? Who was X? Was somebody trying to tell him something? Up to this point there had been nothing particularly eventful in his life. Oh, he had had the usual childhood and adolescent problems, but they were the normal kind. He had never thought of himself as a neurotic, and people told him he was mature for his age. Put it all together, he reflected, and the life and times of Peter Proud had been fairly cut and dried. No big waves. No particular crisis.

He'd been born in Los Angeles and had lived there all his life. His parents had named him Peter, and he was sensitive about the name. Peter Proud. It sounded like something out of Mother Goose, and people were always making little jokes about it. His friends called him Pete. He was a descendant of an old California family. His father, John R. Proud, had made a fortune in real estate, buying choice land, when it was low, on Wilshire and in Orange County and the Valley. Nobody had dreamed California would have the tremendous migration after the war, and John Proud had sold high. He was now more or less retired and lived with Peter's mother in a house in Palm Springs, complete with sauna and swimming pool and facing a golf course.

For some reason he, Pete Proud, had always been passionately interested in Indians and Indian history. Not because of his remote heritage in this regard. It was something more than that, something deeper. He felt some kind of definite identification with them, some kind of real kinship. As a boy he had read every book that concerned Indians he could get his hands on. He went to the movies and saw every film that was made about them. At ten he could name most of the principal tribes in the nation.

As an undergraduate at Berkeley, he had taken courses in the history and anthropology of the North American Indian; he had spent two years as a teaching assistant and had got his doctorate after a brilliant dissertation on the Plateau tribes. It had attracted considerable attention, and he became somewhat of a name in his field.

Finally he received an offer to teach at UCLA, and he accepted, passing up the opportunity to work in his father's real estate business. He had two brothers who were already engaged in running the Proud Corporation, and he simply had no interest in the building and selling of condominiums or shopping centers. His father was disappointed, but generous, and settled a healthy income on him. And so he was able to live comfortably and still teach.

He was now twenty-seven and had never been married. He was reasonably good looking and attractive to women. There had been a couple of affairs of some duration, and he had lived with a psychology major at Berkeley for a while. He had liked many of the women he'd known, and had thought he loved a few, but never enough for a permanent relationship.

He had developed a taste for classical music; he liked an occasional game of chess and bridge; and in golf his handicap was five. He had played football at Berkeley, but tennis was really his game.

Actually, he thought, it was all pretty damned dull. And, when you come right down to it, rather empty. Without any particular purpose or future. Everyone was going to the same place anyway.

Solomon Grundy, he thought. How did it go? Solomon Grundy. Born on Monday. Christened on Tuesday. Married on Wednesday. Took ill on Thursday. Worse on Friday. Died on Saturday. Buried on Sunday. And that was the end of Solomon Grundy.

And the end of us all. Amen.

Today, he thought, I am not only a dreamer. I am, God help us all, a philosopher, too.

He continued to drive west on Sunset. He entered the campus by turning left on Hilgard. Then he drove to Parking Structure Number Three.

A striped barrier blocked the entry. It could be raised electronically by reaching out of the car window and inserting a sensitized card into the slot. He reached into his inside pocket for his yellow car card, but it wasn't there. He swore softly as he remembered that he had left it in another jacket. A hell of a way to start the day, he thought. It always meant a certain amount of inconvenience, time lost. The parking situation on campus was impossible. The first thing you always made sure to remember was that damned card.

Well, no help for it. He backed out and drove around until he found one of the open parking lots. There was a windowed kiosk there, with a guard in attendance. The guard gave him a token. Then he returned to Parking Structure Three, waited for five minutes until a line of other cars went through, dropped his token into the slot, and passed under the gate.

Even in his irritation, he couldn't help smiling wryly *Score One for Edna.*

He parked the Mercedes on the second level. It looked somewhat conspicuous among the Volkswagens and Datsuns and Toyotas and Pintos. Most of the faculty drove small cars. A couple of professors, getting out of their cars, stared at his vehicle and then at him. They seemed to resent both it and him. Ordinarily he might have been a little embarrassed. Today, in his present mood, he didn't give a damn.

He walked out of the garage and over to Bunche Hall. It stood on huge stilts, its entire façade made of some metallic-like material reflecting the other buildings and trees. It was a beautiful day, clear and sunny and very warm for December. Groups of students, the boys in beards and levis, the girls also in levis, with hair long-flowing, sprawled on the grass, or near the gnarled old olive trees on the south side of Bunche Hall, or on the low brick wall bordering the parterre in front of the building.

He walked into the lobby, then paused briefly to study some of the cards tacked up on a student bulletin board. There were the usual announcements: Pad to rent. Roommate needed, female, nonsmoker. Charter trips to New York and Europe. Somebody wanted to sell a Showman Kustom Electric Bass Guitar. Somebody else wanted to unload a rebuilt Yamaha motorcycle, CASH, Must Sacrifice! The Kung Fu Club was meeting again.

But these were far outnumbered by announcements pertaining to the occult and their practitioners. Tarot Readings by Cassius. The Voice of Isis, Cosmic Mother. Tanya Sings Poems of Myth and Infinity—Small Gatherings Only. Guru Ram Das, Karmic Reader. Spiritualist Center—Expand the Brotherhood of the Source. Cosmic Joy Workshop. Christ on the Tree of Life. Breath, the Key to Spiritual Attainment. Bio-Energetic Anal Workshop. Hexing, Institute of Human Abilities. Astro-Psycho-Logical Encounters. And THE TRUTH SHALL SET YOU FREE Workshop.

Everybody was Edna, these days. The world was full of idiots, all of them looking for answers.

And so was he.

Peter's second graduate student of the day, Ed Donan, came in for his dissertation interview. He was tall and bearded and a little uneasy. He carried a thin folder containing a brief outline of his proposed dissertation subject.

"Sit down, Ed."

"Yes, sir."

Peter could never quite get used to the "sir" part. Or the Doctor Proud part. He was only a couple of years older than Donan.

"Now," he said, nodding toward the folder. "Tell me all about it."

"The area I'd like to examine is the parallel between Freud's *Interpretation of Dreams* and the divinity-of-dreams culture of the Iroquois."

My God, he thought, *what is this?* First Nora, now Ed Donan. This is going to be some day.

"Tell me about it."

"Well, there's no evidence that Sigmund Freud had ever heard of the Iroquois divinity-of-dreams idea. Yet their dream rites offered the same 'therapeutic strategy' of catharsis. They had ritual opportunities for wish fulfillment through dreams. They had dream guessing games, and they were a dream gratification society."

"What's your documentation, Ed?"

"The reports the Jesuit missionaries sent back to their superiors. From 1611 to 1768."

"You mean *The Relations?*"

Donan nodded. "And particularly the *Relation* sent back by Father Regueneau in 1649. He uses language that might have been used by Freud himself."

"Go on."

"The Iroquois knew, just as Freud did, that the dream might conceal, rather than reveal, the wish of the soul. I'm talking of both their personal and visitation dreams. Their idea of therapy was to actually reenact their dreams—make them come true. If the dream desire was not granted, it revolted against the body, causing various diseases. They called it *Ondinnonk*, a secret desire of the soul manifested by a dream. I could give you a few examples . . ."

"Yes?"

"For instance, the personal dreams of the Senecas, as reported by a Father Fremin."

Yes, sir. This is going to be some day.

"A Seneca warrior dreams during the night that he was taking a bath. Just as soon as he wakes up, he runs naked to the other cabins. There, he asks them to throw kettlefuls of water all over him, no matter how cold the weather may be. Some Senecas have been known to go as far as Quebec, a hundred and fifty leagues away, according to Father Fremin, just to get a dog which they have dreamed of buying there. The same idea runs through the other nations of the confederacy—Mohawks, Oneidas, Onondagas, and Cayugas. And even their relations, the Hurons of Canada." Here Ed Donan checked his folder. "In 1656 an Onondaga dreamed that he slept with two married women for five days. Other men willingly gave their squaws to him so that the dream could be fulfilled and thus satisfy *Ondinnonk*. In 1642, a Huron dreamed he was taken alive in battle by non-Hurons. This was a bad dream, and there was a tribal council held to discuss it. The dreamer, with his consent, was tortured and burned with flaming sticks. Another Huron dreamed he had been taken by enemies and that they had cut off his finger. He then cut off his own finger. Another dreamed his cabin had burned down. The chiefs, after due deliberation, ceremoniously burned down his cabin to satisfy the dream command. And so on." He peered at Peter through his thick glasses. "Well? What do you think?"

"Sounds fine. Only there's one hitch."

"Yes?"

"I vaguely recall that a man named Anthony Wallace has already done considerable work in this field."

"Yes," said Donan hastily, "I know Wallace. I'd use his stuff as source material and give him proper credit, of course. The thing is, I want to go deeper, research the *Relations* further, elaborate the parallel to Freud."

"You're still on somebody else's ground, Ed," said Peter. "Unless you can *really* make a number of new points. Tell you what. Why not investigate some of the other tribes? The Plateau Indians, maybe.

Or the tribes of the Southwest. Or the Great Basin. Maybe they've got some kind of *Ondinnonk* of their own. Then you'd have something quite different."

Donan blinked through his glasses, apparently unsure whether he was happy about Peter's suggestion or not. But he said, "Good idea. You might have something there, Dr. Proud. I'll look into it."

When Donan left, Peter leaned back in his chair and closed his eyes. He felt very tired and a little shaken. He picked up the phone and dialed Nora's number.

"*Ondinnonk*," he said.

"What?"

"Indian word. It means 'Somebody up there is playing games with me.'"

"Oh."

"How about lunch?"

"I can't," she said. "Got two conferences." Then: "Pete, I did some reading this morning. On the subject of somniloquy."

"What?"

"Somniloquy. Sleep talking. And I really feel a lot better about it now. They don't know too much about it yet, but they've drawn *some* conclusions. For example, some people talk in their sleep almost every night. Some even when they take a nap, or daydream. Women talk in their sleep more than men do."

"That figures."

"Don't be funny," she said, "I'm serious. Anyway, some sleep talk is slurred. I mean, it's gibberish nobody else can understand. Some people whisper; some yell out, the way you did. And some speak in different voices entirely. The way you did. So . . . it isn't that unusual, after all."

"Exit Mr. Hyde."

"Yes. Even though I still get gooseflesh thinking about it, I feel a lot better. And I hope you do."

"Oh, I do," he said. "I do."

Just as he hung up, the pain hit him. It came suddenly, as always. And, as always, in the same place—on the left side, just above the hip-bone.

It was excruciating. As though some assassin had plunged a red-hot dagger into his side.

He arranged with his teaching assistant to take the class, then called Dr. Tanner's office. He told the girl that it was an emergency—the same crazy thing as before—and he was coming right over.

He hung up. Then he leaned back in his seat and closed his eyes.
Score Two for Edna.

Chapter 4

A nurse led him into one of the cubbyhole examination rooms. Finally Dr. Charles Tanner came in. He was a few years older than Peter, a friend, and also a tennis buff.

"Hello, Pete. Back again, I see."

"And sitting here like a dummy for half an hour."

"Sorry. Heavy traffic today. I understand it's the hip again."

"Yes."

"Bad?"

"Murder."

"Let's have a look."

He probed the area in and around the hip with his fingers.

"Any reaction to this? More pain? Or less?"

"No. Just the same."

He put Peter through a series of bending and leg-raising exercises. "Any new strain?"

"No. Just the same."

He looked at the folder. "Let's see. You first came in with this about six months ago. Then two more visits. Two x-rays, the last one taken only a month ago. Negative. No evidence of any intrinsic pathology. No objective evidence of any disease. All good healthy bone and tissue."

"Then why the pain?"

Tanner looked puzzled. "I'm damned if I know. There's no history of previous injury in the area. It doesn't occur during, or as a result of, any active exercise." He looked at the folder again. "Just comes and goes at random. Duration, one to three hours. And then, suddenly, it isn't there anymore." He stared at Peter. "How did it happen this time?"

"I was just sitting at my desk. Talking to someone. Hung up the phone. And bang."

"And that's all?"

"That's all."

Tanner shook his head. "Look, this may sound like some kind of copout. It's barely possible the pain could be psychosomatic. But this particular area would be a very unusual place to get a reaction of this kind. People usually get psychosomatic pains in the back or legs. Or they suffer from headaches, stomachaches, chest pains, ulcers. Still, I suppose any area of the body is vulnerable." He laughed. "Now, if you had a wooden leg, I could come up with a *real* diagnosis."

"Yes?"

"Amputees sometimes feel pain. In a phantom limb. A leg they don't have anymore. Their experience has been so traumatic that they imagine they have the same kind of pain they'd have in a real leg. The same with women, in post-mastectomy breast phantoms. But hell, Pete. I don't know what to tell you. Except that you're absolutely sound, organically, in that particular area. Look, I'll give you a shot. Maybe it'll relieve the pain." Then, as he prepared the needle: "How about some tennis this coming week?"

"Okay. When?"

"Wednesday. Doctor's day off. When else?"

He walked out of the office and got into the elevator. Going down, he suddenly remembered the scar on X's hip.

He lay back in the dentist's chair.

His mouth gaped open like that of a dead fish. His jaw was numb from the Novocain. He kept his eyes closed as the drill burred into his tooth. The fingers of Martin Stein, D.D.S., smelled antiseptic, slightly peppermint, as they pried into his mouth. The burring stopped.

"All right, Pete. You can rinse now."

He had almost canceled this appointment. But the pain in his side had vanished ten minutes after he had left Charlie Tanner's office, and he had decided to keep it after all. This, apparently, was his day for the doctors.

Before the injection, Stein had given him a liquid tranquilizer, some pink stuff in a paper cup. Now he felt relaxed, a little sleepy.

"Open wide."

He felt his mouth being stuffed with hardware. The plastic saliva drain, some cotton batting, something metallic, a clamp. Finally Stein told him to bite down and hold it. It would take a while, he said, before it hardened.

The dentist walked out to attend to another patient in the next room. Peter suspected that there was still another in a third room. Probably had everything timed perfectly. Inject one, drill two, fill three. And be sure and send out all the bills on the first of the month, Miss Delaney.

24

The sound of Muzak filtered through the offices, vapid but soothing. His eyes grew heavy. The streamlined chair glided along the curve of his spine. He lay almost flat on his back, an astronaut waiting for blast-off. The red of the California sunset filtered through the half-closed shutters of the window and glinted off the stainless steel tubes and chrome gadgets.

He stared up at the rectangular band of light in the fixture just above him. The name of the manufacturer was inscribed on the panel: Castle. It seemed to him he had seen this name inscribed on the equipment of every dentist he had visited.

C-A-S-T-L-E.

White letters on a dark background. He stared at them hypnotically. He started to break them up into four-letter words, the way you played those word games they sometimes featured on the puzzle page of newspapers.

Cast, case, cleat, cale, Celt, stale, steal, scat, seat, last, least, lest, east . . .

It gets dark early in December. Through the shutters of Marty Stein's window he could sense that night threatened the sunset. He could barely make out, between the shutters, the roof of a high-rise building farther down on Wilshire Boulevard. There was a sign on the roof. He could not make it out clearly, but it seemed to advertise a bank. Bank of America? United California Bank? He was not sure.

Then the shutters opened, and he saw that he had been mistaken. The big sign on the rooftop actually read: PURITAN.

However, it was rather hard to see the sign because it was snowing. Coming down hard, whipping against the windowpane. A big blizzard. He could hear the howl of the wind. It rattled the walls. The window was frosted now. It felt cold as he pressed his nose against it, trying to peer through. But he could no longer see the sign. There was too much snow.

It was piled on the street in high banks all about him. He was on a busy street. Traffic and shops. He could make out a few signs: Puritan Dress Shop, Puritan Lunch. People passed him, jostled him. They wore boots and galoshes and were buried in big coats against the cold. He saw their faces clearly, but he didn't know anyone. Farther down the street an arched railroad overpass built of gray stone spanned the street. At the moment a train was rumbling over it. And beyond that, he saw a kind of municipal tower.

Now the snow had gone away. It was a beautiful, hot summer's day. He was standing on the observation balcony of the tower. He was quite small, and he could barely see over the guard rail. It was high, very high above the city. From here he could see the broad river, its shape a reverse "S" lying in the sun. Across the river were buildings and factories, their chimneys tracing delicate patterns of smoke across the parchment-blue sky. By looking down between the guard rails, he could see the cars crawling below, and what seemed to be some kind of public square. There were two monuments in the square, each with a figure on a pedestal. From this high up he could not identify them. There were diagonal walks and benches.

Then, quickly, one sequence after the other:

He was no longer in the open, but in some kind of small, restricted area, behind bars, as though he were in a cage or prison, and he was counting money.

And then, beyond the cage, HE appeared. The Puritan. The one he thought of as "Cotton Mather." A giant, frightening figure towering over him. It stared down at him with cold, dead eyes. Every detail of him was clear. He wore a tunic of dark red caught at the waist with a leather band. Over this, a sleeveless jacket of dull gray. A doublet and leather hose lined with oilskin. A large conical broadbrim hat. Broad white collar of linen. Half boots with shining silver buckles. The face hard and stern . . .

Then he was outside. Again, a hot summer's day. He was playing tennis with Marcia on a clay court. There was a small pond or lake to the left, a big, low rambling building of Cape Cod design to the right. Beyond that, the sweep of a verdant golf course, green rolling hills, immaculate fairways, white sand traps bleaching in the sun. Marcia was wearing a white skirt, white blouse, and sneakers, white bandanna around her black hair. The lady in white. They were not playing a regular game, but simply volleying. He was dominating the game. Shouting instructions at her. *Hit it back*, he kept saying; *hit it back*. She showed no pleasure at what he told her. Her face, shining with perspiration, was taut, serious in its concentration. *Hit it back*, he yelled at her. *Hit it back*. . . .

Suddenly he was driving a car. Moving fast over a narrow road lined with tall, stately trees. The car had its top down. A woman was in the seat beside him. It was not Marcia, but some other woman—a redhead. They were going very fast. The moon was a thin crescent. The woman's hair was flying back in the wind. She was as beautiful as Marcia, but in a different way. She seemed ecstatic with the sensation of speed and the wind. She had her head thrown back, and she was singing an aimless, nameless tune. But it was the car that really interested him. It was an absolute beauty—red leather upholstery, black broadloom carpeting, burled walnut-grain instrument panel, a color-indicator speedometer needle that changed color according to speed. The needle was green from zero to thirty miles an hour, yellow from thirty to fifty, and red over fifty. He even noted the exact mileage. There was a pushbutton radio mounted in the center of the dash. The car was long, low, racy. It had a long vertical grill with small horizontal bars, big disc hubcaps, large, curving fenders. The steering wheel was low and below the cowl. Overlarge tires, whitewall. Classic design. He looked at the redhead, smiled at her. He stepped on the gas and they started to fly.

Suddenly a bell was ringing, steady and insistent. He opened his eyes. Through the window he could see the red sky. The timer had just gone off, and now he was aware of Marty Stein standing over him. The peppermint fingers pried into his mouth again.

"All right, Pete. Let's have a look."

They were all very familiar. The Window Dream, the Street Dream, the Tower Dream, the Prison Dream, the Tennis Dream. And, of course, the Cotton Mather Dream, the one with the big Puritan staring down at him. Funny thing about that one. The giant figure never moved. Maybe it was a clue of some kind. It seemed to suggest a still life. A painting perhaps? It could be. He'd ask his father. Maybe there was a portrait of his Puritan ancestor somewhere around. Old Increase Proud. The old hypocrites may have been short on tolerance, but they were long on ego. He knew, because once he had gone to the Research Library and dug up a rare volume on the Puritan oligarchy in America. Everybody who was anybody in the Old Massachusetts Bay Colony seemed to have had his portrait painted.

He'd had all these dreams before, and he knew he would have them again. But this time something new had been added. A new entry in this crazy pantheon, a shiny new hallucination to add to the others he kept in his black book. Instantly, he gave it a name: The Automobile Dream.

He sat there in the dentist's chair, shaken. The small fragments in his unconscious, the mysterious but familiar pictures, always seemed to hover over him like roosting vultures. But this time they hadn't come in deep sleep. For the first time they had slipped in just over the edge. For the first time they had invaded a daydream. And for the first time there had been another woman, someone else besides Marcia.

Score Three for Edna.

Later that night, after Nora had gone off to a meeting, he decided to work on the book he was writing: *The Red Man: Origins and Culture. His Ethnic Role in America, Present and Future.* He hadn't done any work on the project in weeks.

He fumbled through his pile of research folders. Finally he made a few notes and wrote a couple of paragraphs on a new raid some Indians had made on the building housing the Bureau of Indian Affairs in Washington. Then he crossed out what he had written and tried again. He liked it even less than before. Finally he threw down his pen, slammed shut his reference books and stuffed his notes and clippings into their designated folders.

Bullshit! He was already way behind on the project. Worse, at the moment he didn't give a damn. Once the book had been an exciting project to him, but he had done little or no work on it for the past six months.

Ever since these dreams, or hallucinations or whatever, had begun, he had noticed a certain loss of energy. At times he was aware of not being with it at all. He simply was unable to concentrate; his mind would wander or go totally blank. Sometimes his eyes would blur, or his physical reflexes would seem to be dulled. He noticed it particularly in the tennis he was playing. And he was unable to summon up much ambition in other areas.

More than this, he was becoming irritable. He snapped at people, his students or his teaching assistant, for no reason at all. So far Nora hadn't noticed, or if she had, she gave no sign. He had tried hard not to give her any hint of what was bothering him. But he knew that sooner or later, if this went on, he would have to tell her.

He admitted that he was frightened. At times he had to steel himself not to panic. At first, he had been sure it was a temporary psychic phenomenon. He was sure the hallucinations would go away. But when they not only continued but became more frequent and began to take their toll of him in his day-to-day activities, he really became concerned. He had no idea what was going on in his unconscious. Nobody seemed to know. And if an analyst like Ludwig Staub didn't know, then it was something to worry about.

If you were sick and there was no diagnosis, then it had to scare hell out of you. A patient who knew he had cancer at least had a diagnosis. Even if it was terminal, he somehow learned to live with it. At least if you knew, you could do something, *try* to do something. But all he could do was take it, like a dumb animal. And each night he hated to go to sleep. Sometimes he fought to keep himself from drifting off. Not that the devils possessed him every night. Occasionally, they gave him an entire night off.

What was more, he felt persecuted, singled out. Why *me?* he thought. Billions of people in the world, and this is happening to me. Peter Proud, psycho. But a very special psycho: superpsycho. Unique. Even your psychiatrist can't tell you. The proof duly recorded in the notebook he kept by his bedside. My dreambook, he thought. *A Diary of My Dreams*, by Peter Proud. It would probably go big in one of the occult magazines. Or, he thought sardonically, how about a scholarly paper on the subject? In the gobbledygook of his profession, *A Dissertation on Unusual Dream Phenomena Totally Unrelated to the Conscious Milieu. A Series of Psychic Hallucinations Defying Known Methods of Analysis: A Challenge to Freud, Jung, Stekel, and the Traditionalists*, by Peter Proud, M.A., Ph.D.

All he wanted was to get rid of these sick hallucinations somehow. Go back to nice, normal, Freudian dreams, like killing his father or raping his mother.

He had, of course, told Nora that sooner or later he was to be one of the subject-patients at Sam Goodman's Sleep Laboratory. Of course he had not told her why. He had said merely that Goodman needed volunteers, and he had obliged. He would be sleeping away from home for a week, ten days at the most. Nora had smiled and told him to hurry home. Meanwhile, she said, she would be terribly unhappy in a cold and lonely bed. She had grown to love the pleasure of his company, but of course she would be brave and try to survive.

He hoped to God that Sam Goodman and his Sleep Lab would come up with something, anything.

That night he had the House Dream.

He was standing before a house. It stood in a row of other houses on the street, all somewhat similar in design. But this was *his* house. It had two stories. The upper story was faced with brown shingles, the lower with white stucco. There was a big tree-arched front porch, and he saw that it was the third house from the corner. Then came the Tree Dream. He was in some kind of park. There was a large square mausoleum behind him. On top of it were the marble figures of a man and a woman, the man's arm curled protectively around the woman's waist. But he himself was standing before a huge tree, about a hundred feet from the mausoleum. He was a boy, perhaps thirteen or fourteen, and there was a girl with him about the same age. Her face was fuzzy, but he knew that she wasn't Marcia. She had freckles, and long brown hair falling down to the middle of her back, and she was laughing. He had a knife, and he was cutting initials into the bark of the tree. The bark was tough, and he worked hard, cutting the initials deep. But he could not see what they were. . . .

Chapter 5

A few days later Sam Goodman phoned him and said they were ready to take him at the Sleep Lab.

He went there on a Monday night, as instructed, at eleven o'clock.

Sam Goodman was waiting for him. He was a partly bald, dark-faced young man with a big military mustache and intelligent black eyes. He wore a bright red shirt and brown corduroys. He grinned and said, "Before you get undressed, I'll give you a short tour of our little dreamland here, courtesy of the house. By the way, we call our sleepers here by number rather than name. Just to make it anonymous and impersonal. And to keep you as a case history statistic. You're sleeper number seven."

He led the way down a corridor, explaining that his staff consisted of five dream researchers. All of them were graduate students working for their doctorates, and they serviced about ten sleepers on any given night.

Sam showed him into a large room filled with a number of boxlike stainless steel machines, each studded with wires and cables. To each was attached an automatic pen that jiggled across a slowly revolving drum of graph paper. Each unit was also equipped with a tape recorder, the tape set in position and ready to go.

"This is our EEG room."

"EEG?"

"Electroencephalograph. What they do is record the dreams of our sleepers without waking them up. They're built with channels for displaying, all on one chart, the sleeper's respiration rates, body movements, brain waves, and rapid eye movements. Follow?"

"Yes."

"All right. We've got ten sleepers in various rooms here. Each has a number. When one of them starts to dream, everything starts to record here. We can tell by the brain waves and rapid eye movements and other data when the dream's just about finished. Then we ring a bell in this room and wake him up suddenly. We call it the arousal bell. At that moment, in most cases, he's able to remember everything in the dream he's just had. He has a microphone in his room, and he passes on the information here. Then we record it on tape."

The staff researchers were sitting at small tables before the individual units. They chatted, smoked, and drank coffee out of paper cups. They all seemed a little bored, but their eyes kept flicking to the revolving drums, where the pens continued to draw jagged strokes. Sam Goodman took him over and introduced him to a sandy-haired, blue-eyed young man.

"Charlie, here's our new subject. Doctor Peter Proud. Charlie Townsend. Charlie, he'll designate as number seven."

Townsend grinned. "Hello, Seven. Welcome to fantasy factory."

"Nice meeting you, Charlie."

"You won't think so. Not after I keep waking you up in the middle of the night." He turned to Goodman. "Shall I prepare him now, Sam?"

"No. It's his initiation. I'll take care of it myself."

As they moved toward the door, one of the researchers called out.

"Number Five coming through."

Goodman motioned to him and they came back toward one of the machines. Together they stared at the revolving drum. The pen was moving furiously now. It was changing quickly from a valley pattern of hills and crags to almost a flat pattern.

"What stage, Paul?" asked Goodman.

"Stage one; EEG indicates breakup of alpha rhythms. Crest and trough flattened. He's lost touch with outer world. REM activated."

"This one won't last very long. Watch it."

The pattern held steady for about a minute. Then Goodman said, "EEG's beginning to change in amplitude. Short bursts at a frequency of fifteen cycles a second. He's on his way into stage two."

"Yeah. And rapid eye movements decreasing. Dream's almost finished."

"All right. Give him the bell. Wake him up."

The researcher pressed a button. From a feedback, they heard a loud bell ring in the sleeper's room. Then it rang again. The researcher turned on the tape recorder. An irritable, sleepy voice came over the feedback:

"Okay, okay, I'm awake, goddamn it."

The researcher turned off the bell and spoke into a mike. "What's the dream, Number Five? Do you remember?"

"Yeah. But maybe we ought to skip this one."

"Why?"

The voice, that of a young man, hesitated. "It's pretty dirty."

"Tell us anyway. If we don't record it, we can't pass it on to your psychiatrist."

"All right. I dreamed I got out of bed. I went into the john and tried to turn on a water faucet. The thing wouldn't work. I kept turning and turning the thing, but no water would come out. Then I called a plumber. A little while later the door opened, and someone dressed in plumber's coveralls came in. At first I thought it was a man. Then I saw that it was a woman. I was pretty surprised. I told her it was crazy—I mean, this idea of a lady plumber. I didn't think she could do this job. She took off her coveralls, and I saw that she was naked under them. Then she went to the basin and turned on the faucet. She just gave it a little flip, and it turned. I waited for the water to pour out. But just before it did, you bastards woke me!" The sleeper sounded aggrieved. "Man, you woke me just before—well, you know. I'm lying here with the biggest hard-on you ever saw."

"Sorry about that, Five," said the researcher.

"You think Dr. Melnicker will like this one?"

"I'm sure he will. Now go back to sleep."

"I'll try. But it won't be easy."

"Try anyway. Goodnight, Five."

Paul turned off the tape. Then he grinned at Goodman. "Would you like a little mail-order analysis, Sam?"

"Go ahead."

"He sees sexual fulfillment as a plumbing conception. The faucet is a symbol of the dreamer's penis, the turning of the faucet is genital manipulation, and the flow of water is ejaculation."

Sam Goodman laughed. "You really spoiled his fun, Paul."

"If I had known, I'd have let him sleep."

They walked down another long corridor which Sam Goodman called "Dream Street."

It was lined with a series of rooms, each occupied by one of the sleepers. Peter could hear gentle snores coming from a couple of them.

"Everybody's already in the sack but you," said Goodman.

He opened a door marked seven and ushered Peter into a small cubbyhole. It was monastic in style—a cot with khaki army blankets, a chair, a washbowl, and a toilet compartment. On the wall next to the sleeper's head was a panel box with electrode leads, a speaker, an ordinary doorbell, and a microphone, all of which communicated to the EEG room. That was all.

Sam grinned at Peter's expression.

"Well? How do you like it?"

"It isn't exactly the Beverly Hilton."

"What did you expect? Wall-to-wall carpeting? Louis Quinze furniture? You're not going to live here, you're going to sleep here. Now pour yourself into your pajamas and we'll get this thing on the road."

When Peter was ready, Goodman pasted the EEG electrodes—tiny discs at the ends of long colored wires—on his forehead, scalp, and ear lobe, and just over the eyes.

"How does this stuff feel?"

"Pretty sticky."

"It's colloidal glue. Used to patch up professional boxers. We've found it works better than adhesive tape."

He patched other electrodes which measured heartbeat to Peter's chest, and still others to his arms. These, he explained, were part of the electromyograph setup used to measure micromuscle activity. He connected a photocell device attached to the bedsprings which would record those periods in which Peter would toss and turn in his sleep.

Then Goodman turned off the lights. "Goodnight, Pete. Happy alpha and delta rhythms."

The door closed and Peter was alone. He lay there feeling ridiculous, like some mechanical man wired for sight and sound. Wires sprouting out of his head like the Medusa.

After a long time, he fell asleep.

He checked in at the Sleep Lab every night for the next ten days.

First Charlie Townsend would wire him up. Then sleep. Then the raucous bell would sound, and he would wake up abruptly. Then Townsend's voice, over the speaker in his cubbyhole:

"Tell us about your dream, Seven."

And always the same answer. "I don't remember any dream."

Each night, they woke him three or four times. Each time he could remember nothing about any dreams. Not at that point. Not at the time they woke him up. He never remembered any dream when he was *supposed* to.

Yet, at the times he wasn't supposed to be dreaming, when his eyes showed no rapid movement and the valley patterns on the EEG showed all quiet, he experienced them all.

By actual count, he had the Lake Dream three times, the Automobile Dream, the House Dream, the Tree Dream, and the Tennis Dream twice, and the rest of them once. Throughout, as always, they were his constant companions.

Whenever he checked in at the lab, he sensed that he was an object of some curiosity on the part of the staff. They stared at him, then turned away. He became increasingly aware that there was something special about his case. He tried to pump Charlie Townsend about it. But Townsend said, simply, "Sorry. I'm not supposed to discuss anything with you. Not until the data's all in and I get clearance from Doctor Goodman."

It was "Doctor Goodman" now, instead of "Sam." Peter found this a little too professional, a little too serious. It made him uneasy. They were all acting too damned mysterious. There was altogether too much hush-hush where he was concerned.

He noted that ever since the first night, Goodman had not appeared at the lab. It was as though he were avoiding some personal confrontation with Peter. Peter called him three times at his office before he finally answered.

"Sam, what's my diagnosis?"

It seemed to him that Goodman's voice was guarded.

"Can't give any results till all the horses are in, Pete."

"When will that be?"

"In a couple of days."

"Look, isn't there *something* you could tell me?"

"Take it easy, Pete. I told you, I'll need a few more days."

He hung up. Something told him Sam Goodman was stalling. There was a certain tautness in his voice, a strain, an evasiveness. Or so it seemed. But then he thought, maybe I'm just imagining all this, looking for some kind of bogeyman.

He slept in the lab ten nights in a row. On the eleventh day he called Goodman again.

"Sam, it's been a few more days. Now, let's talk about it, okay?"

There was a long pause at the other end. Then he heard a sigh.

"Okay, Pete. My office. Four o'clock this afternoon."

Sam Goodman put a match to his pipe. It went out. He tried another.

"Pete, we've come to some conclusions. Or, rather, conjectures."

"Yes?"

"At first we thought you were simply an extreme case of dream amnesia. But after a few arousals, it's clear to us that you're suffering from what we call dream deprivation. A certain amount of this isn't unusual. But yours is total. You're a man who doesn't dream at all. You had practically no rapid eye movements. Your REMs barely recorded. Same with the EEG. Your brain waves were very small, gave only very weak signals."

"But I did dream, Sam. I had the same ones I told you about."

"Maybe. But they didn't register as dreams."

"Then what the hell *are* they?"

"I don't know. I've been in sleep research for years, and they're unique in my experience. Staub called them hallucinations, didn't he?"

"Yes."

"All right. Then that's what they must be. Or they could be memory plants, visions, revelations. Hell, I don't know. Pete, you're going through some kind of wild psychic experience. That's all *I* can tell you."

"No," said Peter. "You know more than you're telling me. Look, give it to me straight. I've got something to worry about here—is that it?"

Goodman avoided his eyes.

"I wish you hadn't asked me that."

"But I *am* asking you."

Sam Goodman's pipe went out. He picked up a book of matches to relight it. Then he threw the matches back onto the desk.

"Pete, first you've got to understand—I'm not very good at playing young Doctor Jones, the way they do on television. All I can give you are certain facts as I know them. A certain amount of normal dreaming is a requirement of any human being. Both physically and mentally. It seems to give immunity against psychosis."

"Go on."

"Nobody seems to really know why. Oh, there are theories. When people are dream-deprived, they're unable to discharge certain tensions, infantile or otherwise. The nightly dream cycle provides release for these pressures. If the cycle is suppressed, then the pressures may be dammed up and at some point could break through. When this happens, the mind is swamped by distorted images. The senses are confused. Ordinary perceptions become blunted. Put it another way. When we dream, it allows us to go quietly and safely insane each night of our lives, instead of each day."

"In other words, I'm on my way. Sooner or later, I've got to crack up. Go crazy. Psycho."

"I didn't say that."

"But that's what you mean."

"Look," said Goodman carefully. "I agree, you have a problem. And it's serious. But all this is premature. We just don't have any precedent . . ."

"Damn it, Sam," Pete said furiously, "will you level with me? If I don't start to dream normally pretty soon, I've got a brilliant future as a gibbering idiot. Is that it? Or *isn't* it?"

"Take it easy, Pete. We've still got some time. There has to be some way to pull you out of this. Somebody will come up with something."

He sat there, shaken. Sam continued talking, but Pete hardly heard what he was saying.

Chapter 6

All that night he was unable to sleep.

The next morning, bleary-eyed and haggard, he flew north to a town in Mono County called Bridgeport. He had been retained by the California Indian Legal Services and the Native American Rights Fund to testify on behalf of a small colony of Paiute Indians who were trying to keep twenty acres of ancestral land. The government wanted it for a federal reclamation project.

It was his job as an expert to testify that the members of the colony were legitimate descendants of the original Paiutes; further, that their ancestors had occupied this land long before the first white man had come to their valley in the high Sierra, and that the occupation of the land was entirely valid, by treaty. If the Paiutes lost this land, and therefore a settled status, they could not qualify for federal housing aid and other programs designed to improve their jobless, welfare-dependent lives.

When he was called upon to testify, he blew it.

It wasn't just that he was tired. Somehow, he couldn't coordinate his testimony. He had lapses of memory. He had to refer repeatedly to files from his briefcase. He shuffled documents interminably, trying to find what he needed. He could hear the restless movements of those in the hearing room, the shocked whispering. He stammered and stuttered through his opening statement. An attorney from the Department of the Interior began to cross-examine him and somehow trapped Peter into contradicting himself. Everything seemed involuted, unreal. Peter's testimony, although sympathetic, turned out to be damaging. He practically conceded that this particular band of Paiutes were squatters on someone else's land. Under a patent issued in 1914 by the old General Land Office and under the Desert Land Act, the land had been sold to a non-Indian who claimed it was unoccupied. Peter knew this was illegal. But because he did not have his wits with him this day, he was unable to prove it.

When the hearing was over, he walked out red-faced. A senator on the Senate Indian affairs subcommittee who was sympathetic to the Paiute cause glared at him. The people who had retained him were hostile, tight-lipped. The few Paiutes who were there simply stared at him. He knew he would remember those hopeless, hurt faces for a long, long time.

He walked out onto the street. He swayed dizzily. He knew he could not travel back to Los Angeles, not now. He was just too tired. He had to sleep.

He found a motel and checked in.

First, he had the Baby Dream. He was in a quiet room, a child's nursery, late at night. There was a white crib, pink blankets. And the sound of a baby's cry. He picked up the baby and held it. He could feel the fretful child's hot cheek against his and smell the odor of feces and urine, and then she appeared in the doorway, wearing a nightgown, staring at him, looking upset, and it was Marcia. . . .

Next, almost immediately, the Cliff Dream. It was night, and he was on a grassy knoll just at the edge of a cliff, and below, in the valley, you could see the winding river and the myriad lights of a city on both banks. He was with Marcia and both of them were naked, and then they sank to the grass and she spread her legs for him, and he was on top of her. . . .

And finally, the Automobile Dream again.

The same as before, to the last detail. It was an open car, and they were going very fast. They could see the branches of the trees flash by overhead. The sky was clear and spattered with stars. The moon was a thin crescent. Around her neck the woman with the red hair wore a red scarf. Her hair was flying in the wind, and there was a look of ecstasy on her face. He could hear her singing, but he could not identify the song. The motor hummed and purred. The ride was smooth, without vibration. He had the illusion that soon they would take off, as though they were on an airport runway. Soon they would leave the ground and fly over the trees and toward the stars. Then the girl's eyes were closed, her head thrown back. She was still singing, but the words were lost in the wind.

But again, as before, it was the car itself that enchanted him. Long and low and sleek. Large curving fenders. Black broadloom carpeting; red leather upholstery. Burled walnut-grain instrument panel. The color-indicator speedometer. He noted the mileage on the speedometer gauge: exactly 18,342 miles. Although from his position at the wheel he could not see the outside, he knew what it looked like.

His passenger continued to sing, oblivious to everything. Her eyes closed, an ecstatic smile on her full, red mouth.

He stepped on the gas. The speedometer needle changed color. From yellow to red. Sixty. Seventy. They were flying now. They were really flying. . . .

He awoke.

He had slept through the whole afternoon, and then the night. He dressed, had breakfast, and drove out to the airport.

On the plane he began to think about the Automobile Dream. It was beginning to obsess him. Of them all, it was the most detailed, the most specific. He could literally *see* that car. It was almost frightening how clearly he could see it. And the exact mileage. Eighteen thousand, three hundred and forty-two miles. How specific could you get?

It was an old car. A quality car, classic, built long ago. That much he knew. But he wasn't a classic car buff; old cars didn't interest him. He had seen an exhibit of them once in a museum; he did not remember where. He'd also seen custom car rallies: the men in those old-fashioned driving caps and wearing big gloves and goggles; the women in wide-brimmed hats with the veils coming down over their faces. He'd see them parade the cars along the freeway—Model T Fords, Pierce Arrows, and the like. They belonged to some kind of club, he knew. Met for lunch, attended auctions, watched the ads for classic cars.

But he had the impression that this one, the car he had imagined in his fantasy, was much newer than these museum pieces. His curiosity started to gnaw at him. He couldn't wait till the plane touched down at International Airport in Los Angeles.

He picked up his car and, instead of driving home, went straight to the campus. He parked his car and walked quickly past Bunche Hall, Haines Hall, and across Dickson Plaza. He felt impelled now, driven. His heart was beating hard, the excitement whipping his blood.

He entered the Powell Library, and went directly to the desk of the Reader's Adviser. There were two students ahead of him. He waited impatiently. One wanted to know where she could find a book on the art of embroidery. The other wanted to know where he could find material on energy transfer processes in chemical kinetics. The boy was politely informed that he was in the wrong place, that what he wanted was the Research Library.

Finally it was Peter's turn.

"Yes?"

"I'd like to find a book on old cars. Classic cars."

"Oh, yes." She thought a moment. "I believe we have several."

She led him to one of the stacks. "You'll find them on this shelf."

There were several books on the subject. He began to go through them one by one. He quickly sorted out those which portrayed the very early cars and others which emphasized the ancient Model T's, the Durants, and the Marmons. *His* car wasn't that old.

He began to go through the others carefully, page by page. *Picture History of Motoring, Cars of the Early Thirties, Treasury of U.S. Cars, Sports and Classic Cars.* He studied illustration after illustration. Cars of the past, with familiar names: Cadillac, Lincoln, Chrysler. Vaguely familiar names: Pierce Arrow, Duesenberg, LaSalle, Daimler, Cord, and Stutz. And exotic and almost forgotten names: De Grand Lux, Hispano Suiza, Isotta-Fraschini, Marmon, Peerless, and Wills Sainte Claire.

Then he saw it. On page 158 of *The Great American Automobile. His* car.

It was an exact replica—beautifully photographed, both exterior and interior. He'd have known it anywhere.

He read the copy under the photographs.

PACKARD CLIPPER. Custom Convertible. Last of the Classic Packards. Construction begun August 25, 1941. Ended February 9, 1942, by government decree, when all new car models were suspended for the duration of the war. In these five months of production, 33,776 units were produced.

These luxurious and expensive eight-cylinder cars were identified by a long vertical grill with small horizontal bars, and by their large wheels with large disc caps. The fenders were large and rakishly curved. The Clipper was popular with those who could afford it, because of its long, low, racy design.

The interior on this model has true red leather upholstery and a black broadloom carpet. It features a burled walnut-grain instrument panel, and a pushbutton radio mounted in the center of the dash. A special feature, and unique to the Clipper, was a color-indicator speedometer. It changed colors as the car increased speed. From zero to thirty it was green, thirty to fifty, yellow, and at speeds beyond fifty, red. . . .

He took the book to the Xerox machine, made a photocopy of page 158, and slipped it into his briefcase.

As he walked out of the library, he suddenly stopped dead still in the middle of Dickson Plaza.

He was dimly aware that he was the focus of some attention. Groups of passing students paused to stare at him curiously. One girl half-turned, as though to ask him if he was all right, then changed her mind, shrugged, and went on.

He stood there for a long time.

It had suddenly occurred to him that he was born in 1946. October 10, 1946, to be exact. About the same time that that car had been in style.

He began to walk toward Parking Structure Number Three. He no longer had any doubt about it. He had lived in some previous life as the man he thought of as X. He wondered what kind of man X was, what he thought about, what he did, what other people thought of him. It struck him suddenly, and with shock, that perhaps X was evil. Perhaps he had committed an unpardonable sin as far as this woman Marcia was concerned. Otherwise, why had she wielded that murder weapon so viciously, with such obvious hatred? Why had she cut him off in the prime of his life?

And before X? Reincarnation meant that you lived many previous lives. That you were born and died and were born again. The soul remained the same, but it inhabited one body after another. Who had he been before X? What kind of man had he been? Good or evil? He considered himself a civilized and decent person now. But for all he knew, back in some previous life he could have been a rapist or a murderer. The thought wasn't pleasant. But of course he would never really know.

Chapter 7

That night, he decided that he could not keep Nora in ignorance any longer. He told her everything, from the beginning right up to his discovery in the library.

"I must have had another life before this one. *Before* October 10, 1946. I *know* I was the man playing tennis, and swimming that lake, and driving that car. And this woman Marcia must have been something to me. Wife, lover, *something*."

"I see. So you've been reincarnated. You died and you were born again. But you don't know your name, rank, or serial number."

"No."

"Well," she sighed, "you're worse off than all those people in the institutions. At least *they* know they're Napoleon, or Joan of Arc, or General Grant."

"Damn it, I'm serious!"

"I know you are, Pete. But really—reincarnation?"

"A lot of people believe in reincarnation, Nora."

"Oh, I know. Thousands, maybe millions. They believe in astrology charts, and tarot cards, and witchcraft, and gurus who'll read your fortune for twenty-five dollars an hour. Most of them are kooks, or just plain simple-minded. I know the kids are going for the reincarnation thing in a big way. But they'll go for anything that gives them an out, a chance to escape reality. They're looking for miracles to make them feel better. Anyway, it's just a fad with them, the way so many of these things are."

Pete's eyes wandered down to Nora's left wrist, on which she was wearing two big copper bracelets. They were supposed to protect you from arthritis, rheumatism, tennis elbow, and sciatica. He had noticed any number of women wearing them, and a few men.

Nora saw his grin. Her face turned red.

"Oh, look," she said. "I just wear these for fun. It's just a—well, it's a gag. *You* know."

"Sure," he said. "I know."

"Oh, go to hell!" She laughed, then grew serious.

"But really, Pete, think about it, and you'll see how ridiculous it is. You die, but you don't *really* die. Your soul doesn't go to heaven or to hell, like the fire and brimstone preachers said it would, but floats around until it finds a home in another body. Maybe that new body was born ten years later, or a hundred years later. And so on and so on. Life is just one big karma trip. Now—can you really buy that? *Really?*"

"I don't know."

"When you're dead, you're dead. When they bury you in the ground, or cremate you, you've had it. You're just a bunch of chemicals turned into ash. And there isn't any more. Period."

He thought a moment. "Nora, there's something I want to try."

"Yes?"

"I'm going to set up a tape recorder next to my bed. If that voice you heard ever comes out of me again, maybe you could record it for me. I want to hear it."

"What's the point of that?"

"I just want to hear it. Or *him.*"

"Pete," she said. "Listen to me. Let it alone. Don't make waves."

"It's something I've got to try."

He felt Nora tugging at him furiously, shaking him out of sleep. He opened his eyes and saw that it was early in the morning. As before, she was pale and shaken.

"Listen," she said.

She turned on the tape recorder. At first he heard what seemed to be someone breathing, then chuckling under his breath. Then it came—a long, piercing, blood-curdling scream. A kind of howl, like a war cry.

He listened transfixed, chilled to his marrow.

"My God," he said softly. "Oh, my God."

"Now there'll be a pause," said Nora. "Nothing happens for a little while."

After a while he heard the Voice. For the first time.

"Look, Marcia. I didn't mean what I said back there."

He listened, stunned, feeling his flesh crawl. The Voice was that of a stranger, deeper than his, with a different timbre. There was a kind of coarseness to it, a slurred quality, and the suggestion of teeth chattering —from the cold of the lake, of course. It had a slight accent. New England?

"I'm sorry. I mean it. I'm sorry."

The tone was apologetic, contrite. Yet a subtle insincerity underlay the words.

"*I was drunk. I didn't know what I was saying. I hate myself for what I did to you back there.*" A moment of silence. Then: "*I love you, Marcia. I always have.*"

Cold. Disembodied. Coming out of the lake he remembered so well.

"There's another long pause here," said Nora.

He waited. Of course he knew what was coming next. He was ready for it, and yet *not* ready for it.

"*No, Marcia. No. NO!*"

The scream was pure agony. High-pitched, primal, eerie.

"Oh, my God," said Peter again.

After that, nothing but silence. He felt sick. Sick to his soul. Nora turned off the machine.

Chapter 8

He knew practically nothing about reincarnation. He was vaguely aware that in the East people believed in it as part of a religion. In the West it was considered nonsense. If you believed in it you were considered a crackpot. Many of the students were into it. They spoke glibly and knowingly of good and bad karma. What you did in some past life had a lot to do with who you were and what you did in this life. And the way you conducted yourself in this life definitely influenced your status and behavior in the next.

He had no instant guru to brief him on the subject, but all the student bulletin boards on the campus told him where to go.

The bookshop, called The Tree of Life, was located on Melrose Avenue. Peter expected to find some little psychedelic type of shop, a hole in the wall staffed by eccentrics in beards and robes. Instead, he found a big, well-lit and tastefully decorated bookshop swarming with customers. Apparently it was one of the occult centers of Southern California. There were three large rooms crammed with books, and a couple of lecture rooms where periodically mediums, astrologers, clairvoyants, tarot readers, healers, and witches scheduled lectures at modest fees. There was even a lecture scheduled by a self-styled Saucerian, for buffs who believed in flying saucers. Here you could get readings on your past lives at twenty-five dollars a session. Or get your aura read. Or learn to cure by the laying on of hands. Or learn about hypnotism, numerology, spiritualism, palmistry, ESP, psychokinetics, and of course yoga. Some of the mediums advertised special deals. A glass of champagne, discounts on certain books, and three readings, all for fifty dollars. At a long table in the rear, the patrons could sample three exotic blends of tea, all on the house.

The bookstore was decorated with wicker screens, Hindu paintings, cabalistic symbols, and signs of the zodiac. It sold such exotic items as handmade Tibetan incense, Black Mesa High Altitude Indian Incense, red ginseng, handmade bamboo flutes and Tibetan prayer flags, natal charts and Malas Sandalwood prayer beads, cedar lavender, and meditation pillows and pads.

What surprised Peter was the fact that the customers were not all longhair. There was a liberal sprinkling of ordinary-looking people: men in business suits, housewives and matrons, well-groomed young girls who looked like stenographers or private secretaries to establishment bosses.

He went up to one of the clerks at the main counter. She was young and fresh looking and wore Benjamin Franklin glasses. She could have been a clerk at Brentano's.

"What can I do for you?"

He felt embarrassed. "I'm interested in something on reincarnation."

She smiled at him. "So is everybody else. Reincarnation's very big these days. We just can't get enough literature on it."

She told him to go to the rear of the shop and then turn right, where he would find three shelves on reincarnation. As he did so, he passed one of the lecture rooms. The door was partly open, and he could see that a lecture was going on. The speaker was wearing black robes and a priest's collar. He wore a pointed goatee, his eyes were penciled so that they looked slanted, and he was totally bald. His audience listened in awe as he declaimed:

"I am a disciple of the Black Pope. The absolute head of the Church of Satan. We believe in the powers of the devil.

"You know why people have all these hangups today? Because they're denying themselves the pleasures of life they deserve. They're guilt-ridden, man, repressed. But in the Church of Satan, there is no guilt. The only sin is *not* to sin. To sin is to act natural. Virtue is bullshit. Love is a loser. The Black Pope issues encyclicals. He says man should enjoy himself now, instead of waiting for his reward in heaven. The Black Church is a religion based on self-indulgence. Go on out. Eat, drink, be merry. Screw all the rules. Men, screw any girl you want, your mother, anybody. Girls, screw any man you want, including your father. Open up. Give your soul to Satan. *Live!* And don't let anyone con you with this bullshit about Love. There has never been a great love movement in history that hasn't wound up killing countless numbers of people to prove how much they loved them. Every hypocrite who ever walked the earth has had pockets *bulging* with love."

The audience laughed. The speaker grinned at them. Then he saw that the door through which Peter was watching was open, and he ordered it shut.

Peter selected two books and came back to the front of the shop.

The same girl waited on him. As she checked out the books she said, "Would you be interested in a reading of your past lives?"

He stared at her. "I don't understand . . ."

"You seem into the subject. I just thought you might like to see a good clairvoyant. Sometimes, if you have hangups, they can really help you clear them up."

"I don't know any clairvoyants," he said.

"I do. It's part of my job here. I know who the charlatans are. Whenever I hear that a new medium has set up practice, I go and have a reading. You see, I happen to know all about the past lives I've lived. And, of course, I know what's happened in this one. I check these people out, and if they don't read me right, then I never recommend them to the people who come into the shop. You might say I'm a kind of occult policeman. A lot of disturbed people pay out their hard-earned money to have their lives charted for them. You know, to show them what decisions they should make. We have clients come in here who are pretty close to flipping their lids. If they don't get truthful readings, there's no telling what they might do. Now, if you want a good clairvoyant, I can recommend one to you."

"I don't know. I haven't thought about it."

"She's marvelous when it comes to reading past lives. Her name's Verna Bird. She's a real psychic, absolutely authentic. The number one clairvoyant in California, maybe in the whole country. Would you believe all the movie stars consult her? I mean the really big ones. And people fly in from all over the country to see her." The clerk reached into a drawer. "This is her card. You can keep it. She's very busy, so you can't just walk in. You have to make an appointment by telephone. You can mention my name, if you like. Say you talked to Janet at The Tree of Life."

Chapter 9

He listened to the tape again and again.

The voice of X taunted and tormented him. Sometimes he thought of X as an obscene aberration of himself. At other times, X was a separate entity, another person entirely who had somehow found a home in his, Peter Proud's body. When he went to bed he was aware that X was standing somewhere in the wings, ready to step onto the stage of his unconscious. Just before he dropped off to sleep, he began to plead with X: *Give me a break tonight. Stay out of my sleep. You and Marcia. Please . . .*

Then, horrified, he would suddenly realize what he was doing and stop. He would lie there trembling, in a cold sweat. Here he was, babbling to the creatures of his hallucinations as though they were alive and could hear him. This, he thought, was the beginning; he was well on his way to becoming some kind of zombie. Ever since his conversation with Sam Goodman, he hadn't been the same. Fear had sucked at the marrow of his bones. He felt he was beginning to slip down into some deep, dark abyss. He became increasingly irritable. Things seemed out of focus; he found it hard to concentrate. He suffered from lapses of memory. Insomnia began to plague him. He fought sleep in order to avoid further confrontation with X.

He tried hard not to panic. The frightening part of it was the fact that no one could help him. Staub, Goodman, Tanner—no one. His disease was terminal, with no apparent cure—unless he could somehow exorcise these strange companions of the night.

He took out the card the clerk at The Tree of Life bookshop had given him. And he thought, why not? It's sure to be a lot of crap, but what can I lose? He'd read all about the great clairvoyant Edgar Cayce and the miracles he'd come up with. Unfortunately, Cayce was long dead, so you had to make the best of what was around. Patronize your local psychic.

The house was located high on Laurel Canyon, near Mulholland Drive.

It was a three-story affair of pink stucco. The style was Hollywood Castilian: red tile roof, overhanging balconies with rusty wrought iron twisted-grill railings; a huge swimming pool, empty of water, its walls and bottom cracked and stained with time; a neglected garden overgrown with weeds. The place was a relic of the thirties. He wondered whether some of the old stars had once lived in this house. Harold Lloyd, or Laura LaPlante, or Carole Lombard. It had that marvelous museum look about it.

There was no bell. He discreetly tapped the knocker on the huge oak door, which was opened by a woman in her middle forties. Her face was plain, her dress frumpy, almost old-fashioned. She peered at him through steel-rimmed glasses.

"Miss Bird?"

"Oh, no," she said. "I'm Elva Carlsen, Miss Bird's secretary."

He introduced himself, and she led him down a dark corridor to a small, windowless waiting room dimly illuminated by a single small table lamp.

"Please sign the register."

She opened a thick registry book and offered him a pen. Peter signed his name.

"Now, then," said Miss Carlsen briskly. "What kind of life reading do you wish?"

"I don't know." Then, feeling a little ridiculous: "What kinds are there?"

"There's the ordinary life reading. That's thirty-five dollars. There's the reading of past lives, with a past lives chart. Fifty dollars. And then there's the Spiritual Healing reading. That includes not only your past lives, but a spiritual message from Miss Bird on your present problems. That's seventy-five dollars."

Live it up, he thought. *Go for broke.*

"I'll take the Spiritual Healing readings."

"I think that's wise, young man," said Elva Carlsen. "Very wise. We have so many problems these days. So many. You wouldn't believe the people who come in here looking for help. Now, if you'll wait a few moments, I'll see if Miss Bird is ready to receive you."

She bustled off, and Peter surveyed the room. The furniture was old-fashioned, Grand Rapids style—upholstered, with antimacassars. Peter was vaguely disappointed. He had expected something more exotic, like lithographs of Indian deities, statuettes of Buddhas, astrology charts, psychedelic sunbursts, incense—anything to illustrate that A Mystic Lives Here.

He knew that Miss Bird could afford a much more elaborate establishment than this. Her fees for her readings were obviously fat. Such fees would be normal, or perhaps above normal, for any respectable psychiatrist. He assumed that this simple and humble setup was calculated. Edgar Cayce had been a simple and humble man, living in very plain surroundings. And Verna Bird, he understood, was a disciple and admirer of Cayce's. If you are an apprentice to the master, you emulate the master. The difference was that Cayce had taken very small fees for his "readings," and sometimes nothing. Verna Bird, on the other hand, apparently knew a good thing when she had one.

His attention was caught by a series of photographs on the wall. They were pictures of some of Hollywood's motion picture stars—the really big ones, the ones whose names were currently seen on marquees all over the country. And each of them was gratefully inscribed with a testimonial. *"To Verna, who saved my life"*; *"To the marvelous Miss Bird, who showed me the light"*; *"To Verna, God bless you. How can I ever thank you, darling?"*

They were interesting, as testimonials go, and in their own way impressive. Yet Peter was somewhat skeptical. Actors and actresses dealt in superlatives. For them everything was larger than life. He would have felt somewhat more reassured if the testimonials had been from scientists or bankers or lawyers, or other more pragmatic types. He himself didn't expect any miracles from Miss Verna Bird. He was a drowning man clutching at any straw.

The secretary came back into the waiting room.

"Miss Bird is prepared," she said. "Please follow me."

They went down another dark corridor and entered Verna Bird's consultation room.

The room was large and bright. Two big windows faced out toward the overgrown garden and the empty swimming pool. The furniture itself, as in the waiting room, was standard and drab. There were shelves full of books, a desk, and a chaise longue. A tape recorder stood on the table. The only two unusual items were a pair of live Siamese cats, both standing on the desk, staring at him fixedly, and a small altar sitting on a movable tea table in the corner. At least he assumed it was an altar of some kind. It consisted of a small marble slab with a candle on each end, one red, the other white. In all other respects, the room was the kind you might find in any middle-class suburb anywhere.

"Verna, this is Mr. Proud. Peter Proud."

"Peter Proud." Verna Bird smiled at him. "What a strange and lovely name. I'm glad you've come to see me, dear."

Peter mumbled something about being glad to be there. The clairvoyant was a tall woman—perhaps six feet tall—and thin. She stood straight as a ruler. She was in her late fifties, Peter guessed, with bright blue eyes and dyed red hair piled up cloudburst style. She wore a long, flowing red housecoat and jeweled red sandals.

"Sit here, dear." She indicated a chair opposite the chaise longue. "Make yourself comfortable. You may take off your shoes and loosen your tie if you like. We're very informal here." She smiled at her secretary. "Aren't we, dear?"

"We certainly are, Verna."

He sat down, feeling a little ridiculous. He felt stiff, like a character in a Victorian English comedy. Any minute he expected them to wheel out tea and cakes à la *Arsenic and Old Lace*. You'll sleep well in the cellar, my dear, after you take a little of this elderberry wine. What an idiot he was to have come here.

One of the Siamese cats startled him by suddenly leaping to the top of a bookcase from the desk. It arched its back, staring down and spitting at him. It was a beautiful animal, black, with agate blue eyes and the classic feline profile you saw on those Egyptian cat symbols.

"Stop that, Yang. You're being rude." Verna Bird smiled at Peter. "You mustn't mind, dear. You aren't unique. He's simply hostile to *everybody*. Isn't that true, Elva?"

"Yes, dear. It's true."

"They're beautiful cats," Peter said inanely.

"Aren't they?" beamed Verna. "My pride and joy. This one's Yang. But you already know that. The other one's Yin."

"Elva," said the clairvoyant, "before we have our reading with Mr. Proud here, do I have another scheduled for this afternoon?"

"Yes. One more."

"Damn," said Verna Bird. "I had a date at the beauty parlor to get my hair done. It's such a mess. Now I'll have to cancel it. You'll have to schedule another appointment, dear."

"I will. I'll take care of it later."

Verna Bird turned to Peter. "I'm sorry, dear. Women's talk." Then: "Now, do you feel you're ready?"

"Yes."

"All right. I want you to simply sit in that chair. Feel perfectly relaxed. It's hard for me to sense his vibrations when the subject is tense. Try to feel in harmony with the world. At peace. You may ask any questions you wish when there's something you don't understand. But do not ask them unless it is important. Do you understand?"

"Yes."

"Very well, Elva. Let's begin."

She lay down on the chaise longue and kicked off her sandals. Meanwhile, her secretary set up the tape recorder. She took a cartridge of tape from its container and marked the container "Reading #1877. Peter Proud." Then she added the date and placed the container on top of a pile of other boxes. Each was labeled with the name of the subject, the number of the reading, and the date. Apparently they kept an extensive tape file on all readings. Then she went to the corner and brought the tea table carrying the portable little altar and set it carefully in front of him. From his seated position he was now looking through the space between the candles and directly at Verna Bird lying on the chaise.

"The red candle represents Evil," said the clairvoyant. "And the white candle, Love. Love and Evil. God and the Devil. And man eternally caught between these two passions."

There was a subtle change in Verna Bird's voice. It had become deeper, more resonant, vibrant. Her eyelids had already begun to droop. Her hands hung limply by her sides. He felt like several kinds of damn fool now, sitting here like some superstitious oaf, staring at her through the area between the two candles.

Now Elva Carlsen took charge. She put her finger to her lips, signaling Peter not to say anything at the moment. She went to the windows, drew the blinds, and pulled down the shades. It was now pitch black in the room. Then the secretary lit the candles.

The flames sputtered for a moment, then burned steadily. Peter stared at the clairvoyant. He was startled. Suddenly she seemed transformed into someone else entirely. She was sprawled on the chaise watching him. Her eyes had become two blue jewels set into two dark holes in the pallid face. They were almost hypnotic. He felt uncomfortable in their stare. They seemed to bore straight through him, through his flesh and somewhere beyond that. She lay absolutely still; not a muscle moved. It seemed to him that she had even stopped breathing. She looked like someone in rigor mortis. The red housecoat fell in symmetrical folds about her. It all looked as though both the body and the drape of the garment had been carefully arranged, for a certain theatrical effect, by a film director, or perhaps by a mortician.

The room was in absolute silence. He stirred uneasily. He told himself that it was all very theatrical, part of the trade. All these people had some kind of ritual, and Verna Bird was no different. Yet, he was disturbed. He wished she would stop staring at him with those unblinking blue eyes.

Finally the lids began to droop over the eyes, and she started to breathe deeply. He could see that she had gone into her trance. He waited.

For a minute there was nothing but total silence. He had to hand it to Verna Bird and her secretary. They knew how to prolong an effect. Candlelight, and shadows dancing in the room. The medium meditating. They were giving him a run for his seventy-five dollars. Another minute passed. He waited for something to happen. He glanced at Elva Carlsen. She was sitting to one side, straight and rigid in her chair, hands folded, watching the clairvoyant. He was about to say something to her, to ask her what happened next, but she shook her head before he could speak. Again, she put her finger to her lips in warning.

Then, suddenly, Elva spoke to the clairvoyant.

"We have a soul here."

"Yes," said Verna Bird. "I see the soul."

"And we have a body which houses the soul."

"I see the body."

"Do you see others before this?"

"I see others. The bodies are different, and they live at different times. They live and they die, according to God's will. And the old soul passes from one to the other."

"Tell us about the bodies you see."

"I now address the body before me, which now possesses the soul. I speak of your past lives. I see you first over three thousand years ago. You live in the land of Egypt, and you are a Hittite slave. It is the time of the nineteenth dynasty. Your name is Chalaf.

"You are a skilled worker in stone, and you labor in the hot sun on such temples as the Great Hypostyle Hall at Karnak and the funerary temple called Ramesseum at Thebes. You are given barely enough to eat, and often you feel the whip of the overseer.

"Then you, and hundreds of others, are put to work on a great statue of Rameses. It stands at Abu Simbel, overlooking the river of the Nile. It is a colossal figure, reaching high into the sky.

"It is a hot day, just after the Nile has flooded, and the valley is green. On the river itself men glide by in reed boats, stopping to set snares in the thickets of papyrus so as to trap water birds for the fattening pens. But you, Chalaf, are not concerned with these. Your task is to labor on the colossus from dawn to sunset. You know only the whip, and the backbreaking weight of stone, and the hot hammer of the sun. The giant figure of Rameses is almost finished on this day. He sits on his throne, majestic and serene, his eyes closed in benediction. There are other carved figures beneath him, clustered at his feet. These are others of the royal family, and it is here that you are occupied—at the moment, polishing stone.

"High above you, men are dragging stone blocks up the ramps by means of reed ropes. Suddenly, they lose control of one of the blocks. It topples off the ramp. It comes bouncing down directly at you. You try to leap out of the way, but it is too late. It does not crush you, but a corner of the stone block strikes you in the hip and knocks you down.

"You lie face up in the sun. There is excruciating pain in your left hip. You try to get up. You cannot move. The chief overseer, known by the name of Bak, comes over to you. He shouts at you to rise. You try, but you cannot. You are faint with the pain in your side. He strikes you with the whip, again and again, but it is no use.

"You, Chalaf, are no longer of any use to Pharaoh. Bak decrees that you will lie at the feet of Rameses until the sun kills you. Then you will be left in the fields to be devoured by the animals and birds of prey.

"But it happens that a lady of the court comes up the river by barge. She is carried ashore by royal litter, and she sees you lying in the sun. In her eyes there is pity. Or perhaps it is something else, because you are a handsome man, with black hair and a curving Hittite nose and a lean young body. She calls the chief overseer and orders that you be offered to the Nile.

"And so it is done. Bak orders men to tie stones to your hands and feet. They place you on a litter of reeds. You smile at the lady; your eyes thank her for her mercy. She smiles back. You are not afraid to die. You remember a previous life in the Old Kingdom, when you yourself were of royal birth, a chief official of the Royal Household. Death is a sleep, and you will live many lives to come. Perhaps in one of them you will again meet this royal princess. She will be some other woman, and you will be some other man, but your souls will know each other. . . .

"Now two strong men lift you and slide you from the litter into the water. And you go down, down, into the dark depths, until you reach the bottom. . . ."

Verna Bird paused. There was no sound except for her long, steady breathing and the slight whir of the tape recorder. Her eyes remained closed. Then Elva Carlsen said, "Are there other bodies you see? Other past lives?"

"I see others. But there are too many shadows to tell much. I see you again as a slave, but this time in a Roman galley. Blond, great of body, from the north, from Gaul. Your name is Vercinex. There is a great storm off Crete, and you perish at sea with all the others. I can see no more of this particular life. . . ."

Again she fell silent. And he thought, sweating, this is wild. Chalaf, Vercinex, it was all nonsense. But then, in both cases, he had ended up drowning. And then there was that bit about getting hurt in the hip. . . .

For a full two minutes Verna Bird was silent. Peter glanced at Elva Carlsen. Finally he said, "Is that the end?" She glared at him for dese-crating the silence. Again she put her finger to her lips. And suddenly Verna Bird said, "I see another body."

"Does the body have a name?"

"Makoto Asata."

"When does this body exist?"

"In the seventeenth century, in Japan. So turns your wheel of karma. You, Makoto Asata, are an outcast, despised by others. You are a *buraku-min*, a pariah. You and your people follow such despised occupa-tions as slaughtering animals to provide leather, burying the dead, beg-ging, and fortunetelling. Like all *buraku-min*, you are forced to stand aside while others pass. You kneel in the standing presence of others. You are a worker in leather, a maker of sandals. Adding to your misery, you have been born a cripple. Your left leg is shorter than your right, and you must walk with a cane. One day you finish a pair of sandals for an employer. When you discuss the price, you must remain on your knees. He throws you your wages, which you must then pick up, so he will avoid contamination.

"All this weighs heavily upon you. And you, Makoto Asata, on this day you find this life unbearable. You decide to seek death, knowing that you will later live another life. If the next life is even a little bet-ter, you will have made a good decision. So you make the pilgrimage to the top of Fujiyama. It is a long and difficult climb, in view of your in-firmity, and the pain in your left side is excruciating. But at last you reach your destination. And you throw yourself into the boiling caul-dron, into the crater."

The clairvoyant paused. For almost a full minute she said nothing. Then Elva Carlsen said, "Is there another past life you see?"

"I see one more," said Verna Bird. "Your soul has traveled far and waited a hundred years before it finds a new home. You are an Indian boy named Red Horse, and you are of the Pawnee tribe. When you become of age, you will be a warrior.

"But one day tragedy comes to you. Your tribe is at war with another. On this day, your warriors bring captives back. Some are tortured and burned. But as is the custom, some are given to the sport of the boys. The prisoners are tied to trees, and the young boys are allowed to kill them by shooting at them with bows and arrows. Thus, they may not only test their skills, but also taste the thrill of killing an enemy. The objective is not to kill the prisoner immediately, but to place your arrows so that he suffers and still stays alive.

"You enter this exciting game, and you are better than all the others. You walk up to the victim to extract your arrows so that you may use them again. As you do so, one of the other boys lets an arrow go too soon. Just as you step in front of the target, you are pierced in the left side, and you fall. Blood gushes from the wound.

"You hover between life and death for many days. Finally, you recover. But now your life has changed. The arrow has crippled you. You can walk only with difficulty. And run not at all.

"After that, you will grow to the age of the young warrior. But you cannot fulfill yourself. You cannot hunt with the others. When the war parties go out, you are left at home to stay with the women. It is more than you can bear. Death is better than a life like this.

"One night, you have a dream. You have dreamed of how you will die. And you know you must reenact this dream. Otherwise your soul in after life will be in torment forever. The following night while all are asleep, you rise. You go to the shore of the lake nearby and pick out a canoe. It is autumn and the water is cold, very cold. You know that because of your infirmity you cannot swim very far. You sit in the canoe and take in your last sight of the world. Then you pick up your hatchet and chop a hole in the bottom of the birch canoe. It sinks. You start to swim, but not far. You want the lake to embrace you. And finally, you go down, down, into the muck and the weeds. And it is the end of this life. . . ."

Peter shivered. My God, he thought. A classic case of *Ondinnonk*. He stared at Verna Bird. How would she know anything about this? Was it just a coincidence? Perhaps. He made a mental note to check the Pawnees, to see if they practiced dream reenactment.

Verna Bird was silent for a long time. Then Elva Carlsen asked, "Is there another life after that?"

"I see none."

Then Peter heard himself say, "There's another one. I *know* there is."

"I see no other. Except the body now present here."

"Before me," he croaked. "A life just before this one. Who was I then? What was my name?"

"There is nothing," said Verna Bird. "I see no one. Only darkness."

He sat back sweating. His collar felt tight around his throat, and he loosened it. His temples throbbed. He had an impulse to go to Verna Bird, there on the chaise, and shake her out of her trance, shout at her, demand that she perform a little more, tell him the rest. Then he heard Elva Carlsen say, "You have told him of his past lives. Now, this body has asked for a Spiritual Healing reading." A pause, and then: "Do you have one for him?"

"I do."

"How can he heal himself?"

"There are ghosts who torment him. He must go back and confront them, and then he will be free."

"And that is all?"

"No," said Verna Bird. "There is more. He has been chosen. Once this is done, he will become a prophet. For he has a message to the world. And it has been given to him by God."

Suddenly the reading was over. Verna Bird opened her eyes. Quickly her secretary blew out the candles, then went to the windows and opened the shutters. The room was flooded with the white-hot light of a Southern California afternoon. Outside, the two Siamese cats, Yin and Yang, were chasing each other around the edge of the empty swimming pool.

Verna Bird stretched her arms and yawned. Then she smiled and said to Elva, "Well, Elva? Was it a good reading?"

"Marvelous," said Elva. She removed the tape from the machine, wrote something on it, and put it into the classified container. "This one was very interesting, Verna."

Peter stared at her. "You don't know what you just told me?"

"I haven't the foggiest idea, dear. I never know what I tell people when I'm in a trance. Once in a while, I'll listen to one of the tapes if Elva says it's interesting. But I couldn't possibly listen to all the readings I've given over the years. After all, there are hundreds." She turned to her secretary. "How many exactly, Elva?"

"Eighteen hundred and seventy-seven."

Verna Bird smiled. "You see? Besides, the readings are important only to my clients, not to me. Whatever it was I said, dear, I hope it didn't upset you."

"No," he said.

"I'm glad. I always give an honest reading, no matter what. I couldn't help it, even if I tried. Only a fraud consistently gives everybody good news—the kind people want to hear. Sometimes people get hysterical, call me a liar or a fake. Film people, for example, get very emotional about their readings. I had a movie star in here the other day, a woman, who almost—well, never mind."

Suddenly her attention was distracted by something going on outside the window, by the two cats running around the edge of the pool.

"Elva, have you noticed? Yang looks a little thin."

"I know. He doesn't eat as well as Yin."

Verna Bird looked worried. "Maybe we ought to try him with that special cat food. The one with the liver concentrate and all those vitamins."

"All right, I'll see if I can pick it up at the supermarket." Then she moved to the door and opened it. "Our next client will be here at any moment, Verna. You'd better prepare yourself."

Verna Bird nodded. Then she smiled at Peter. "Goodbye, dear. And good luck."

The secretary led him down the corridor. He followed her in a kind of daze. He heard himself mumble "goodbye" and started to open the door. Then he heard her say gently:

"Mr. Proud, you forgot something."

"Yes?"

"The fee. That'll be seventy-five dollars."

Chapter 10

When he got back to the Summit Plaza, Edna handed him a phone message. It was from Sam Goodman, and marked *Important*. Sam wanted to meet him for lunch the next day. He suggested the Sunset Room of the Holiday Inn just off the San Diego Freeway. If Peter could not make it, he was to call Sam's office and leave a message to that effect. Otherwise, Sam would go directly to the motel.

When Peter walked into the Sunset Room the next day, Sam was already seated at a table. When they had ordered a drink, Sam came quickly to the point.

"Pete, I've been thinking of your situation. You've gone the orthodox route, and nobody's been able to help you. But I think there's another approach."

"Yes?"

"Ever hear of Dr. Hall Bentley?"

The name sounded familiar—it was a name in the news—but he couldn't place it. He shook his head.

"Bentley's one of the top parapsychologists in the country. Used to be at Berkeley but split off to conduct his own private practice and research. He has an office right here in Los Angeles, and he's just back from some research project in Europe. He's an expert in Psi phenomena."

"Psi?"

"Stands for psychic phenomena. Men like Bentley, and Rhine at Duke, and Ian Stevenson at the University of Virginia are working in studies of the human mind, but far beyond anything we already know. That is, anything we can prove by any known methods or define by known physical laws. Areas like clairvoyance, telepathy, hypnosis, ESP, psychokinesis, telekinesis. I suppose you can define these fields as occult. But parapsychologists like Bentley are solid scientists and highly respected by their peers."

"Interesting," said Peter. "But how can he help me?"

"He's an expert on hypnosis. The important thing is for you to kick these fantasies you get in your sleep. Maybe he can do it for you."

Peter stared at Sam. "You really think it's possible?"

"Could be. People have been hypnotized into getting rid of all kinds of problems that bug them. Maybe it would work in this case. Anyway, it's worth a try."

Peter thought about it a moment, then shrugged. "Why not? I've tried everything else."

"Exactly. I'll set everything up with Bentley. He's not a close friend of mine, but I know him. He's a very busy man, and I'm not sure he'll take on any new patients. But I've accepted some of his people at the Sleep Lab, and he owes me a favor. I won't tell him what it's all about —you go in cold and tell him in your own way. Okay?"

"Okay."

"Incidentally, he's written an article that might interest you. You'll find it in last month's issue of *Parapsychology*." There was a little grin on Sam Goodman's face. "It's called 'The Case for Reincarnation.' As you may gather, he's interested in the subject."

"By the sound of the title, he believes in it."

"Not exactly. He simply says he's got an open mind on it. Makes a number of assumptions, and then—well, you'd have to read it for yourself. Anyway, he's already alienated a lot of his peers—those in the orthodox establishment, I mean. This in spite of the brilliant work he's done in his field. Some of them have been calling him a charlatan. But the fact is, they really don't like an open mind. It frightens them."

He picked up the magazine at the library and read the article.

Bentley began with a prologue—his own gut reaction to the subject, purely personal, purely subjective.

"It seems incredible to me," he wrote, "and it depresses me to find the western world clinging to the dread of death instead of the hope of life. I am not a religious man, and nobody has proved to me that God exists. But it's hard to believe that we simply are born, we suffer, and we die. Ashes to ashes, and dust to dust. It is hard to believe that this is all there is.

"For if this is so, what are we doing here in the first place? For what purpose, what reason? Simply to eat, sleep, defecate, fornicate, love and hate others, suffer pain, enjoy a little pleasure, and then die? Must life be so hopeless, because no matter how we live it, death ends it?

"When we die, we die, we are told. Death is the end. But *is* it?

"I, frankly, do not believe it. I believe, as a rational man, that we must

61

be here for some higher reason, some greater and continuing purpose. Men have always been aware, on some deep and mystical level, that there is another part of him that has nothing to do with logical thinking, but is something far beyond that."

But all this, wrote Bentley, was simply an expression of faith on his part. What he proposed now was to examine the entire idea of reincarnation as a scientist, coldly and objectively.

First, he said, the idea of reincarnation was older and better established than any of the present religions. It was just as believable, and even more logical, than any of the existing religions. Even today over one billion people on the planet believed in it. Most of them were from the East, but it was rapidly spreading through the western world. Reincarnation was not simply a comforting superstition for idiots; many men of intelligence and reason passionately believed or had believed in it. Among them were: Gandhi, Benjamin Franklin, Henry Ford, Masefield, Yeats, Robert Browning, Schopenhauer, Nietzsche, Thomas Huxley, Voltaire, Goethe, Ibsen, Spinoza, Plato, and Oliver Wendell Holmes.

"The professors in our universities, the scientists, regard the occult groups, the fringe societies, as absurd, way out, immature, fuzzy, unsubstantiated and fraudulent. The fringe groups see the so-called Establishment as rigid, arrogant, intolerant, and condescending. Both are partly right and partly wrong, but each can learn from the other. Some day they may fuse their efforts in a constructive way. And the catalyst may be reincarnation.

"The materialist says that only that which you can see or measure, or otherwise identify by your senses, is real. But this kind of materialism belongs in another age. Any child with a primary scientific education today knows that no one has ever seen an atom. It exists only by inference. But we accept it as there. Yet most psychologists, most of my colleagues, will not accept the idea that a soul exists. Why? Because nobody has ever seen one. I am defining 'soul' here as a living thing that leaves the body at death and goes on to exist elsewhere.

"Those who ridicule the concept of rebirth try to bury any evidence of reincarnation. They call it wishful thinking. It is, to use the parlance, a 'copout,' a refusal to face the future on rational grounds. But let us now examine this concept on a rational basis. An orthodox scientific approach to any problem is to make a number of reasonable assumptions and then either eliminate or prove them by the application of logic. There are three assumptions we may make here. The first is that when you're dead, you're dead. The soul, if it exists at all, dies with you.

The second is the idea that you do have a soul, but when you die, your soul goes to heaven or to hell, depending on how you behaved in life. And the third is the idea of reincarnation. Your soul is immortal and is carried from one life to another.

"As to the first assumption," said Bentley, "nobody has ever proved that when you're dead, you're dead. I know that most people insist this is true, but there is no real evidence to prove it is so. As to the second assumption, nobody has ever proved that your soul has gone to hell, or to heaven, either. But consider the third assumption, the idea of reincarnation.

"Here, we must consider certain phenomena. Not real evidence, perhaps, and by no means scientific proof, but interesting nevertheless. These consist of observation, testimony from living persons, and memory phenomena no one can explain.

"First of all, there is the phenomenon of *déjà vu*. The skeptics argue that if we have indeed lived before, why can't we remember anything of our past lives? But the fact is, many of us seem to do just that. Almost everybody has had the experience of going somewhere he has never before visited in his lifetime, and yet having the eerie feeling that he has been there before, has seen the place before: a hillside, a road, a village, a view. There are thousands of case histories of people, rational and intelligent people, who have claimed *déjà vu*. Orthodox psychiatrists have put this down simply as a process of 'opening a false memory door.' But they never explain the basis of this 'false memory.'

"There is another phenomenon—one that is truly universal. You meet a stranger whom you like or dislike intensely on first sight, even before you've exchanged a word. And you can't explain why. In a boy-meets-girl situation, there is often instant attraction, or 'love at first sight.' Why does this happen? Some call it a mysterious chemical attraction. Others say the stranger reminds you of someone in childhood you loved or hated or feared. The children of Aquarius call it vibrations. But nobody has really explained it. Could it be possible that these likes or dislikes have come from buried memories of someone you knew in a past life? This, to me, is at least as good an explanation as any of the other theories, and probably better."

But the evidence for reincarnation, Bentley pointed out, was most startling in the behavior of children.

"Researchers all over the world have recorded hundreds of instances in which children seemed to remember some past life. They insisted they were someone else, an adult in some previous life, and they described places where they have never been. Usually, this is put down to childish prattling or fantasy. But the fact is that the people and places named by these children and some of the happenings they recounted have later been verified by trained and disinterested investigators."

He cited some famous cases of prenatal memory in children—that of Shanti Devi; and the Japanese boy, Katsugoro, first reported by Lafcadio Hearn, as well as others. Also, there was the work done by Stevenson of Virginia in the prenatal memory of children. It was interesting that in India, when children talked about being somebody else or having once lived in some other place far from their native village, they were listened to seriously. Here in the West, when children spoke about the same thing, it was considered childish fantasy and either dismissed or actively discouraged. Children became inhibited about reporting these prenatal memories and ultimately repressed them. In this way the memories became "lost" to them.

A third phenomenon, Bentley continued, was the existence of child prodigies—for instance, Mozart and Mendelssohn, who wrote great symphonies at a very young age, or the great chess master Samuel Reshevsky, who, at the age of five, played three European champions at the same time and beat them all. Some people tried to explain this in terms of genes, but, again, this has not been conclusively demonstrated. A more interesting explanation would be reincarnation. Could these prodigies have actually learned these skills as adults in previous lives, and simply brought them into their present ones? Again, it is as good a hypothesis as any other, if not better.

"Finally," wrote Bentley, "parapsychologists like myself have been able to regress people under hypnosis—not just to the point where they remember their very early childhood and even their babyhood, but way beyond that, where they remember, or claim to remember, some previous life. Some, while in regression, have even spoken foreign languages totally unknown to them.

"Unfortunately, we have never been able to document these past lives. The reason for this is that the subjects regress to periods too far in the past for their experiences to be reliably corroborated. It is this lack of documentation that makes it ultimately impossible to offer conclusive proof of reincarnation. . . ."

Chapter 11

Bentley's office was on Rodeo Drive. It was modest in size and tastefully furnished. The parapsychologist smiled a welcome and waved Peter to a chair.

"Sit down, Dr. Proud."

He was a big man, about fifty, with iron-gray hair and penetrating gray eyes under heavy brows. To Peter, he looked more like a football coach than a parapsychologist.

Bentley offered him a silver cigarette box.

"Smoke?"

"No, thanks."

"Sam Goodman was very mysterious about your problem. All he would say was that you were going through some curious psychic experiences and that they were upsetting you pretty badly. He called them fantastic, absolutely unique. And Sam isn't a man given to superlatives." He smiled. "Naturally, I'm hooked."

"Dr. Bentley, I'm in trouble. Frankly, I'm scared."

"Suppose you tell me about it."

"I don't even know where to begin."

"Go back a little first. Tell me something about yourself. Who you are, what you do, who your parents are. Then you can get into the nitty-gritty. Just tell it the way it happened, and don't leave out anything."

Peter glanced at the clock. "It's going to take some time."

"Relax. We've got plenty of time. And I'm a good listener." He motioned to the small tape recorder on his desk. "Mind if I use this?"

"No."

"Good. It seems to upset some people. But I like to have everything on tape." He picked up the small microphone and said: "February fifth, 1974. Initial interview with Peter Proud. Referred by Dr. Samuel Goodman." Then Bentley leaned back and signaled Peter to begin.

Through it all, the parapsychologist sat perfectly still. He never took his eyes from Peter's face. When Peter got into the dream sequences, Bentley seemed particularly fascinated. Peter told him about everything except his visit to Verna Bird, which he omitted out of embarrassment. He was afraid Bentley would think him an idiot.

When he had finished, Bentley continued to stare at him.

"Well, I'll say this. You're a pretty unique bird."

"Yes?"

"I've had a lot of people come in here and tell me they've lived past lives. They sailed with Ulysses, or spoke to Christ as a shepherd in Galilee, or fought the Gauls with Caesar. But you're the first one who's walked into my office and claimed prenatal memory that's really recent." He paused. "You're sure these dreams never vary? There's never anything new?"

"No."

"Interesting. I'll use a better word than that: fantastic. Sam Goodman was right."

"The question is—can you help me?"

"I don't know. I'm still trying to digest what you've just told me."

"I wish to God I knew what was happening to me. If you have any idea at all . . ."

"Let me put it this way. If men like Staub don't know, then I can't illuminate your problem any further. That is, not on *their* terms. But without going into a long song and dance about some of the work we've been doing in the Psi area, I can tell you this. We have some reason to believe, in our limited frame of reference, that recurring dreams like yours may be an indication of genuine prenatal memories. The fact that the same details accurately repeat themselves over and over makes the possibility even stronger. And the fact that they are almost contemporary makes them even more intriguing. However, from your point of view, they're tormenting and debilitating, both mentally and physically. And in time they could be dangerous. It's important to penetrate through to them, if we can. My suggestion, Dr. Proud, is that we try regressive hypnosis."

"Regressive hypnosis?"

"Yes. Once in a great while, we're able to regress people in a trance state back to prenatal memory. Presumably, they're able to remember details of their previous lives. I'd like to try that with you. If it works, we may open up a very important door."

"What do you mean?"

Bentley took a deep breath. "Dr. Proud, in every case I've ever known about in which a subject regressed to a prenatal state, the 'memories' have always gone far back in time—so far back that nobody can check to prove the reincarnation. Even the celebrated Bridey Murphy goes too far back for easy and conclusive proof. She is supposed to have been born in 1798 and died in 1864. The controversy about her is still going on, and it'll go on for a long time, because there's no way of checking it out."

Bentley paused. "Now you walk in here and drop a bombshell in my lap. Without any regressive hypnosis at all, you've experienced dream fragments just a few years away from being contemporary. All of them fall into the same time frame—according to The Automobile Dream, as you call it, sometime in the forties. Mind you, that's what the hallucination says. That doesn't mean it's true. I'm not buying it, at least not all the way. It's still possible you saw a picture of that car, or even the car itself, a long time ago and stored it in your memory bank. In none of your dreams can you recall any names whatever—names of people, the town, anything we could follow up and *prove*. But *if* we can regress you back into prenatal memory, and it's a very big IF, then maybe you'll come up with something—the name of this town you lived in, your own name, or, rather, the name of the man you call X. If you knew the name of the town, for instance, you could go back and visit it. Find some answers. Obviously, if it exists in reality, it'll still be there."

"My God," Peter said softly. "That's—frightening."

"I know," said Bentley dryly. "It's an interesting scenario. But don't count on it. We ran out of miracles long ago, and I don't think anything's changed. But if you agree, I'd definitely like to try it. And if it doesn't work, we'll try to attack your problem through suggestion hypnosis. That means that I'll try to get rid of the hallucinations through suggestion—exorcise them, so to speak. Well, what do you say?"

"I'll try anything at this point."

"All right. Suppose you be in my office tomorrow morning at ten o'clock."

When the door closed, Hall Bentley leaned back in his chair and shut his eyes.

It was enough to stagger the imagination.

Listening to Proud's story, he had at first been incredulous, then shaken. He had fought to stay cool, to present only his professional face to Proud. He didn't want his patient even to sense the excitement churning around inside of him; it might upset him. Any effective use of the trance itself was contingent on the trust and confidence the patient had in the hypnotherapist; without it, there would be resistance to the induction of the trance itself. Further, the hypnotized subject was very sensitive to everything in his immediate environment, especially the emotional configuration of the hypnotherapist.

He canceled all his appointments for the rest of the day. And that night he was unable to sleep.

Chapter 12

The next morning, Bentley saw that Peter was tight, tense.

"What do I do first?"

"The first thing you do is try to relax."

"That's pretty hard to do. I've got a lot riding on this."

"The idea of hypnosis bother you?"

"I guess it does, a little."

"No reason for it. If you respond, you'll find the whole experience quite pleasant. Now, suppose we get started. That is, if you feel ready to begin . . ."

"As ready as I'll ever be."

"All right, Pete," he said, slipping into the first name casually and easily. "Take off your shoes and loosen your tie. Lie down on the couch and put your head back on those pillows. Let your body go slack. Take a few deep breaths . . ."

Then he spoke into the tape recorder.

"This is Wednesday morning. The date is February sixth, 1974. The hypnotist is Dr. Hall Bentley. The place is my office on Rodeo Drive, Beverly Hills, California. The subject is Dr. Peter Proud, age twenty-seven, a professor at the University of California, Los Angeles. I have never hypnotized or regressed this patient before."

He clicked off the mike. Then he went to the windows and closed the blinds. He walked back to his desk and turned on a small desk lamp. Then he sat down in one of the easy chairs, lit a cigarette, and looked at Peter.

"Still uptight?"

"Yes."

"Take it easy. Just lie there. Try to empty your mind of everything. Take a few more deep breaths."

There was silence for a while. Bentley sat in the chair as motionless as a Buddha, watching him. The clock on the shelf, next to the sailing trophies, ticked away the seconds. Peter felt his muscles loosen a little. He began to get a little drowsy.

Bentley reached into his pocket and took out a flat gold disc about the size of a half-dollar suspended on a thin chain. He held the disc up to the lamp. It glittered in the light.

"Now, I want you to take ten deep breaths. In and out, in and out, slowly. Deep, deep. Now fasten your eyes on this disc. Keep looking at it. That's it. Relax, relax . . ."

His voice was soothing, tranquilizing. He started to revolve the disc on the chain. Peter continued to stare at the spinning disc. Bentley's face faded. So did the rest of the room. He saw nothing now but the glittering gold disc.

"Now close your eyes. Listen to my voice. I am going to count to ten. At ten you will be fully relaxed."

Bentley began the count in a slow beat. It seemed to Peter that his voice was receding. It sounded disembodied, far away.

"Your arms and legs are getting heavy. Your whole body feels as though it were sinking down in the couch. You are alone now. You hear my voice, but it comes from a distance. I am going to count to ten again. When I reach ten, you will float out into the distance. Far from where you are now. It will be a pleasant place, but far away. And you will always hear my voice."

Bentley's voice slowly counted to ten. It seemed to move even farther away. But he could still hear it distinctly. It didn't seem to belong to anyone in particular. It was just a voice.

"You can still hear everything I say. Now listen to me. You are free, and you are floating away. You are alone. You are happy, relaxed and alone. There are no more problems. Do you still hear my voice?"

"I hear you."

"You cannot open your eyes. Try to open your eyes." The voice was calm. It was serene, soothing. He did not even try to open his eyes. He did not want to.

"You are asleep now. You will not awaken till I wake you. And you will answer all my questions without waking. Do you understand?"

"I understand."

Suddenly the faraway voice seemed close in his ear.

"All right. You can open your eyes. You will awaken now."

He opened his eyes. Hall Bentley was sitting in the same chair, watching Peter as before. But now he was in his shirtsleeves. The ashtray next to him was full of butts.

"How do you feel?"

Peter stretched. He was deliciously relaxed. "I feel great. It's all over?"

"Yes."

"How did I do?"

"I'll say this much. You were a good subject. Very responsive. At least to hypnosis."

"What happened? What did I say?"

Bentley did not answer at once. His face was expressionless. He went to the window and opened the blinds. The sunlight came flooding in. Peter blinked in its glare. He lay back on the couch limply. He felt marvelously rested, as though he had slept around the clock.

"Well? What did I say?"

"You might as well hear it from the tape. Verbatim."

Bentley turned on the tape recorder. First, the parapsychologist's voice asked Peter a few routine questions. His name, address, age. His interests outside of teaching. Then, suddenly:

"Now, Pete, you are still asleep. Deep asleep. Now we are going to turn back. We are going to move back through time. And through space. When I speak to you next, you will be eight years old. You will be eight years old, and you will be able to answer my questions. Now you are eight years old. You go to school now, don't you?"

"Yes."

"What school?"

"Larkin School."

"Who sits in front of you?"

"A girl. A girl with black hair."

"What is her name?"

"Elizabeth."

"Elizabeth what?"

"Rhodes."

"And who sits next to you?"

"A boy."

"His name?"

"Ernie. Ernest Harris."

"Who is your teacher?"

"Miss Ellis."

"What does she look like?"

"Red hair. Fat. And she has a wart on her cheek."

"What is your favorite subject?"

"Indians."

"You like to study Indians?"

71

"Yes."

Peter listened to the tape, startled—not only because he was able to remember these long-forgotten details, but because his voice had changed. It was that of an eight-year-old boy—high, a little squeaky. He shivered a little.

The tape went on.

"Now, Pete, when did you first learn to play tennis?"

"When I was seven."

"We are going back, Pete. When I talk to you next, you will be a year younger. You will be seven. You understand?"

"Yes."

"Now you are seven."

"Yes."

"How are you learning to play tennis?"

"I take lessons."

"Who is giving you lessons?"

"A tennis instructor."

"What is his name?"

"Corrigan. Mr. Corrigan."

"Do you play well?"

"Very well."

"*How* well?"

"The tennis instructor was surprised. He said he couldn't believe it."

"Did he say anything else?"

"He said it was—uh—there was a word he used."

"What was the word?"

"Incredible."

"You mean, he was surprised at how well you learned?"

"Yes."

"Whom did he say this word to?"

"My father."

"Can you tell me what else he told your father?"

"He told my father that my form was terrific. He asked my father whether I had ever played before."

"And what did your father say?"

"He said no, it was my first time."

"And then what did Mr. Corrigan say?"

"Well, he shook his head. He used this word—incredible. He said I must have been born with a tennis racket in my hand."

"He said that? Those were his exact words?"

"Yes."

Pete glanced at Bentley. He had no memory of this conversation. He remembered Corrigan only vaguely. The tape went on:

"Now you are six. Do you understand? You are six years old now."

"Yes."

"Do you remember your friends?"

"Yes."

"What are their names?"

"Joe Morris. He has freckles and blue eyes. Steve Marks. He's dark and kind of fat. Ollie Peters. He's the biggest, and can run the fastest. Jimmy Drummond. He's Scotch."

"What kind of games do you play?"

"All kinds."

"Is there one you like best?"

"Yes."

"Which one is that?"

"Cowboys and Indians."

"Where do you play that?"

"Around where I live. Pacific Palisades. Thirty-two Vista Street."

"Which do you play—cowboy or Indian?"

"I always play the Indian."

"Why?"

"I like it. I like being an Indian. All my friends want to be cowboys."

"Are you any particular kind of Indian?"

"Yes."

"What kind?"

"A Seneca."

"You know about Senecas?"

"I know a lot of tribes. But when I'm an Indian, I'm always a Seneca."

Peter sat frozen, listening. God, it was weird. He had forgotten about these kids years ago. About the games they played, and their names. He wouldn't have remembered them in a million years. But there they were, coming out of his mouth now. In a six-year-old voice.

The tape went on:

"Now, rest and relax for a little while. I will not ask you any questions for a while. But I want you to go back by yourself now. You are going back into time and space. Now you are five years old. You are five years old. Think about the time you are five years old. Think about some scene then. Think about something that happened to you then." A pause. And then: "Now you are four. You are four years old. Think about something that happened to you then. You don't have to tell me about it; just think about it. Now, go back a little more. Turn back, turn back. See yourself when you were three years old. You are three years old now. What do you see when you were three years old?"

The voice was babyish.

"I have a puppy dog."

"A real puppy dog?"

"No. It's a toy."

"What does it look like?"

"It's black. And it has a bushy tail. And little red eyes. And a white collar."

"What is its name?"

"Blackie."

"Where are you now?"

"In a car with my father and mother. I'm holding Blackie. We're riding in the car."

"And then what?"

"I lean out the window. And Blackie falls out of the car and on the road. And then another car runs over it."

"What do you do?"

"I cry."

"Now you are two years old. Two years old. See yourself as two years old. Now, go back further. You are one year old. One year old. Think of something that happened when you were one year old. Think about it a little while. All right. Now, keep going back and back and back in your mind. Go back to when you were born."

No answer. And Bentley's voice again:

"Think. Go back to the day you were born. What do you feel?"

"I am very tiny. I am curled up. In a dark place. I cannot see . . ."

Suddenly Bentley stopped the tape. He showed Peter a photograph.

"Took this picture of you with a Polaroid. Thought you might find it interesting."

Bentley had apparently opened the blinds in order to get enough light to take the picture. It was very clear. Peter was curled up on the couch in the posture of a fetus.

Then the parapsychologist turned on the tape recorder again. And Bentley's voice:

"Do you hear anything?"

"I hear a noise inside of me. Something beating. My heart. And I hear another noise. The same beating sound. Outside of me."

"Your mother's heart?"

"Yes."

74

"And then what?"

The squeaky little voice suddenly became filled with terror.

"Something is gripping my head. Cold. Hard. Squeezing. It starts to pull me out of the dark, warm place. Everything hurts me. I like the dark, warm place. I don't want to leave it. I keep moving forward. It's hard to breathe. Then I come out head first. Something lifts me up, holds me by the legs. I hurt all over. I start to cry. There's something around my neck. I begin to choke. I can't breathe. Then they take it away . . ."

Peter listened, amazed. Suddenly he remembered a conversation his mother had had long ago with friends. He had been only a child then. They had been talking about someone's pregnancy, and his mother had remarked that Peter had been a forceps baby and had been almost strangled by the cord which had become caught around his neck.

Then Bentley's voice came in. It was still calm. There was no feeling or urgency in it.

"Now you're going to go further back. You're going back, back, back. *Before* you were in that dark, warm place. Yes, you can do it. You can go back, back, further back. Look into your memory. It is before this life you are about to begin. Look back into some other lifetime, some other time, some other place. You will remember certain things, things that happened. You will be able to tell me about them. Think now. Long ago. What do you see?"

There was a long silence. Suddenly, a voice:

"A lake. I see a lake."

Peter almost jumped from his chair. Now he heard the voice of X. The transition was startling.

"You're at this lake?"

"Yes."

"What is your name?"

"I don't know."

"Try to think. What is your name?"

A pause. Then: "I don't know."

Bentley's voice was insistent. "Try. Try to think. Try to think."

"I don't know. I don't." X sounded querulous. "I don't know my name."

"All right. You are at the lake."

"Yes."

"What is the name of the lake?"

"I don't know."

"Try to think."

"I don't know."

"All right. Are you there alone? Or with someone?"

"With someone."

"Who?"

"Marcia."

"Marcia who?"

"I don't know."

"What is her last name?"

"I don't know."

"All right. Tell me what you *do* know."

"It's night. I come out of the cabin. I'm naked. The wind is cold. I shiver a little. But then, I hardly feel it . . ."

"Go on . . ."

"The moon is out. It's almost full. I feel good. Very good. I walk down to the dock. I do a little war dance. . . ."

From this point on, the voice of X related the entire incident, down to the last detail—just as he, Peter Proud, had dreamed it again and again. Right up to the hideous end. There was a pause of several minutes.

He felt entirely different, separate from X. They were two different people. After the moment of birth a stranger had come into the picture. A familiar stranger, but a stranger, nevertheless.

Then Bentley's voice broke in:

"Is there anything more? Can you go even further back?"

There was a pause. Then:

"I see an automobile."

"Yes?"

"I'm driving this automobile. The top is down. There's a girl beside me. She's singing."

"Where are you driving this car?"

"I don't know."

"What is the girl's name?"

"I don't know."

"What is your name?"

"I don't know."

"All right. Go further back. What else do you see?"

X then related, in succession, the Baby Dream, the Tennis Dream, the Prison Dream, the Tower Dream and all the others, right up to the Tree Dream. In none of them did he come up with any names, any new facts. The Tree Dream would be the last possibility.

Bentley's voice took on even greater urgency. "Now tell me what you see."

"I see a tree."

"Yes? Where is this tree?"

"It's in a kind of park. Just outside a town."

"What is the name of the park?"

"I don't know."

"What is the name of the town?"

"I don't know."

"Try," Bentley's voice persisted. "Try to think."

"I don't know the name of the town. I don't know."

"You were there. You *must* know."

"No." The voice became querulous again. "I don't know. I don't know."

"All right. What do you see?"

"I am there. And with a girl."

"The girl is Marcia?"

"No. Some other girl."

"What is her name?"

"I don't know."

"How old are you now?"

"I'm young."

"*How* young?"

"I don't know."

"What are you doing?"

"I'm carving my initials—and hers—in the bark of the tree."

"What are the initials?"

"I don't know. I can't see them."

"Try to see them."

"I can't, I can't see them!"

After a few minutes of silence, Bentley turned off the tape recorder.

"Well, that's that. Nothing we can use. Nothing new. Not a name anywhere, not a clue."

"Why couldn't I remember anything else?"

"I don't know." The parapsychologist took out the spool of tape and slammed shut the cover over the machine. Clearly he was disappointed. "We can only theorize. Obviously, you developed a deep resistance, even under hypnosis, to opening yourself up. For some reason, you didn't want to open the door. Or in another sense you didn't want to open a Pandora's box. Afraid, perhaps, to explore this weird mystery, to reveal yourself to yourself. Afraid, perhaps, that it would be too much to handle, that you might go insane . . ."

Peter was still stunned by what he had heard on the tape. All the names he had remembered, right up to the day of his birth. And after that, nothing. *I'll just tell you so much and no more*, X had said. *If I don't want to remember, there's nothing you can do about it.*

"Look," said Bentley reluctantly, "we could try again. Maybe we can get you down into a deeper stage. . . ."

It was easy to see that Bentley didn't have much hope in this possibility.

"You don't really think it would work, do you?"

"If you pin me down to it, no." Then, hopefully, "But there is another method we might try."

"Yes?"

"Electroshock."

"Shock treatments?"

Bentley nodded. "There's a theory that applied electroshock before hypnosis may produce some interesting results, change some memory patterns temporarily, so that the patient evidences less resistance. Of course we'd experiment with a very mild current . . ."

"Experiment? You mean, this hasn't been tried on anyone before?"

Bentley hesitated. "Well, yes. It has."

"On whom?"

"On schizophrenics."

Peter stared at the parapsychologist. "I don't think I'm a schizo, Hall."

"I didn't say you were," Bentley said hastily. "It's just something we might possibly consider."

"No. I don't want to be anybody's guinea pig. And I don't intend to have my brains scrambled to prove *anything*."

"Okay," said Bentley. "I don't blame you. I guess I was reaching a little. Let's forget all that and try to get this monkey off your back another way. We'll try suggestion hypnosis. Suppose you come in tomorrow morning, same time."

"You think there's a chance . . . ?"

"I don't know. In hypnotherapy, it's foolish to make any predictions. We've had some success with certain traumas involving certain sleep disturbances, amnesia, and the like. All we can do is try."

After his patient had gone, Hall Bentley went to a cupboard and poured himself a drink. He felt very tired and very depressed.

Christ, he thought, what a letdown. For a while his hopes had soared, especially when he had found out that his patient was able to go, first, into a trance state, and, second, into regression. For a while he had believed that here, on this day, Peter Proud would turn out to be the living proof of reincarnation. That here history would be made, that they would shake the world. The prospect was a thousand times more exciting than walking on the moon.

But his patient had come up zero.

He had pursued this wraith hopefully for years. But it always came down to the same roadblock. Theories, conjecture, even a certain logic. But no hard-nosed proof. At this moment he was convinced that there never would be any. And anybody who really thought so was only deluding himself.

If you believe it's so, fine. But just try proving it, doctor.

The next morning, Bentley put Peter under hypnosis again. When he had gone under, the parapsychologist began:

"You have been having these dreams. The same dreams. But they are really hallucinations. They are harmful. They are nightmares that hurt your sleep. They exhaust your energy. Now, you must get rid of them. You have had enough of them. You will forget all about them. They never existed . . ."

Miraculously, the dreams vanished.

Night after night passed dreamlessly. Peter awoke feeling rested, completely refreshed. The man he thought of as X had apparently died for the last time. He no longer walked the streets of the mysterious city, or played tennis, or drove the big Packard, or counted money in his prison.

In time, he began to dream again. But these dreams were different, the kind everybody had. Dreams identified with childhood memories or authority figures. Dreams in which the cast of characters was familiar: his father, his mother, his friends, Nora. And in locales he recognized in present memory.

In time, the hallucinations themselves became one big dream, a series of nightmares he had had at one time. Now and then he would refer to the notebook he had kept. He could read about them now in a curious, detached way. Their content seemed the wildest fantasy.

He became his old self again. He worked well, teaching, doing his research. He completed four chapters of his book. His appetite was good. He played even more tennis than before, and his game and reflexes were much sharper. It seemed to him that he had twice as much energy as he had ever had before. He felt marvelous. And at peace.

His relationship with Nora improved. He knew it had been badly shaken recently—that, in fact, she had been on the verge of leaving him. He knew he hadn't been easy to live with. She had gone along with him, but it had been an ordeal for her, too. And their sex life had suffered. Now everything was normal again.

Occasionally they would talk of marriage, but in a deliberately vague way. Perhaps, they said. Someday. But they both knew it wasn't really there, not for the long run. They appreciated each other, both physically and intellectually. They more than just liked each other, but someday, they knew, it would end, with deep regrets and a great sense of loss on the part of both. But in the meantime they enjoyed each other from day to day.

Then one night, out of nowhere, without warning, his pleasant, peaceful existence was shattered.

Chapter 13

It was about two months after his last session with Hall Bentley, during the spring midterm break. He was sprawled on the couch in front of the television set, indifferently watching the end of one program and the start of another. The program just coming on was one of those documentaries the networks occasionally produced, the kind they put together to convince the FCC that they were indeed operating in the public interest and vitally interested in raising the cultural level of the American people. This one, according to the opening title, was on "The Changing Face of America."

He had played three hard sets of tennis that afternoon and was on his second martini. He felt pleasantly tired and drowsy. He had to struggle to keep his eyes open as he stared at the screen. Nora was in the kitchen broiling steaks. She was complaining to him about her job. He only half-listened as she went on irritably:

"That bastard I work for—Dr. Lohrman—he's been impossible lately. Having some trouble with his wife or something. I think she left him. Anyway, he's taking it out on all his teaching assistants, particularly me. It seems I can't do anything right. And do you know what I found out about him?"

"What?"

"He's dishonest. Intellectually dishonest. I happen to know that he found an article in some obscure German publication, paraphrased it a little, and he's going to use it in his own work. Publish it without credit. . . ."

On the television screen, a narrator came on. He stood on a huge floor map of the United States. This was a program, he said gravely, about contemporary America. The America you and I live in today. The America most of us love. We are going to show you how its face has changed, where America has gone, where it is now. How it has changed in population, in regional economics, and in other ways during the past fifty years.

Peter drained the last of his martini. He was getting sleepier. Nora's voice continued from the kitchen. Vaguely he heard her saying that she had had it up to here with being a T.A., especially for a demanding idiot like Lohrman. He was impossible. Here she was, a Ph.D. candidate, treated like a child, paid a pittance, and still paying tuition. On top of all this, she had gone before the doctoral committee to present her dissertation subject and the chairman, a pompous son of a bitch, had rejected it. He had told her that she needed a more problem-oriented subject. And what the hell did *that* mean?

Her voice drifted off. It became a babble from a distance. He stared fixedly at the television screen. Pictures were flashing on the screen now, quick cuts of various towns and villages. Grainy pictures taken long ago, the kind they would call Americana now. The narrator was talking about the Northeast now—specifically New England. Many years ago, he said, it was a vital industrial area. Here, in these towns and villages, were silk, paper, tool and die, textile, and small arms industries. It was an area full of skilled craftsmen, many of them immigrants from the old country, as well as native Yankees. But times had changed. Many of the industries had closed and moved south, where labor was cheaper.

The pictures went on and on, a montage of shots, one after the other —towns and cities, circa 1920, from Maine to Connecticut. They showed principal streets, factories, residential sections, monuments, public squares and so forth, none of them identified by name.

Suddenly he sat bolt upright. There, on the television screen, he saw it. His town.

He was sure of it. There was one quick picture of the main street he knew so well. The stone railroad bridge over the street, its underside curved in the shape of an arch. Then a shot of the square he remembered. And the tower, an exact replica of the one he had seen so many times in the Tower Dream.

They were only glimpses. The name of the town hadn't been given. But it had been there, right on the screen. *His* town.

He sat rigid, staring at the screen. The narrator was talking about the South now. Pictures of other cities, other towns, flipped by quickly. He sat there in a cold sweat. Then he yelled:

"*Nora!*"

She came running from the kitchen, looking alarmed. "What is it?"

He told her what he had seen. He babbled it out, the words coming out in a rush. She stared at him.

"Pete, you're crazy."

"I *told* you. I saw it!"

"You couldn't have."

"I swear I saw it."

"All right," she said. "You think you saw it. Maybe you did—in your imagination."

"No."

"Darling," she said patiently, "there isn't any such town. Not the one you dreamed about, anyway. You were just lying on the couch, you had had a couple of martinis, and you were half asleep. You know—daydreaming. You saw all these pictures flashing by, and you just identified with a couple of them. Had a kind of hallucination . . ."

He stared at her. Now he was a little uncertain.

"You think so?"

"I don't think, I *know*."

"I could have sworn I saw it, Nora. That railroad arch. That street. Right there on the screen. Staring me in the face. And that public square, and the tower . . ."

"The next time, darling," she said, "I'd go easy on the martinis. Especially when you're so tired. Now why don't you go in and wash up? Those steaks are almost ready."

Later he was unable to sleep. He tossed and turned, trying to re-create those few moments in front of the television set. Now he didn't trust his memory. Maybe he *had* been dozing, or just seeing things.

Still, he had been so damned *sure*.

There was only one way to find out. Somehow, he had to get another look at that film.

He called the network offices in Burbank. They did have a copy of the film, but it was locked up in a vault. It was against network policy to show it privately. However, if he wanted to put his request in writing, they would see that it was directed to the proper channel. In short, it was a dead end.

Peter tried another tack. He had a few friends in the television industry, and one of them knew the producer of the show, a man named Paul Daley. Daley was located in the New York office of the network. The producer would certainly have an air copy of the film, and if Peter wanted him to, his friend would volunteer to call Daley personally.

Peter called Daley in New York, mentioned his friend's name, and told the producer a vague story of trying to trace his childhood hometown and thinking he'd seen shots of it in the film. He explained casually that he was going to be in the East on other business and would appreciate a chance to see the film. Daley was agreeable.

Following that, he talked to Hall Bentley. The parapsychologist heard him out without comment. He told Bentley everything—his planned visit to the network, Nora's reaction.

"You know, Pete, maybe she's right. It could have been just an illusion."

"But I swear I saw that town."

"One hundred percent sure?"

"No."

"Then you *thought* you saw it."

"Yes. But at the time, I *was* sure . . ."

"Look. It's possible you *did* see it, in a manner of speaking. You were drinking, and tired, and almost dozing. You're staring at the screen. All these pictures are going by—pictures of New England cities and towns. You've got a mental picture of *your* New England town, the one you dream about. It's very vivid. You want to *see* that town—so much, it's coming out of your ears. So you simply thrust it up there on the screen—among all the others."

"All right. I see what you mean."

"Another possibility. Maybe you actually dozed off and then hallucinated. As you did before."

"I haven't done that once since you put me under . . ."

"I never said the results would be permanent. You could slip back at any time."

"But why *then*? Why would I have that particular hallucination at the exact time I was watching that particular program?"

"I don't know. Unless the pictures you saw while you were still conscious triggered it."

"Still, it's quite a coincidence, isn't it?"

"I'll quote you a much bigger one," Bentley said dryly. "You dream about a particular town. And then, miracle of miracles, you see it on a television program."

They were silent for a while. Then:

"Hall?"

"Yes?"

"Suppose it isn't a coincidence at all. Suppose it's true. Suppose it was all arranged."

"*Arranged?*" Bentley stared at him. "I don't follow."

"I don't know how to put this. I realize how strange it must sound. But it's a feeling I have. That somebody or something is trying to tell me something. Otherwise, why did I have these hallucinations? Why *me*? And why did I just *happen* to turn on that program and see what I saw?"

"We haven't established that you saw anything."

"There's a simple way to find out."

"Yes?"

"I'm going to New York. The answer's there, on that film. Either I saw it or I didn't."

Bentley was silent for a while. Then he said thoughtfully, "Pete, I don't want you to get me wrong. I'm not trying to put you down. I'm a scientist. It's my nature and my business to be skeptical, to prove any story out by picking holes in it and still finding it doesn't leak. But I'm not *that* pure a scientist. You say you have this feeling that somebody is trying to tell you something. Maybe it's true. After all, these hallucinations of yours are absolutely unique. I've interviewed thousands of patients, as I've said, and I've never come upon any case even remotely resembling yours. Even an idiot has to admit there are things happening all around us which no one understands. Just because they happen to be beyond our limited comprehension doesn't mean they're not true. We're cracking new frontiers in human perception all the time. You've dreamed of a town, and now you think you've seen it on television. Maybe you did—just by chance. Which reminds me of something that Anatole France said about chance. You know the quotation?"

"No."

"'Chance is the pseudonym God uses when he doesn't want to sign his own name.'" Bentley was silent for a while. Then he stirred.

"When are you leaving?"

"Tomorrow morning."

"There's something I want you to do. And do it today, before you leave."

"Yes?"

"Where's that notebook, the one in which you recorded all those dreams?"

"At home. Why?"

"Go home and get it right after you leave here. Then get two Xerox copies. Mail one to me, registered mail. When I get it, I'll put it, unopened, into a vault. Along with the tape we made while you were under hypnosis."

"What about the other copy?"

"Get to a bank today, before they close. Take out a safe deposit box in your name."

"I've already got one."

"I'm sure you have. But take out a *new* box in some other bank. Put the other copy in that box. Then don't make another visit to that vault. Don't go near it again until I tell you. Your name and today's date will be registered on the vault clerk's admittance card. It'll be the only entry, proving that you never made a second visit." He glanced at his wristwatch. "You'll have to hurry to get all this done."

"Why all this?"

"I'll give it to you in one big word: proof. If something happens, we're going to need all of it we can get!"

That night he told Nora he was going to New York. And as he packed, he told her why.

"You're out of your mind," she said.

"Maybe."

"You must see that what you're doing is completely irrational."

"I don't think so."

"I do." She was angry now. "You didn't see anything on that television set. Not one damned thing. Except what you *wanted* to see. There wasn't any town that you recognized. Certainly no town that you dreamed of. It was all fantasy. Can't you understand that?"

"I'll find out when I get there."

"Pete, listen to me. Stay here. Here you were, feeling fine. No more hallucinations. Cured. Now you're getting involved again, opening up a whole new can of beans. Let it alone, Pete. Don't go exploring now. Stay here."

"I can't. I've got to see that film."

"Then you've made up your mind. And nothing I can say is going to change it."

"I'm sorry, Nora."

"All right," she said. "I tried, but I've had enough. Frankly, you scare me, Pete. I don't think you're rational. I think you're going over the edge and don't realize it. Anyway, you won't find me here when you get back."

Chapter 14

He caught an 8:45 A.M. flight and arrived at Kennedy airport a few minutes before five. He picked up his bag and stepped out onto the curb. It was cold and raining hard. He had forgotten to take a raincoat, and he shivered as he hailed a cab. The traffic was snarled up as they came out on the Van Wyck Expressway. For a long time, they crawled along. Outside, the city was almost blanked out in a gray murk. The rain slanted hard against the windows of the cab. He felt tired and depressed.

He checked into his hotel and had dinner in his room. He had no desire to go out. He could hear the wind howling and whining through the steel and glass canyons outside. It was still raining hard. As he stared out of the windows the city outside seemed hostile, set on another planet. He felt as though he were a stranger here, a displaced person. More than that. He felt like a fool.

What am I doing here?

Like an idiot, he had come all this way just to pursue a fantasy. Now he was sure that he had seen nothing, that it was just another hallucination. The conviction had begun to grow on him when he had boarded the plane. If the flight hadn't been nonstop, he was sure he would have turned around and flown back home. Even Bentley had been skeptical. And Nora thought he was mad. Now he had lost her. When he had gotten up that morning, she was already up and packing. He had begged her to stay, but she remained stiff, remote. She had simply told him she would be back for the rest of her things later that day. Then she had walked out.

He went to bed, more depressed than ever.

That night they came again, for the first time in many weeks. One after the other. First, the Tree Dream. Then the Tower Dream and the Money Dream and the Tennis Dream and all the others. And ending, as always, with the Lake Dream.

Paul Daley, the producer of "The Changing Face of America," was young. He greeted Peter in his office, then took him up to the editing room. He had an assistant editor thread the Movieola, then turned to Peter.

"I'll start it going. I'll be looking into the eyepiece here. But if you stand just a foot or two behind me, you'll be able to see what's going on, too. When you see the town come up, tell me to stop. Then I'll be able to freeze the scene, so you'll get a good look. Okay?"

Peter nodded. There was a tight feeling in his chest. Then panic seized him. *There isn't going to be any town,* he thought. There never was a town. Not on this film, and not anywhere else. And since there was no town, how could he tell Daley to stop the machine? Where? At what point on the film? It was absurd. He, Peter, would be caught with egg on his face. *I thought the town was there. Sorry I wasted your time, Mr. Daley. It must have been something I just dreamed up.* He wouldn't blame the producer for throwing him out of the place.

"All right. Let's roll it."

Daley stepped on the foot pedal. There was a loud, whirring sound. Looking into the eyepiece, over Daley's shoulder, Peter saw the title come on, then the narrator standing on the huge floor map of the United States. The narrator's mouth was moving, but no sound came out. Vaguely, Peter remembered the gist of what he was saying. The America you and I love. And how its face has changed. Where it has gone, and where it is now . . .

"That montage is coming up now," said Daley. "Keep your eye peeled."

Suddenly the pictures came on the screen, grainy, old. New England towns. Factories belching smoke. Main streets. Forests. Mountain ranges. Rivers and fields. Farms. Closeups of faces. Parks and monuments. White Colonial churches. Public squares. Workers swarming out of factories. Pedestrians crossing streets. First one town, then another. Then another.

To Peter they seemed endless. At any moment, he knew, the locale would switch to the South, and it would be over. Not only the sequence, but his hope. He would have to tell Daley . . .

Suddenly he saw it.

"*Stop!*"

Daley stopped the Movieola abruptly. The producer said, "That it? The one I just passed? The one with the tower?"

"Yes."

The word came out of him in a croak. Daley glanced at him curiously.

Peter had broken out into a cold sweat. He continued staring into the eyepiece, but the town was no longer there. Some other place was on the screen.

"I overran it a little," said Daley. "I'll reverse the film, and then freeze the frame for you."

He stepped on the foot pedal again. The pictures slipped back into reverse. Then Daley froze the picture.

His town. There it was. It was real. The picture had been taken from the tower. There was the river in the distance, lying there in that reverse-S curve. There was the square just below, the familiar monuments and walks, the benches where people sat. Just as he had seen it so many times in the Tower Dream.

Daley moved the film back a couple of frames more. Now he saw what appeared to be a main street, with the stone railroad bridge with the archlike curve on its underside. He'd know it anywhere. Crowds of people were on the street. They were wearing old-fashioned clothes. This must have been taken sometime in the twenties. In his dream, of course, he had seen it in a much later period, the forties. But it was his town; there was no doubt about it. The picture on the tiny screen swam before his eyes.

"I guess that's it," said Daley. "There ain't any more."

He called over the assistant editor, and the man began to unthread the Movieola. Daley looked at Peter again.

"You seem upset," he said. "Was it *that* big a shot of nostalgia?"

"I guess it was. Look, I can't tell you how grateful I am."

"No sweat. Glad to be of help."

"Now if I only knew the name."

"Maybe I can get it for you."

"Yes?"

"That was a piece of stock film. The name may be on the film log. Let's go downstairs and find out."

They took the elevator and went back to Daley's office. He withdrew a folder from his file, glanced through a few pages, then stopped and frowned.

"Nothing here. No name. It's just identified as *General Shot, Day, New England Town*. And *General Shot, Day, Main Street of New England Town*."

"I see."

"Wait a minute," said Daley. "Let's try something else. We bought this stock footage from a firm called Apex. Maybe they'd know something."

He phoned them and told them the name of the show, the date, and the numbers of the shot, and asked if there was any identification of that particular town. He waited a long time. Then he said, "I see. What about the producer? Or cameraman? Any idea who shot that film?"

He listened a moment more. Then he hung up and looked at Peter. He shook his head.

"The town was never designated by name. And the producer and cameraman involved in those pictures are listed, but they've both been dead for a long time. That footage was taken way back in 1925."

"Then there's no way I can find out the name."

"No," said Daley. "No way."

He went back to the hotel and booked a flight for Boston. He packed and checked out, then took a taxi for LaGuardia. At four o'clock that afternoon, he was in Boston.

He rented a car at the airport, picking up a detailed road map of Massachusetts and another for all of New England.

He checked in at a nearby motel. It was after dark, too late to start out now. He would get a night's sleep and start down the highway early in the morning.

After dinner, he studied the map of Massachusetts. The word "Puritan" had cropped up constantly in his hallucinations. It seemed to be a key, a symbol, a signpost. He had read up on the Puritans. They had founded Massachusetts in the 1640s where they had originally set up their meeting houses and churches, their freehold houses, their gristmills and sawmills and smithy shops. They had created an austere, Bible-reading oligarchy, held their town meetings, punished their drunkards in the stocks, and, later, burned their witches. Massachusetts had been their stronghold, although later they had spread to other parts of New England.

Massachusetts, then, was his best bet. If he failed there, it would be only the beginning. If he had to, he would cover every damned city and town in all of New England. He had a lot of ground to cover, and it might take him days to find it, even weeks. But he knew it was out there somewhere. And he would know it when he found it.

If he found it.

Chapter 15

Early in the morning, he took to the highway. In studying the map, he had plotted a rough attack. First, he would cover the ring of cities and towns forming an arc around Boston itself. Then he would continue in a kind of north and south pattern, gradually tracking westward toward the Connecticut Valley and the Berkshires.

His prime landmark would be the tower. And, of course, that arching railroad span over the main street.

He drove through Medford, Malden, Woburn, and Melrose. Then Lynn, Wakefield, Peabody, Salem, Beverly, and Danvers. He avoided the thruways and the parkways, using only the heavily congested secondary arteries connecting one town with another. Only in that way, by driving up the main streets of each city and town, could he make the identification he looked for.

After that, farther north. Middleton, Newburyport, Amesbury. Then away from the coast, moving southwest—Haverhill, Methuen, Lawrence. And south, back toward Boston again. Reading, Burlington, Bedford.

He saw nothing even remotely resembling his town. There were any number of railroad bridges spanning streets, but none of the shape and color that he sought. There were a few towers, but none that resembled the one he knew. But everywhere he saw the signs: Puritan Motel, Puritan Restaurant, Puritan Barber Shop, Puritan Drugstore.

He drove south from Boston. Quincy, Braintree, Weymouth, Brockton, Taunton, New Bedford, Fall River; he avoided Cape Cod. From his dreams, he knew that his town was not surrounded by the sea. His feeling was that it was inland somewhere.

Attleboro, Norwood, Framingham, Marlborough, Shrewsbury, Worcestei.

He slept only a few hours each night. He barely paused to eat. A quick hamburger, then straight through the city, a quick look around, and then off again to the next city. He drove hour after hour. He stopped for a million red lights. Highways danced before his eyes; the white lines in the road wobbled. By darkness, weariness engulfed him. He drove like a robot, by sheer instinct. He slept exhausted, in motels and hotels, and awoke at dawn to continue his search.

Leominster, Fitchburg, Gardner, Greenfield, Northampton.

Ultimately, they all looked the same. The same gas stations, drugstores, department stores, roadside stands, souvenir shops. The same shopping centers, the same traffic, the same bowling alleys, the same golf courses, the same traffic signals, the same people on the streets. Each town with the same face, but with a different name.

Holyoke, Chicopee, Springfield, Westfield . . .

Gradually he began to see that his quest was almost hopeless. A fool's errand.

He had seen nothing remotely resembling his town. The film log had said: A *New England Town*. It could be anywhere, not necessarily in Massachusetts. It could be in Connecticut, Rhode Island, Vermont, New Hampshire, even Maine. He could spend weeks trying to find it. And he didn't have weeks. He had another four days before he had to fly back to the Coast.

There was another, more chilling, possibility. He may have already driven through the town, and never known it.

True, he had a picture of the place. God knows, it was frozen clearly enough in his mind. But he knew it the way it had looked sometime in the forties. This was the seventies. Who knew how it looked now? Thirty-five years, and maybe forty, had passed. That was long enough to change the face of any city. There had been the postwar population boom, great new housing developments, new high-rise buildings, vast shopping centers, retail complexes. Familiar landmarks had been torn down, streets widened, entire neighborhoods razed and rebuilt.

Maybe he'd already been there and never knew it.

On the next day, he drove through the Berkshires. Great Barrington, Stockbridge, Pittsfield, North Adams. Nothing that he recognized.

He followed the signs, found the Massachusetts Turnpike, and headed east for Boston. He would turn in the car there and grab a plane for the Coast.

He was deadly tired of the state of Massachusetts. He'd really traveled it, upward and downward, backward and forward. He'd hardly slept or eaten. And how many times had he told himself, this isn't the town, but it could be the next. Or the next. Or the next.

Now, he didn't even care anymore. Maybe someday he'd come back, take another look, go through the rest of New England. He'd take his time, do it leisurely. Or, on the other hand, maybe he'd never come back. What was the use? What was the point?

Let sleeping dreams lie.

Still, he knew he never could. His curiosity would never let him rest. He'd missed this time. But he knew the town was there, somewhere.

It was a hot spring day. The broiling highway slipped under the wheels of his car, an endless strip of shining white concrete. He was tooling along at a steady seventy. The sound of the motor and the singing of the tires mesmerized him into a kind of stupor. He had to fight to keep his eyes open. On the right of the turnpike, the great green roadsigns loomed up and then whooshed by, their bold white letters shimmering in the heat haze. There were still a hundred miles to go before he reached Boston. Once on the plane, he would sleep.

A big river appeared on the left. He had not been in this particular area before, but he knew it was the Connecticut River. At the moment it lay supine, a broad gray snake dozing in a bath of faint mist, its shiny skin rippling and glinting a little in the sun. Beyond, on the other bank, was a city.

Suddenly he was wide awake.

He stared at the river. Here, from this elevation, he could see that it had a peculiar reverse-S curve. And beyond it, the city.

It looked like any of the other cities he had seen. Yet, it did not. There was something about it, something in its contour, the way it was designed. The way the hills rose beyond the city. Farther down, three bridges spanned the river. One, an automobile bridge, white in color. Another a railroad trestle. And the third, an old steel bridge, its girders painted red.

In the dream, the river in the distance had this same reverse-S curve. Still, that wasn't particularly unusual—the river probably made a lot of similar curves as it meandered down toward the ocean from the north. Yet this particular reverse-S was near the city.

In the dream there had been two bridges, not three. But the white bridge looked comparatively new. He seemed to remember the trestle, and the bridge with the red girders. But maybe he was simply reading them into the dreams.

He looked for the tower, the tall, delicate Florentine rectangle towering over a public square. The one with the spectator's balcony where he had stood, in his hallucination, and looked out over the city and down on the square itself.

But there was no tower. And without the tower, it wasn't the town.

Yet—yet—there was *something* about the place. He saw the big turn-pike sign rushing up on his right: Riverside. Exit One Mile.

Riverside. It meant nothing to him. It jogged no memory. It was just another name. The smart thing was to go right by it, and get on to Boston. And from there, home.

But he found himself easing down his speed and moving over to the right lane and toward the exit ramp. Almost as though his head were saying one thing, his hands another.

He crossed the big white bridge and drove into the city. Bridge Street. River Street. Columbus Avenue. The names on the street signs meant nothing to him. There were the usual gas stations, used-car lots, whole-sale houses, cafeterias, and drugstores. The usual crowds on the streets, the usual buses, the usual traffic. Just another town.

But again, there was something about it. He saw an occasional build-ing that seemed to look familiar. The curve of a street. The way the river and the opposite bank looked from here. The factories on the other side, smoke eddying from their chimneys. They seemed familiar, and yet they did not. And he thought again, Take it easy. This isn't the place. It can't be. You want to see something badly enough, you can see it.

He was hungry. He decided he'd have a bite and push on. Parking the car on what seemed to be a main street, he remembered that he had run out of cash. He'd have to cash some traveler's checks. There was a bank just across the street. The sign said: Puritan Bank and Trust. He walked inside.

And then Peter saw him. *Cotton Mather.*

The big Puritan stood on a pedestal at the rear of the bank. He was a huge effigy, larger than life size, perhaps ten feet tall. He looked exactly as he had in the dream. Dark red tunic, caught at the waist with a leather band. Over this, a sleeveless jacket of dull gray. A doublet and leather hose lined with oilskin. A large conical broadbrim hat. Broad white collar of linen. The face hard and stern. The eyes cold and dead.

Well, old friend, thought Peter, it's you at last. We have finally met. . . .

He walked toward the rear of the bank, toward the effigy. He heard his steps echoing on the floor. Dimly, he was aware of the business of the bank going on around him—the people standing in lines to complete their transactions, the cashiers behind the glass wall, the buzz and hum of voices. The area in which the Puritan stood on his pedestal had been roped off. Peter looked up at the effigy. The old Puritan towered above him, gigantic, frightening. Exactly as he had in the dream. The cold eyes seemed to be looking down, glaring at him.

"Everything all right, sir?"

Peter whirled around. A uniformed bank guard was staring at him curiously. Peter was shaking. He tried to pull himself together. Finally he managed a smile.

"That figure up there. I've never seen anything like it before. It's very—impressive."

The guard smiled. "That's one word for it. A lot of people around here think it's just plain ugly. The directors of the bank have been talking about getting rid of it. But I don't know—people in town are used to seeing it here. You know—it's part of the bank, tradition, and all that. Some of 'em would miss old Cotton if they took him away. Looks real lifelike, doesn't he?"

"Yes, he does." He stared at the guard. "Is that what everybody calls him—Cotton?"

"Yes, sir. After Cotton Mather. It's kind of a nickname, I guess."

"How long has he—it—been here?"

"Well, of course, it's a kind of trademark for the bank, you might say. Been here ever since the bank has. That would be about forty years. I'll tell you this much. Old Cotton up there is a real dust collector. About every five years we have to throw away his clothes and get him a new set."

"I see." He wanted to turn again and take another long look at the effigy. It wasn't every day you could stare at a dream come true. He knew the Puritan's eyes were only glass, but he had the curious feeling that they were alive and boring into him. He was in the aftermath of shock now. He could feel the gooseflesh all over his body, and he knew he was still shivering. The guard stood there, watching him.

"Where can I cash some traveler's checks?"

"Over there, sir. Any one of those windows."

He walked toward one of the windows. He did not look back; he didn't dare. Sweat broke out on his forehead. He knew there couldn't be another figure like that anywhere else in the world. And he had found it. Or had it found *him*?

This, he thought, was the place where I lived. Before I died. No doubt about it now. Riverside, Massachusetts.

The clerk behind the glass partition cashed Peter's check.

"Noticed you staring at the old witchburner."

"Yes."

The clerk grinned. "Every stranger who walks in here usually stops to take a good look. Catches your eye, if you know what I mean. A great attention-getter." He smiled ruefully. "But how would you like to have that ugly devil staring you in the face every day? The way I have to." The clerk shook his head in distaste.

Peter walked out of the bank and onto the street. He got into the car and started to drive north. Somehow he knew there was a curve just ahead, and then beyond that the intersection of two main avenues. Now he knew he had been here before. Some of the buildings, the older buildings, seemed familiar to him. He drove around the curve, paused for a traffic light, and then without hesitation took the street to the left. State Street, the sign said.

Another turn, this one to the right. And then he saw it. The arched railroad bridge spanning the street just ahead. It was made of gray granite and supported by a small turretlike structure at each end. Just as he had seen it in the dream. Except that now it seemed much grayer than he remembered it.

He drove under the arch and, without hesitation, took the next left. Chestnut Street. It was strange, he thought. He could remember the name of no street in his dreams. Yet, now that he was here, he seemed to know exactly where to go. And he knew precisely what would appear when he turned right on Chestnut.

The public square was there, just as he expected. There was the same green lawn. The same green park benches lining the diagonal walk. The same two statues. The sign said: Court Square.

But there was no tower.

He parked the car and walked into the square. On the site where he had seen the tower, there was now another building. It looked fairly new and was modern in design. Functional, all stainless steel and glass. He saw that it was the town's municipal building. It housed the Superior Court, the Riverside Police Department, the City Clerk's Office, the Department of Parks.

His immediate reaction was one of anger. He had wanted to find that tower there; he had expected it. It had been one of the artifacts in the museum of his memory. Now they had destroyed it, and it seemed like some kind of desecration.

An old man was sitting on a bench reading a newspaper. He wore bifocals and was neatly dressed. Peter walked up to him.

"Excuse me, sir."

The man put down the paper and stared up at him with rheumy blue eyes.

"Yes?"

"Wasn't there a tower here a few years ago?"

"Sure was. They used to call it the Municipal Tower."

"When did they tear it down?"

"Oh, along about 1950. Or maybe it was '51."

"I see."

"They had another name for it, too. The Campanile. Designed it after some tower in Italy. Florence, Venice, somewhere like that. You could see it for miles around. But it was pretty old. The engineers figured it was unsafe, so they tore it down."

"Wasn't there some kind of observation balcony at the top?"

"Yep. Sure was. Great view from there, too. Used to take my grandchildren up there. Personally, I think it was a damned shame they tore it down. The tower looked pretty, standing there. I mean, it made the town. But then, what can you do? The stupid bastards are always tearing down something beautiful and putting up something ugly. Said they had to do it in the name of progress. The real estate was too valuable." The old man snorted. "The same old story. When a fast buck is involved, nobody respects anything."

The man went back to his newspaper. Peter found an empty bench and sat down. He felt faint, giddy. His heart was pounding violently. He thought, All right, let's try to put it together now. Let's try to put it all together.

This is where I lived before I died. Riverside, Massachusetts.

But who was I?

PART TWO

Except that a man be born again, he cannot see the Kingdom of God.
CHRIST

God generates beings, and then sends them back, over and over again, till they return to him.
THE KORAN

After all, it is no more surprising to be born twice than it is to be born once. Everything in Nature is resurrection.
VOLTAIRE

Death is but a sleep and a forgetting. If death is not a prelude to another life, the intermediate period is a cruel mockery.
GANDHI

Were an Asiatic to ask me for a definition of Europe, I should be forced to answer him: "It is that part of the world which is haunted by the incredible delusion that man was created out of nothing. And that his present birth is his first entrance into life."
SCHOPENHAUER

My doctrine is: Live, so that thou mayest desire to live again—that is thy duty. For in any case, thou wilt live again!
NIETZSCHE

Chapter 16

He had no idea how long he had been sitting there.

But after a while his head stopped spinning. The buildings surrounding the square came out of the blur and into focus, etched sharply against a darkening sky. The wind had sharpened, and he felt cold. Gradually he became conscious of the noise of traffic on the streets bordering the square. The old man had left his nearby bench. The newspaper he had been reading lay forlornly on the wooden slats, the wind whipping its pages. The noise of traffic was heavy now; horns were blowing. He had the impression that it was the rush hour. A flock of pigeons settled at his feet, waiting hopefully.

And again, the questions came pounding through his brain, tormenting him.

Who was I? What was my name? How did I come to live here? What kind of man was I? And who was Marcia? Wife? Lover? What kind of woman was she? A murderess, yes, but before that? Why did she cut off my life while I was still young? Did they ever find out her crime and convict her for it? Perhaps not. Perhaps they never even found out that she murdered me. Is she dead? Perhaps. But the chances were good that she was still alive. She would be somewhere in her fifties now. It was possible that she still lived here.

And if she did, he would find her. No matter what it took, or how long it took, he would find her.

It was possible that at this very moment, as he sat in the square, his murderess might be walking along the streets, or shopping in one of the stores, or driving one of those cars he saw. Perhaps he and Marcia had even passed each other on the sidewalk as he came out of the bank, drove down the street and into the square. Perhaps they had looked each other in the eye and gone on, without recognition. She would not know him, of course; he was sure he bore no resemblance to his previous incarnation, to X. He was a different body, with a different face and a different name. His soul was the same, but you could not see a soul. You could not describe it. A soul had no face and no fingerprints. And after all, the man she knew was dead. She had killed him herself.

He wondered whether *he* would recognize *her*. He knew the chances were against it. After all, in his dream world she was a young woman. Now she would be much older—some thirty years older. She could be ugly now. Fat. Her youth obliterated by time. He might pass her on the street and never know her. He shivered at the thought.

Funny. He was confused about his own identity now. Sometimes he thought of X as an entirely different person, and at other times he thought of X as himself. It depends on how you look at it, he thought. If you saw it in purely physical terms, X's body had died years ago in the slime and weeds at the bottom of that lake. And my body, the body of Peter Proud, is very much alive. Yet we have the same souls. In that sense, we are one and the same. And perhaps that is the most important sense.

The wind became sharper. What he had to do now was check in at a hotel somewhere. He remembered there had been one near the bank.

He rose and started to walk out of the square. Then something caught his attention—a large rock, or boulder, the top of which had been flattened out. On the flat area a bronze plate had been riveted. He read the inscription:

> Here stood the Parson's tavern
> where George Washington was
> entertained, June 30, 1775,
> traveling in the saddle from
> Philadelphia to Cambridge to
> take command of the American
> forces, and on October 21, 1789,
> riding in his coach through
> the New England states as
> President.
>
> ERECTED BY THE GEORGE WASHINGTON
> CHAPTER, SONS OF THE AMERICAN
> REVOLUTION, 1914.

He read the inscription on the boulder a second time. George Washington drank here. He wondered whether Washington was alive now in some other incarnation. It was entirely possible. The Father of Our Country might still live, in some other body, some other house of flesh, somewhere in the world. In his reading, he had learned that many men had claimed they had been George Washington in some previous incarnation. Or Napoleon, or John the Baptist, or Caesar. Most of them, he presumed, were in insane asylums. But the idea was no longer ridiculous to him.

He himself was the living proof of that.

The hotel was called the Riverside.

Vaguely, Peter recalled it from one of his dream fragments, although in the hallucination it looked much newer than it did now. It was an old building, perhaps fifty years old now, and it seemed out of place amidst the new shops along Main Street. It was perhaps ten stories high and built of the time-darkened granite that apparently was indigenous to the region. Under its roofs and cornices were fancy flutings and small gargoyles of what appeared to be dirty marble.

When he entered the lobby, he knew he had been there before. It was all vaguely familiar: the green carpets, the palms, the dark mahogany reception desk, the heavy leather furniture, the doors to the restaurant and the rest rooms, their upper halves made of Tiffany glass. He even seemed to recall the oaken grandfather clock standing at the entrance to the dining room.

Clearly, the place was doing very little business. There was nobody in the lobby. Probably on its last legs, he thought. They'd tear it down any day and build another new and sterile high-rise office building in its place, or maybe another bank.

The eerie feeling persisted that he, in the form of X, had frequented this place. Back in the forties, it must have been quite fashionable. It was possible that X had taken Marcia here for a drink and dinner many times. Certainly he could afford it. In the dreams he seemed prosperous enough.

There was no one at the reception desk. He punched the bell on the counter. A clerk came out, a man of about sixty, white-haired, with a seamed face.

"Yes, sir?"

"I'd like a room."

"For how long, sir?"

"Oh, about two days."

"I think we can accommodate you. We've got a big room high up and at the front, for eighteen dollars. And a smaller room at the rear, for fifteen."

"The room at the front will be fine."

He signed the registration card. Peter stared at the elderly clerk. Then he asked, "How long have you been with this hotel?"

The man was startled by the sudden question. He stared at Peter. "Why do you ask, sir?"

"Just curious."

"Why, let me see. Came here in 1940. Been here thirty-five years."

"I see." Peter looked around. "Must have been quite a place back then."

"Yes, sir. It was."

He had been here long enough then. Long enough to have met X. He must have known what X looked like. Known him by name—and Marcia. Suddenly he had a desperate desire to say to the man, *I am someone you used to know. A long time ago. Someone who probably came into this hotel. With a woman named Marcia. But I don't know my name. Can you tell me who I am?*

Crazy. The man would think he was crazy, and with good reason. Yet he almost blurted it out.

The clerk, still looking at him curiously, rang for a bellboy.

He lay on the bed, drained of all energy, his nervous system still in shock.

He remembered the clairvoyant, Verna Bird, lying on her chaise longue in her long flowing red housecoat, frozen in her trance. And Elva Carlsen, her secretary, sitting rigidly with folded hands, acting as conduit to the beyond. "We have a soul here." *Yes, I see the soul.* "And we have a body which houses the soul." *I see the body.* "Do you see others before this?" *I see others. The bodies are different, and they live at different times. They live and die, according to God's will. And the old soul passes from one to the other.* And himself, listening, fascinated, as he peered at Verna Bird through that ridiculous altar.

Ever since his visit to the house on Laurel Canyon, he had been confused about Verna Bird. Was she just an aging female charlatan conducting a little mumbo jumbo for fat fees? Or did she have genuine insight, the kind that transcended logic itself? She had told him he had lived a number of lives before, back through the centuries. Chalaf, the Hittite slave, the Japanese outcast, and so on. But this was pretty safe ground. Who could call her a liar? Who could possibly prove her wrong or right? It was significant that she had stopped short of any reincarnation that might possibly be documented as true or false. She had claimed she knew nothing about X.

Yet, curiously, all his previous lives had come to an end by drowning, in one way or another. So, too, had his last life. But he had told Verna Bird nothing of the dream. It was strange. And frightening.

Then he recalled what she had said in her Spiritual Healing reading, about his becoming some kind of prophet. He had instantly dismissed it as pure nonsense. But now, in view of what had just happened?

He shivered a little. It's crazy, he thought. Death was not the end of everything, it was just the beginning. In effect, nobody died. Death was a long sleep from which you always awakened. A man didn't live just one life; he lived many lives.

The body, of course, was mortal, a temporal covering. It was also changeable. The flesh we began with when we were born wore out and was continually replaced by new flesh. New tissues replaced the worn-out ones. In a sense, your body was reincarnated even during the same lifetime. It underwent birth and rebirth in its material form. He recalled reading that the cells in a human body change completely every seven years. When you were a child you were in one body. When you became a teenager, you were still *you*, but your body had changed completely. When you became a man, you had a whole new body. But inside of all these bodies, there was still the original *you*. When the body got too old to function anymore, you simply shed it. The flesh decayed and became dust.

But the soul goes on. To another body, newly born. And after that, still another. And so on, according to some divine design. There is no end to it. And the principle is immutable: *I will be tomorrow, or some future day, what I establish today. I am today what I established yesterday—or some previous day.*

He, Peter Proud, knew this now, knew it for sure. But nobody else did.

He wondered what would happen if he ran out onto the street and proclaimed what he knew. *Don't be afraid to die, good people. Because you'll live again.*

He imagined the incredulous faces, the jeering laughter, the names: kook, nut, weirdo, crazy. In earlier times, he would have suffered the fate of other prophets. The mob would have torn him apart or stoned him to death. Today they'd probably call the police, judge him insane, and lock him up.

But there was someone he could tell it to: Hall Bentley. He reached for the phone, and stopped. He decided that he might as well wait a little while. Possibly in the two days he had before he left, he might accumulate more information. He might as well give it all to Bentley at once.

He rose and went to the window. It was a moonless night, and the city of Riverside was ablaze with light. He could see the traffic moving along the cloverleafs and the parkways on the other side of the river, like a series of jeweled snakes, and the myriad of lights blinking in the suburbs of the city. He thought about Marcia again, wondering whether she was living down there somewhere among those lights.

He decided the chances were very much against it. Thirty-five years, give or take a few, was a long, long time. People died, or they moved away, or they got lost. Yet, in a very real sense, she was the only clue to his own identity. Find her, and he'd know who he was.

That, he thought, was going to be some trick.

He undressed slowly, and finally he fell asleep. His sleep was plagued by the dreams. He had them all, except for four: The City Dream, the Tower Dream, the Cotton Mather Dream, and the Prison Dream.

Chapter 17

The next morning he had breakfast in his room. Then, unable to think of anywhere else to start, he began to go through the telephone directory.

In the short time he had been here, he realized that Riverside was a fairly sizable city, its population perhaps two hundred thousand. The phone book itself included not only the subscribers of Riverside itself, but those of many of the outlying districts and towns.

He began on three assumptions. First, that Marcia had never been convicted of his murder. Second, that she was still alive. And third, that she still lived in Riverside. He started to check off every Marcia listed in the phone book. Vaguely, he hoped that one of the surnames might hit a memory nerve somewhere, might open some tiny hidden compartment.

By the time he got through the letter F, he had checked off some twenty names beginning with the name Marcia. None of the last names conjured up anything. Besides, there could be fifty or a hundred more Marcias in Riverside whose identities would be hidden because only their husbands' names were listed in the phone book. He closed the directory in disgust and threw it on the bed. He was reaching for nowhere.

Still, the key was Marcia. If he found out who she was, he would find out who he himself was.

He went downstairs. The elderly clerk was on duty at the reception desk. He smiled as Peter approached.

"Good morning, sir."

"Good morning."

"What can I do for you?"

"I'm looking for a lake somewhere in the area."

"Yes? What lake?"

"I don't remember the name. I used to live around here as a small boy, and my folks used to have a cottage there . . ."

The clerk looked at him dubiously. "Well, we have a lot of lakes around here . . ."

"I realize that. But I do remember something about this one. There was a big hotel on it, called Puritan. Puritan House, Puritan Inn, something like that . . ."

"Oh, you probably mean Lake Nipmuck."

"Nipmuck?"

"Yes, sir. There used to be a Puritan Hotel on the north shore. But when they built the new parkway near the lake about five years ago and got all that traffic going through, they tore it down and put up a Holiday Inn there."

"I see. Where can I find it?"

"Here," said the clerk. "Let me show you on the map." He picked up a folder on the desk. "It's about twenty miles from here. But once you get on the Miles Morgan Parkway, it'll take you no time at all."

Nipmuck. The name was familiar enough. The tribal word itself meant "fresh water fishing place." The Nipmucks were one of the inland tribes of central Massachusetts. They had followed the hostile tribes at the outbreak of King Philip's War and later fled to Canada or westward to the Mohicans and other tribes on the Hudson. Nipmuck. One for the book, the one he would finish someday—maybe.

He drove down Main Street. The arrows indicated that there was an entry to the Miles Morgan Parkway on the other side of Court Square. He drove past the Municipal Building and then stopped the car for a moment near the curb. A sign on a separate section of the building caught his eye: Riverside Police Department.

It struck him suddenly that the answer might be in there. Maybe part of the answer, maybe the whole answer. If the girl in his dreams had been caught and convicted of her crime, they would surely have some kind of record. Even if it went back thirty-five years.

He started to circle the square, looking for a parking place. Through his windshield the traffic was a moving blur. Sweat soaked his collar. It was very simple—just go in there and ask.

Then he thought about it. It wasn't simple at all. In fact, it could get pretty damned complicated. He began to write a scenario in his mind. The red-faced police sergeant sitting behind the desk stared at him:

"What can I do for you, mister?"

"I wonder if you could give me some information, sergeant."

"What kind of information?"

"Do you have any record of a murder committed at Lake Nipmuck, sometime in the forties?"

He pictured the sergeant, hard blue eyes suddenly alert, watching him now with interest.

"In the 1940s, you say?"

"Yes."

"That's a long time ago. We'd have to look it up. What kind of homicide was it?"

"Well, it probably looked like an accident. But it was a murder. The victim was a naked man. They probably dragged the lake for him, or found his body floating . . ."

"What was the name of this victim?"

"I don't know his name."

"You remember the name of the killer?"

"I don't know that, either. But it was a woman."

"I see. A woman."

"Yes."

"You know a woman murdered a naked man, but you don't know her name."

"I told you, I don't. I don't even know whether the police ever found out about her or not. If they did, it'd be in your records."

It was easy to imagine the way the sergeant would stare at him now— as though he were dealing with some kind of kook. But more than that: the hard eyes would become suspicious.

"What's your name, mister?"

"Peter. Peter Proud."

"What's your interest in all this?"

"I—I'm just interested."

"You haven't answered my question, Proud."

"Look, sergeant, all I wanted was some information . . ."

"Just how did this homicide happen? Can you give us any details?"

"Well, the man was swimming in the moonlight. The woman came up in a boat. Her name was Marcia. She hit the man over the head with her paddle two or three times. He sank . . ."

"How do you know all this happened?"

"Well, I dreamed it. I just dreamed about it."

"I see. You saw it all in a dream."

"Look, sergeant, I'm sorry I bothered you. Forget it . . ."

"Hold it, mister. Not so fast. Maybe you'd better tell your story to the lieutenant . . ."

He squirmed as he let his imagination run on.

"*I saw it all in a dream, lieutenant. It's true, it really happened. How do I know? Well, I was the man who was murdered. In my previous life, that is . . .*"

Say that again, Proud. And see how crazy it sounds.

They might do any number of things—simply throw him out, or hold him for observation. They might, out of curiosity, even take the trouble to go back into their files. Suppose they found no record of any homicide at Lake Nipmuck in the forties. That would prove that Marcia had gotten away with it, of course. But the police might be interested enough in what he had to say, no matter how wild it was, to start some kind of investigation—of him. Who had really told him about this? Where had he gotten his information? What was his real interest?

It was late morning, and the sidewalks were crowded with shoppers. Through his car window he stared at the people passing by. He had developed the habit now of peering at faces, trying to match them with the faces he had seen in his hallucinations. Particularly the faces of women in their late fifties.

He headed for the lake. He had originally intended only to visit it, to see how it compared with what he had seen in his hallucination. Now he realized that his search might very well end there. At Nipmuck, it was possible he might find out who he was. *If* he had any kind of luck.

He turned the car into the Miles Morgan Parkway and then cruised at a steady sixty.

The excitement grew in him. The more he thought of it, the surer he was that his answer waited for him at the lake.

It was a beautiful, clear spring day. To the west he could see the eroded remains of what were once the lofty Berkshires, to the east the ridges of the central Massachusetts hills. Here, in the valley between, there were small farms, the land just being plowed for planting, and tobacco fields. Much of the land was strewn with rocks. Vaguely he remembered from some long-forgotten course in geology that this region had gone through a great glacial period. Enormous ice sheets had ground their way toward the sea. Like giant battering rams, they had pushed tons of rubble and stone before them, strewing the rocky waste all over the region. In places, he saw these deposits piled in rounded drumlins or left in long ridges of gravel. He saw two or three abandoned quarries filled with water.

Again, he had the same eerie feeling *I have been here before.*

He wondered whether, as X, he had been born and brought up in this Riverside area. It was entirely possible. In the dream, he pictured X as about his own age when he died—twenty-seven. If that were so, and he had died sometime in the forties, as the dream indicated, then he must have been born sometime between 1910 and 1920. Maybe, as a small boy, he had clambered over these rounded hills of traprock or run along the ridges of gravel. He might have gone skinny-dipping in the cold, clear spring water that filled the quarries, and dived from their tilted rocks, taking care not to break his neck on some rocky protuberance concealed by silt or weeds. Here he might have known the feel of rounded pebbles on bare feet as he waded brook or stream, and heard the singing of water as it rushed down the granite crevasses in the floods of the New England spring, and perhaps he had snagged many a fishing hook on the stony bottoms.

The roadsign caught him dreaming. He was almost upon it when he saw the direction: Exit 16. Lake Nipmuck. He put on his brakes hard. The tires screamed on the pavement. Someone blew a horn at him angrily from behind.

In a few minutes he was at the lake. He drove slowly along the narrow, two-lane blacktop as it twisted and turned, following the contour of the shore. He saw the patch of smooth-faced stone on the mountain, exactly as he had seen it in the Lake Dream. The Holiday Inn was standing behind the same grove of pines, built on the site of the Puritan.

But he could not find the cottage. In the Lake Dream he had seen it all so clearly: the outdoor fireplace, the picnic table, the graveled walk lined with whitewashed stones leading down to the dock. And, of course, the dock itself. He remembered the place with woods on each side and a sprinkling of other cottages around the lake. He had been sure he could go directly to it.

But now he was totally confused. The lakefront was jammed with cottages, one next to the other, with very little land between them. In the last thirty-five years or more, the building boom had come here. In some places, there were two or three cottages between the lake shore itself and the road. Almost all of them had the same kind of dock he had seen in the dream. To his eyes, they all looked vaguely the same, as though the same developer had thrown them all up at once. They were homey folksy places, with small signs saying: "The Wilsons Live Here" or "George and May" or "Fred and Alice" or "Charlie and Joan." Now, in April, they were all closed. They were all forlorn, looking a little shabby, wearied by the winter.

He drove around slowly. None of them looked the least familiar. Vaguely, he knew it was directly opposite the hotel, somewhere on the south shore. But you could stand at a hundred places on the south shore and be opposite any point on the opposite side. Moreover, he had never seen the *part* of the cottage he had dreamed about that faced the road, and he couldn't go tramping around every cottage on the south shore. And in three decades or more the cottage could have gotten a new dock, new walk, new outdoor furniture. The old place could even have been torn down, and a new one put up in the same spot. Despite the fact that some refurbishing seemed to be needed, many of these cottages seemed fairly new, as though they'd been put up in the last five or ten years.

It had all seemed so simple. He had planned to find the cottage, then find out who the owners were. They could tell him who had owned it back in the forties, or tell him where he could find out. Then he would know his own name. But there was no chance of that now.

He drove slowly along the blacktop until he came to a public beach. There was an open area here where he could see the entire lake. He parked the car, got out, and walked to one of the picnic tables on the grassy area just behind the sand itself. He sat on the table and stared out across the lake.

It seemed so quiet here, so empty, so desolate. In a couple of months, Nipmuck would come alive. This beach would be crowded with bathers, laughing and chattering, pretty girls toasting themselves in the sun, children running round, screaming and splashing in the water. The surface of the lake would be covered with small boats, their motors desecrating the silence. And beyond them, on the other shore and the mountain beyond, the naked trees he saw now would be clothed in rich summer green.

But this was April and it was quiet, and there was still a chill in the air. An errant breeze started and stopped at intervals, rippling the surface of the lake.

He fixed his eye on a point toward the middle of the lake. There, he thought, is where I died.

He wondered what had happened after that. Had they found him? Had they dragged the lake for him? Or had his body floated to the surface? Had Marcia reported him dead? Or missing? Maybe he'd been caught in the weeds down there. Maybe he was still down there on the bottom, rotted to the bone, eaten by the fishes.

He continued to stare at the point in the lake where he estimated he had gone down. Then the sun ducked behind a cloud. Suddenly he couldn't stay there any longer. He got up and walked slowly back to the car.

He stopped for gas at the juncture of the lake blacktop and the road linking the lake to the parkway itself.

The sign said: Pop Johnson's Place. It was a combination gas station and country store. The owner came out of the store. He was about sixty-five, and his walk was slow and deliberate. He wore a stained baseball cap and a heavy lumberjacket shirt of plaid design.

"Afternoon."

"Good afternoon."

"Fill 'er up?"

"Please."

The proprietor set the pump, inserted the gas line, and then came around to clean the windshield. As the man sprayed the glass with a spray can, Peter studied the wrinkled, wind-beaten face. Maybe he would know.

He'd have to give the man some kind of cock-and-bull story, of course. He got out of the car, went to the soft drink dispenser in front of the store, and dropped the required coins into the slot. A bottle of Coke rattled down. He pinched off the cap and drank while he figured out his approach. The man looked simple enough. There was no reason why he shouldn't buy it. He walked toward the proprietor.

"Are you 'Pop'?"

"That's right."

"Been here at Nipmuck long?"

"All my life. Born near here."

"I wonder if you could give me a little information."

"I'll try."

"Well, you see, I'm a writer. I write true mystery stories. Right now I'm doing a series of articles on, well, famous murders of the past here in New England. For one of the Boston papers."

The old man stared at him.

"What do you know. Murders, eh? My wife's crazy about that kind of stuff. Watches all those programs on television. Personally, I don't care for 'em much."

"Someone told me that there'd been a famous murder here at Nipmuck. Happened a long time ago. Way back in the forties, I think. Got a lot of publicity, they tell me. But this someone who told me about it couldn't recall the name. I thought maybe you'd know . . ."

The proprietor thought for a moment, pursing his mouth.

"Back in the forties." Then his watery eyes lit up. "Yep. Now I remember. That must have been the Grady killing."

"Grady?"

"Man named Charles Grady. Had a cottage here at Nipmuck."

"Yes?"

"Found his body floating in the lake. It was something terrible."

Peter held his breath. He heard himself say, "What happened?"

"Nobody knows. They never found who done it. But Grady's throat was cut, and he'd been hacked in about ten places with a knife. Some maniac, they say. No reason for it at all. Everybody liked Charlie. Anyway, scared the devil out of people around here for weeks. Bolted their doors, wouldn't go out nights. They were afraid the maniac would come back and try it again. But he never did. It was in all the papers. I forget the year exactly, but you could look it up."

"Thanks. I will. And that was the only homicide?"

"Yep. Can't think of any other. If there was, I'd know."

Peter swallowed his disappointment.

"I suppose there've been plenty of accidents around here."

The old man peered at him. "Accidents?"

"You know. People drowning."

"Oh. Yep. Get a lot of drownings over the years. The thing is, there are cold springs out in the lake. People get cramps. Then, someone's always tipping over a boat or canoe and going down and getting caught in the weeds. There are some pretty thick weeds on the bottom there. Things like that. But that isn't exactly what you're looking for . . ."

"No."

The old man glanced at the register on the gas pump.

"That'll be $4.85, mister."

He paid the man, thanked him again, and drove away. And he thought, that's that.

Good, sweet, beautiful Marcia. She had gotten away with it after all.

As he started his drive back to Riverside it began to rain. In a few minutes it was coming down in sheets.

He had one more card he could draw. This was Saturday. He had to be back in Los Angeles on Monday. The final quarter would begin soon, and he would be heavily involved in all the administrative detail before actual classes resumed. But before he flew home the next day, he had to try this one last possibility. Rain or no rain, he had to check out the Tree Dream. He didn't give it much of a chance, but he had to try.

He came off the parkway at an upper exit to Riverside itself. The exit spilled out onto a busy four-lane highway. Again, as he drove, he had the same eerie feeling: I have been on this street before. Only then I was driving a Packard Clipper, not a rented Pontiac.

The rain continued coming down in torrents. He looked at his watch:

2:30. He realized he was hungry. He turned into a big shopping center, parked the car, and ran through the rain into a big super drugstore with a lunch counter. He ordered a hamburger from a waitress whose badge said her name was Joan.

"Terrible day."

"You can say that again."

"Joan, wonder if you could help me with something. I'm trying to find a certain park here in Riverside."

"*Which* park?"

"I don't know the name."

"Stranger here, huh?"

"Yes."

"Well, we've got three parks in town. If you don't know the name, you've got a problem." She glanced at his coffee cup. "Another cup, while you're waiting?"

"Thanks. As I said, I don't know the name of this park, but I have an idea it's a pretty big place. And there's a mausoleum somewhere on it."

"A *what?*"

"A burial tomb. This one's got a couple of figures on it. You know, statues. A man and a woman. The man has his arm around the woman . . ."

"Oh, yeah. You're talking about the Bannister tomb. Frederick Bannister. He gave half the park to the city. Woodland Park. That's him and his wife standing on top. They're buried there."

"Woodland Park."

"Right."

She stared at him. "If you knew about the Bannister tomb and all, you must have been there. How come you didn't know the name of the park?"

"I used to live here when I was a little kid. I remember the tomb, but I forgot the name of the park."

"Oh."

"How do I get there?"

"You're not too far away now. Go straight down Central about half a mile, turn right on Oak. You'll run right into it." She turned, picked up his hamburger on the serving counter, and then moved a tray toward him. "Mustard and relish?"

"Thanks."

"This is a pretty lousy day to be walking in the park," she said. "If that's your idea, you'd better wait till tomorrow."

"I will."

He bolted down his hamburger. As he left he noticed that the store sold cheap umbrellas, and he bought one. Walking toward his car, he found that it helped, but not much. A hard wind had come up, blowing the rain almost horizontally. He was wet by the time he reached the car.

At Woodland Park he entered the main gate. Rain spattered on the tiny puddles already forming on the clay tennis courts located on each side of the entry road. The downpour was so hard that it made visibility almost impossible. For a moment, he considered canceling the whole idea and going back to the hotel. Maybe he could come out here early the next morning, then catch his plane.

But he decided against it. He was here, and the time was now. He knew if he went back to the hotel now, he would be unable to sleep. It was better to get it over with.

The trees whipped in the wind. His tires splashed through puddles on the road. He passed a wading pool. Beyond this was a series of buildings which he took to be a zoo.

A sign with an arrow pointing to the right said: Bannister Tomb.

He passed a series of baseball diamonds and a bowling green. The citizens of Riverside, he thought, were well provided with recreational facilities. He drove down a road lined with elms and bordered with lily ponds. Then he saw the tomb.

It was perhaps two hundred yards from the road. It stood on a grassy hill, a square, massive structure. The two statues, man and woman, looked sad in the rain. Bits of the statues had already eroded with years of weather. The stone was chipped and worn in places and covered with the white stains of bird droppings. Both figures were leaning forward, as though leaning into the wind. The woman's long hair was blowing backward. The stone face of the man was half turned toward his wife. In the sense that a face made of stone could show love, the face of Frederick Bannister did.

And inside the thick walls of the tomb they lay in caskets, dead. At least, so everybody thought. But he, Peter Proud, knew better.

Maybe they had already been reincarnated into some future life. He wondered whether they would meet again, as strangers. And whether they would be attracted to each other again, as they had been in this life.

From his memory he focused the Tree Dream. He was about thirteen or fourteen. There was a girl with him about the same age. He had a knife and was cutting some initials into the bark of the tree. The bark was hard, and he worked hard, cutting the initials deep. But he could not see what they were.

The tree was about a hundred yards from the mausoleum. He rolled down the car window, stared out for better visibility, and was suddenly brought up short. In his dream he had seen only one tree. But now he saw a dozen scattered about, all about a hundred yards from the tomb. They were all big trees, old, gnarled. Their high branches, leafless, rattled in the rain. The bark on their trunks glistened with the sheen of it.

The trick was to find the right tree. It had to be one of them, but which one? He tried hard to think of the angle from which he had seen the mausoleum in the dream. But nothing registered. He simply did not know.

Worse, thinking of it now, he saw the odds pyramid against him. He, or X, had been only a boy when he had carved those initials. In that case, the incident would have taken place almost fifty years before. The chances were that the bark had grown completely over the initials, wiping them out completely. Still, there was no way of knowing, at least not from here. It depended on how deep they had been cut.

He stepped out of the car and raised his umbrella. The wind howled about him, slanting the hard rain under the umbrella and onto his body. In a few moments he was soaked. The umbrella, bellied by the wind, fought against him, twisting in his hand. It threatened to collapse at any moment. He decided it was useless and threw it away. It bounced and spun on the ground, gyrating crazily under the gusts.

He picked out one of the trees at random. Rain whipped his face and drenched him as he ran to it. He walked around the tree, staring at the bark.

He ran to the second tree. Nothing. And the third. Nothing.

This is crazy, he thought. He was insane to be out here, running around in this park like some grotesque and drenched zombie. If he had any sense, he would go back to the hotel.

The fourth tree. The fifth. The sixth. Nothing.

Then he realized he had made a mistake. *Stupid, stupid. Idiot, idiot.* He had been looking at the tree bark from the eye-level of an adult. He was six feet tall. But it had been a boy who had carved the initials. That meant the initials would be carved perhaps a foot lower down on the bark, it they were visible at all.

The rain was relentless. He had to get close to each tree so that he could see the bark at all. Then he saw them—the initials.

They were very faint, so faint that he had almost missed them. They were bare impressions in the bark. And, as he had calculated, about a foot lower than his actual line of vision. But he knew instantly that these were the ones he had carved almost half a century ago. He stood there in the rain, staring at them stupidly. It was an old tree. It must have been an old tree when he had carved the initials. And he must have cut them pretty deep. Otherwise, the new bark would have grown completely over them.

He reached out his hand and traced the outline of the initials with his forefinger. There were two sets.

J. C. — E. K.

As a boy, he would have carved his initials first. The name of the boy always came first. Steve loves Sally. Tom loves Elaine. Tony loves Rosa.

His initials then, had been J. C.

X equals J. C.

Chapter 18

When he got to the hotel, he peeled off his wet clothes, then soaked in a hot bath for an hour. After that, he asked room service to bring him two double Scotches.

He called the reception desk and was delighted to find that he could get a direct flight to California leaving from Bradley Field, between Hartford and Springfield. The drive there wouldn't take too long, and he could turn in the rented Pontiac at the airport.

The whiskey began to warm his stomach. He felt a pleasant glow. He had been uptight too long, and this was the first time he'd really felt relaxed. He drank the second double, thinking, *this* is where I began— Riverside, Massachusetts. No, that's wrong. I started from a lot of places, way way back to the beginning of time, probably. Or when Man, with a capital M, first began. Maybe in my first reincarnation I was some kind of Neanderthal—dodging mastodons, throwing spears at wild pigs. Dragging my woman by her hair to my dark and stinking cave, beating her with a club if she didn't behave. Making noises instead of words.

Many lives. I have lived many lives. So has everybody else.

Say that again, and see how foolish it sounds. Nobody, but nobody, will ever believe me.

He felt very good now. J.C., he thought. I wonder what that stands for? The initials seemed familiar. J. C. Penney, the chain of department stores. J.C. . . . J.C. . . . Could be anything—John Carroll, Jacob Cohen, Jackson Coolidge, even Jesus Christ. He laughed.

Suddenly he remembered. He had never called Bentley. Old Hall ought to know what had happened here. He dialed the parapsychologist's private number.

"Hall. Pete Proud."

"Yes?"

"I found it. The town."

"You're sure?"

"I'm positive. A place called Riverside, Massachusetts. X lived here. George Washington slept here . . ."

There was a silence. Then:

"Pete. You sound as though you've been . . ."

"Drinking? I have. I'll admit I've had a few. But I know what I'm saying, Hall. I'm sober enough for that. I used to live here. Right here . . ."

Again, silence. Then he heard Bentley breathe into the phone:

"If this is really true . . ."

"I *told* you it's true. I'm flying home in the morning. Tell you all about it when I see you."

"What flight are you taking?"

"The morning flight from Bradley Field."

"What time does it get in?"

"Twelve o'clock noon."

"I'll meet you at the airport," said Bentley. His voice shook a little as he said goodbye.

The voice coming over the PA system was nasal.

"This is your captain speaking. We are approaching an area of moderate turbulence. Please fasten your seat belts."

Peter buckled his seat belt and stared out of the window. They were somewhere over the Rockies. The plane trip seemed interminable. He remembered somewhere that it was an hour longer flying west to Los Angeles than east to New York. Something about the winds.

He'd have to figure out some way to get back to Riverside soon. This was the first week in April, and the spring quarter at UCLA didn't end until the tenth of June. He knew he couldn't wait that long. He had to start digging again, like an archeologist looking for artifacts that might clue him in to some lost civilization.

He leaned back and closed his eyes. He thought of what had happened to him in the last few days. Who would ever believe him? Hall Bentley. The people who took reincarnation on faith. But nobody else. He had a message to the world—nobody dies forever. But nobody would believe it.

The stewardess came down the aisle to see that they were buckled in. She had that clinically clean, sterile look that all airline stewardesses seem to have. He had the feeling that she had been delivered to the airplane in one of those refrigerated trucks and then unloaded, wrapped entirely in moisture-free cellophane to preserve her freshness. Her uniform clung to her as tightly as a bandage, as though her body had been melted down in some furnace, poured into this mold of cloth, annealed, and then allowed to cool.

He wondered about *her* reincarnation. Had this magnificent body once belonged to an ugly old hag? A witch? In her previous life, had she been someone repulsive? A cripple perhaps? Whatever she had been, she had been blessed by a benevolent karma. But her young body would someday age, wither, and die. He hoped she would do as well in her next life.

He had caught a whiff of her perfume as she walked by. It reminded him of Nora. He missed her. He'd call her when he got in; that would be one of the first things he'd do. He wondered what she would say when he told her. But he didn't really wonder. He had a pretty good idea . . .

The big jet began to rear and pitch. It seemed to rise several feet and then plummet with a sickening drop. Some angry monster had seized both wings and was shaking the plane as a child would shake a toy. He could feel the seat belt bite into his stomach. The captain had said the turbulence would be moderate. It was a lying, mealy-mouthed word.

Somewhere in the galley, objects clattered to the floor. Dishes perhaps, glasses, bottles. It seemed to him that every seam in the curved wall of the cabin was straining and ready to rip apart, every rivet in the aluminum skin outside crying to be free. It was easy to imagine the entire tail assembly breaking up. That somewhere, some fatal area of tired metal would give way, and they would plummet straight down.

He had never really been a hundred percent comfortable in an airplane. His imagination, he supposed, was too vivid. He thought of all those nuts and bolts and screws and wires and generators, all those gallons of highly combustible fuel yearning for just one stray little spark. Not to mention lightning bolts, and bombs in the luggage compartment, and of course hijackers.

But this time he felt totally relaxed, absolutely without fear. It was remarkable how calm he was.

He watched the other passengers. All conversation had stopped. Some gripped the arms of their seats and stared out through the window apprehensively. Others sat stiffly, their eyes closed, moaning softly as the great plane dipped and rose.

Just ahead of him, a woman seized a paper bag from the seat pocket in front of her and retched into it. Across the aisle, another woman sat next to her husband, her face the color of chalk. He could see her lips moving. Her eyes were closed and she squeezed her husband's hand, sitting rigid in terror, as though waiting for some painful injection from a long, sharp needle.

He wanted to lean over and tell her that she had nothing to fear. The plane, of course, would get through. It almost always did. But in case anything happened, her death wouldn't be the end. Just the prelude to another life. She would be given another ticket. He imagined her reaction if he told her that. She would think he was crazy.

Then, as quickly as it had come, it was gone. They were flying levelly again over the desert. After a while, they were over the city, and the jet began to circle lazily before its final approach.

Now, through the layer of smog, Peter could see the gas stations and the blinking neon lights, the tiny blue and green swimming pools, rectangular and round and kidney-shaped, the arid hills and canyons climbing in craggy patterns like the ribs of a starved lion, and the hundreds upon hundreds of houses, pastel pink and yellow and blue and beige, sprawled through the valley, crowding each other like vivid toadstools.

He could see the freeways with the sun glinting off the tops of the moving cars. He could not see the drivers, but he thought of them now as old souls in new bodies. Now they drove Chevrolets or Pontiacs or Fords or Cadillacs, whooshing along at sixty or seventy miles an hour, on an engineered highway in this so-called Age of Aquarius, in the last part of the twentieth century. But at some time past, in their previous lives, they might have been Roman centurions, driving chariots; or early Christians riding asses; or disciples of Mohammed, riding camels on their pilgrimages to Mecca, across vast deserts. Knowing what he did, it was easy for his imagination to carry him away.

But somewhere on those freeways, sometime today, a couple of those cars would crash and end up as flaming hulks. The bodies of their drivers would lie mangled or burned. But not the old souls. They would simply leave, to find new homes. They would join all the thousands and millions of other old souls, all restlessly flying around to the mountains and far beyond, to infinity itself, all seeking new habitats in which to rest and produce a new life.

Old souls never die. Nor do they fade away. They merely go on, forever and ever . . .

The plane landed with a bump, bounced once, hit down hard again, and started to roll. The engines reversed with a banshee roar, and the canned music came on.

A few minutes later he came off the ramp to find Hall Bentley waiting for him. The parapsychologist would not even let Peter take the time to pick up his luggage. "You can get it later," he said. There was a strange light in the gray eyes. He led Peter to the airport cocktail lounge.

"All right," he said. "Let's have it."

Chapter 19

When Peter had finished, Bentley was silent for a while. Then:

"Pete, I don't know what to say to this. I guess I'm still trying to believe it."

"So am I."

"As of now, you're unique. You're the living proof of reincarnation. You know it and I know it. But nobody else does—yet. I know this sounds facetious. But the important thing is for you to stay alive until you can really prove it. You ought to be kept in an isolation ward to protect you from sickness. You should be forbidden to drive. Right now, your life is precious. Right now, you're a bomb with a million times the explosive power of any nuclear bomb we've ever invented." His voice shook. "God, it boggles the imagination. One man, and you've got the power to shake the world, reshape the thinking of the whole human race. But surely you've thought of all this."

"Not on those terms."

"Well, think about it."

"It scares hell out of me. My God, what'll I do?"

"What you set out to do. Go back to Riverside. Find out who you were. Get the rest of the proof. When we think we have enough, in terms of real documentation, then we'll release it. And let everybody take it from there."

"I'm trying to think of what'll happen. When people find out . . ."

"It's hard to say. We can only try to project. First, I can imagine a kind of worldwide shock, traumatic. For a while, suspended belief, then exhilaration. After that, a mass release from fear. There won't be that emptiness anymore, the hopelessness we all feel, knowing that no matter what we do in this life, it all ends up in dust and eternity. Death, or the fear of it, haunts us all from the day we are born. But when people realize they're going to get another chance—Christ, who knows what will happen to them then?"

Bentley went on, speculating. Everyone would find new meaning in life, not just in his own, but in the lives of those close to him, those he loved. People who suffered in life would not be afraid to die. They might even welcome it, knowing they might have it easier in the next life. There could even be a wave of suicides among these people, hopeless cripples, or people with terminal diseases, for precisely that reason. If a loved one died, it would ease the pain of bereavement. It might even be that man's greedy drive for power and wealth would lose its attraction when he accepted the premise that the worldly goods he acquired in one lifetime wouldn't do him any good in the next. If he accepted the karmic interpretation of reincarnation, the only carry-overs would be either the good that he had done or the evil he had created. He would be rewarded or punished in the next life according to how he had lived this one. The dog-eat-dog philosophy might very well disappear from the face of the world. People would try to pile up credits for the next life. They would turn away from hate and show compassion for each other, maybe even love. Bentley continued, "But all that's in the future. Let's talk about now."

"Who's going to believe it?"

"A good question. We're going to need proof, of course. As of now, we have those tapes in the safe deposit boxes, proving the detail of your hallucinations before you ever knew about Riverside. We have reliable witnesses to the same thing: Staub, Sam Goodman, and even your girl-friend . . . what's her name?"

"Haines. Nora Haines."

"Yes. No problem at this end. The important thing is to prove your former identity at the other end. Hopefully, to meet people who knew you in your previous incarnation."

"Like Marcia."

"Like Marcia. If you can find her. If she's still alive. And others. Prove that you knew things about them that nobody else would possibly know, except in some previous life. It might be wise to tape an account of what's happened so far and put it in a safety deposit box, too, in still another bank."

"Even with all that, will people really believe it?"

"No. Not everybody. No matter what proof you show them, and I mean documented proof, hard-nosed proof, there are always going to be skeptics who are going to call this a fraud, a hoax, a gigantic put-on. The world is full of people with a kind of deep-seated masochistic pessimism. They have an unconscious hatred and fear of life and a deep wish for its permanent cessation. And then, of course, there'll be the others . . ."

"What others?"

"Those with preconceived notions and fat positions to protect. The Church. You're going to establish a whole new religion, Pete, and the Church is not about to see that happen without a battle. And reincarnation *will* create a new religion; there's no doubt about that. Then, there'll be certain scientists who think that if you can't draw it on paper, or see it in a test tube, or prove it by an equation, it can't be so. And, of course, some psychiatrists and psychologists who've laughed at the new Psi sciences. Frankly, I'm looking forward to shaking some of *them* up. Sure, there'll be some disbelievers. But they're going to be swamped by millions of true believers. Billions.

"But never mind all of this for now. I could spend days like this— making all these dreamy projections. When do you plan to go back to Riverside?"

"I don't know. Soon."

"Why so vague?"

"I've got to make some arrangements. Talk to the head of my department at the University. I've still got to teach the spring quarter."

"My God," said Bentley impatiently. "All this, and you're worrying about a few classes?"

"It's still a commitment."

"If I were you, I'd get back to Riverside tomorrow. *That's* where the commitment is. But all right. If they've been trying to prove reincarnation for thousands of years, I don't suppose a few weeks more will make much difference." He paused. "Any idea how you're going to proceed when you go back?"

He discussed the House Dream and the Tennis Dream with Bentley, and the possibilities behind them. Bentley nodded.

"It might work out."

"On the other hand, I might draw a blank."

"No," said Bentley. "I think you'll find what you're looking for."

"What makes you so sure?"

"Because I think it was meant to be. Ordained."

Peter stared at Bentley. "What does *that* mean?"

"I'm not quite sure. I'm not a religious man, Pete, but everything that's happened to you seems—well, as you yourself said—*planned*. As though you've been tapped on the shoulder by some divine finger. Chosen to deliver this particular message. As a—well, as a prophet."

Prophet. He thought of Verna Bird. A chill crept up his back.

"Hall, suppose, just for argument, that what you say is true. There are billions of people in the world. Why one Peter Proud? Why *me*?"

"I don't know. There's no answer to that question. Maybe there was a big raffle and your number came up. I'll answer your question with a question. Of all the people in the world almost two thousand years ago, why a simple carpenter from Nazareth?"

They said nothing for a long time. Travelers came in and out of the cocktail lounge. Muted chatter rose and fell. There was an occasional laugh. The voice over the airport public address system intruded insistently. Flights were arriving, flights were leaving, last call for Flight So-and-So, and would Mister So-and-So please report to the information desk.

Finally, Bentley stirred and started to rise.

"I guess we'd better pick up your luggage. Then I'll get the car and . . ."

"Hall, wait a minute. Sit down." Bentley sat down, staring at Peter. "There's something we haven't discussed."

"Yes?"

"If all this really does come about—what becomes of me? What happens to my personal life?"

"I'm sure you can guess."

"I can. But I'd like to hear what you think."

Bentley smiled weakly. "I was afraid we'd get into this sooner or later."

"Let's get into it now."

"All right. I suppose we can make some reasonable speculations. First, as soon as all this is announced, you'd become an instant world celebrity, a controversial figure. You'd put Bridey Murphy in the deep shade. To some, you'd become the Man of the Century, or any other century. The man who brought this world a new revelation, who solved the mystery of death. To some, you'd be kind of a new Messiah.

"Does all this sound pretty high-flown? Maybe it does. But it's impossible to exaggerate it. In a sense, to some you'd be the founder, or at least the prophet, of a whole new religion. To others, you'd be a liar and a fraud. To yet others, some kind of Satan, bent on destroying the whole idea of Heaven after death, and other concepts the Christian church holds dear. You'd be both one hell of a hero and one hell of a villain."

Peter felt faint. His head whirled.

"Hall, I still can't absorb all of this. All I have is a gut reaction."

"Yes?"

"I'm afraid of it. I don't want any part of it. My instinct is to pass. Forget it. Not get involved at all."

"You don't have any choice."

"What do you mean?"

"You don't belong to yourself anymore," said Bentley. "You're in too deep, and you've gone too far. You're committed. I appreciate how you feel, Pete. But look, your personal life isn't important anymore. It's what you know, and what you have to tell."

They paid their bill and walked out of the lounge. As they did, Hall Bentley looked at Peter. There was a small smile around his mouth, but his eyes were serious.

"Remind me to drive carefully. *Very* carefully."

As they drove away from the airport the traffic was bumper to bumper. It reminded Peter of the last time he had been here. Then, hundreds of kids with painted faces and wearing saffron robes had tied up the traffic. They were beating drums, clanking finger cymbals and chanting the Hare Krishna. They had come to meet their guru, the Supreme Person, Lord of all Lords, The Cause of all Causes, the Ultimate Truth of all Truths, the Perfection of all Endeavors of Perfection.

He knew they were part of the whole growing occult scene. Most of them had already tried all the psychedelic drugs. They knew all about mind expansion, and they were interested in anything that promised a fourth dimension. It wasn't much of a step to go from acid travel to soul travel. And it wasn't only the kids who were part of this renaissance of mysticism. It was the older people, too. Everybody wanted answers. People everywhere, he reflected, were suffering from the same frustrations. We could fly men to the moon, but it took years to get our men out of Vietnam. We knew how to blow all mankind to hell, but we couldn't get rid of the rats in our slums. We could climb the highest mountain, but we couldn't keep muggers away from a few square miles of city parks and streets.

This didn't make sense to the cultists. To them, what made sense were ideas or movements based on faith or emotion. Brother, we've all been locked in the jail of technology. We've had our minds computerized. And what has it done for us? Nothing. It's turned out to be a desert. Now, we're looking for answers way out there, because there's nowhere else to look.

At the time, the Krishna kids had amused him by the way they had honored their prophet. The Great Guru, the Supreme Person, the Ultimate Truth of all Truths.

Then he shivered a little. My God, that could be me.

Chapter 20

When Bentley dropped him at the Summit Plaza, he still felt a little lightheaded.

When he walked into the lobby Edna was at the switchboard. He found the familiar sight reassuring. He'd been doing too much heavy thinking, been involved for too long in the unreal, the bizarre. He needed to divorce himself from all this for a while. He had a hunger now for the ordinary, the inconsequential.

"Well! Welcome back!"

"Thank you, Edna. Glad to be home."

"We've missed you around here. Did you have a nice trip?"

"Very nice."

"Lots of phone calls for you."

She reached into his message box and gave him a sheaf of pink slips.

He saw that her astrology book was open in front of her.

"What's my horoscope for today, love?"

"Let's see. You're a Libra, right?"

"Right."

"I love Libras," she said. "Libras are usually very interesting people. Very sensitive. You should know some of the *other* signs we get around here." She ruffled the pages of the book and found the reference she wanted. She took a moment to read, and then: "Oh, my. You're going to find this interesting."

"I can't wait," he said.

"Mars and Neptune are approaching your fifth solar house. Neptune is in the third house, and squaring Mars. This is a good time to study your various financial interests and enlarge your sphere of action. Analyze current insurance policies, contracts, and other legal documents to be sure they are to your satisfaction. Follow up any opportunity there may be to do public speaking . . ."

"Nothing very earth-shaking about that."

"Oh," she said, "I haven't finished. Here's the interesting part. Your life is about to change radically. Soon you will meet a new lover. The experience will be deep and profound. Look for a whole new future."

"Well, Edna," he said, "that's more like it."

He grinned at her and walked toward the elevator. His horoscope for today wasn't bad, except it was screwed up in one detail: He was looking for an *old* lover.

The apartment had a faint musty smell. He opened the curtains and threw the windows wide open. Down below, he could see three or four girls lolling in beach chairs and mats on the pool patio. Now, he thought, they're tanned and languid young naiads baking themselves in the California sun. But who were they once? Handmaidens to Cleopatra? Camp followers to the armies of Napoleon? Ladies-in-waiting to Queen Elizabeth? Queens or slave girls?

He swore softly at himself. It was getting so that he couldn't look at people without speculating on their past lives. He'd have to cut it out.

He dialed Nora's number, but there was no answer. He felt very tired. The plane trip, the talk with Bentley at the airport, everything.

He stretched out on the couch without unpacking. He dozed awhile, then fell asleep. He had two dreams, the House Dream and the Tennis Dream. When he awoke it was getting dark. He went to the telephone and dialed Nora's number again. This time she was in.

"Nora, Pete."

"Oh. You're back." She sounded cool, distant. "I hope you had a nice trip."

"Listen, I found it. The town . . ."

"Congratulations."

"It's a place called Riverside. In Massachusetts."

"How nice."

He was silent for a moment. "You *still* don't believe me."

"Why, of course I do, darling."

"Nora, let's have dinner tonight."

"I'm sorry. I have a date."

"Tomorrow night, then?"

"No," she said. "I can't make it then, either."

"I see. You're pretty busy."

"Very busy."

"We'll make it some other time, then. I'll phone you."

"You do that, Pete. Some other time."

He hung up and thought, that's that. Curiously, he felt no sense of loss. He grinned.

Soon I'm going to meet a new lover. I've got it straight from Edna.

The next day he saw the head of his department and got permission to stay for only the first four weeks in the quarter and have his teaching assistant handle the rest of the course. He gave as his excuse some urgent research he had to do on some of the tribes in the East. The department head was unhappy about the request but finally agreed, reluctantly, provided he was back in time for the exam period.

The time dragged. He taught his classes, got through his conferences, worked on his book. It was hard for him to maintain any level of interest. Los Angeles was where his body was, but the rest of him, the most important part of him, was three thousand miles away. At times he was on the verge of quitting ahead of time and taking the next plane for Riverside, even if it meant placing his whole career in jeopardy. But he resisted the urge.

Meanwhile, the hallucinations continued. The Lake Dream was, as always, the most frequent and the most intense. But five of the dreams were missing, seemingly banished to some permanent limbo. The City Dream, the Tower Dream, the Tree Dream, the Cotton Mather Dream, and, curiously enough, the Prison Dream.

He talked to Hall Bentley about it. And the parapsychologist said, "I'm not sure what's happening. It seems to be some kind of expiation process—release through some kind of reenactment or contact, no matter how vague. You've seen the streets of the city. You've been at the site of the tower. You saw the Puritan effigy. Once you come in real contact with the subject of your dream, the hallucination itself disappears."

"But how do you account for the Prison Dream? That's gone too."

"Go over it again for me."

"I'm in a prison, and I'm counting money."

"Maybe you saw it and didn't recognize it."

"No. I never even saw any prison in Riverside."

"Funny about that. It's the only hallucination that isn't realistic. I mean, you don't normally count money in a jail cell."

Something else puzzled him. He had seen the lake. But the Lake Dream still continued.

Suddenly he remembered Ed Donan's dissertation subject. *The Relations*. The Iroquois divinity-of-dreams, their therapeutic strategy of catharsis. You have a dream; you live it again, act it out. The Seneca dreams he buys a dog in Quebec, the next day he travels to Quebec to buy a dog. The Huron dreams he is tortured by an enemy, the next day he gets his friends to torture him. If you fail to do this, the sickness comes.

Ondinnonk.

Chapter 21

He flew to Bradley Field, rented a car, and then drove to Riverside. It was early evening when he checked in at the same hotel as before.

He felt the key to X's identity lay in the House Dream. His best chance of finding out who he had been was in finding that house. If he could locate the house, he could find out the name of the person who had lived there. *If.*

He remembered it clearly, every detail of it. He knew he would recognize it immediately if he saw it. It was a two-family house, the upper part brown shingles, the lower white stucco, with a big three-arched front porch. It was the third house from the corner.

He would start looking for it the next day. He decided to go to bed right after dinner so that he could get an early start in the morning. There were hundreds of streets in Riverside, and it might be weeks—even months—before he found it. But he had to find it—it was his only chance.

The next morning, he bought a detailed street map of the city at a bookshop. Then, with a red pencil, he systematically marked off specific sections. His idea was to cover a section a day by driving up one street and down another till he had covered the entire area.

Suddenly he had a chilling thought. Suppose they had torn it down long ago? They'd torn down half the town already. Maybe there wasn't any house left. Maybe they had put some goddamn gas station or apartment house in its place. . . .

He did have a few things going for him. In the Window Dream, he had been able to see the big sign on the roof of the Puritan Bank before the blizzard obscured it. There had been no river in between. This indicated that the house had been located somewhere in Riverside proper, not across the river in West Riverside. From the distance and the perspective in which he had viewed the sign, he was quite sure the house wasn't located in the central or business part of the city but in one of the many residential areas. And, finally, he was under the impression, from the House Dream, that the location was on a side street, not a main avenue with traffic lights and stores.

Not much. But it was a beginning.

He began to cruise the streets. He had to drive slowly, for fear he would miss the house. *If* it still existed. Up one street, and down another.

After a few days it became a nightmare. His eyes ached from watching not only both sides of each street, but the traffic ahead. He put innumerable miles on the car. And one by one he crossed off the sections he had covered. *The North End. The Eastwood Section. Hungry Hill. Riverside Heights. The Pilgrim Square Section. Winchester. Manor Park. The South End.*

Some of the streets were solid with apartments, and he drove through them swiftly. Others were obviously new developments. Still others were hodgepodges, a mixture of the old and the new. He saw a number of two-family houses, but none that remotely resembled the house of his dream.

The Belmont Boulevard Section. The Oak Avenue Neighborhood. The Central Avenue Area.

By the third day, he realized the futility of what he was doing. More and more he was convinced that the house no longer existed. But grimly he hung on. He had to remind himself that this was his last chance. He had no other options, no way to backcheck any of the other dreams.

On the sixth day, he stopped the car on a street in the Armory section. He sat there for a long time, resting his head on the wheel. He was bone weary, and in the middle of a black depression. He told himself that perhaps he was better off not finding that damned house. After all, he had been messing around in something he didn't really understand. And even if he found the house and, through it, his identity, there was no guarantee he would like it. It could be hideous. It was possible that if he took the cover off this particular Pandora's box, he might start screaming.

He made up his mind then to go back to his hotel and take the first plane to Los Angeles. *Goodbye, J.C., whoever you were.* Enough was enough. Hall Bentley would be disappointed, of course. Well, that was just too damned bad. As for himself, he'd just have to stay curious for the rest of his life. Now he felt relieved. He wouldn't have to play the horrendous role Bentley had pictured. Let someone else bring messages to the world. It occurred to him now, that deep in his unconscious he had really *wanted* to fail all along.

He felt better now. He started the car.

He was on the opposite side of town from where his hotel was located. Checking his map, he found a shorter way to get back. Instead of going down Highland Avenue, with all its lights and traffic, he could cut through Albemarle Street and hit a main artery called Bridge Avenue. This would lead him directly to the downtown section and his hotel.

At the junction of Albemarle and Bridge he found himself in a Negro section. A solid ghetto of blacks. He had gone only a few blocks down Bridge when, suddenly, he stopped the car. His skin began to prickle. He knew he had been there before. He recognized the red brick school building down the street. The big gas station on the corner. And opposite the gas station, a small shopping area that looked familiar. Very familiar. There was a supermarket there now, and a pizza parlor, and a bar called Hi-de-Ho. But he seemed to remember, through the gauze of some veil, a candy store, a shoe repair shop, a bakery.

The signpost said: Almont Street.

This was my old neighborhood. This was where I lived. This was my street.

He had no doubt about it. He simply knew it. It had never occurred to him to look in this area. He had overlooked the fact that white neighborhoods often changed radically during the years, some of them becoming all black. And he knew that old houses in slum neighborhoods often were the last to be torn down. They simply deteriorated until even the ghetto tenants abandoned them.

Dimly he heard the raucous blast of automobile horns behind him. Angry voices shouted at him. He became aware that he had stopped the car in the middle of the street. He drove to the next street, went back, and like a homing pigeon headed down Almont.

Then he saw it. The third house from the corner, on the left-hand side.

No. 28 Almont Street. It had aged tremendously. The white stucco was stained and cracked. Someone had painted the rotting shingles white, but the paint was peeling, exposing the brown underneath. The wooden frames around the windows were warped and weather-beaten. The neat lawn he remembered was now a tangle of weeds and crabgrass. The whole place was shabby, neglected.

He stopped the car at the curb directly in front of the house and sat there, staring at the house. He hardly noticed the three black men sitting on the upper step of the rotting porch. They were watching him intently, their faces hostile. Finally one of them got to his feet and walked slowly down the broken sidewalk toward him. He was a huge, hulking black with great, hairy arms. He stuck his head through the open window of the car.

"Whut you want, man?"

"Nothing."

"Whut you stopping here for, then?"

"Just looking."

"Lookin' for *whut*?"

"That your house?"

"Yeah."

"How long have you been living there?"

"Man, who are you? What in shit are you doin' here? You the fuzz or somethin'?"

"No." The black man was glaring at him. He felt the man was on the verge of opening the door and yanking him out. The other two men sauntered forward now. They stared at him coldly. Other blacks, passing by, stopped to watch what was going on. He was aware of their hostility too. "All I want to know is . . ."

"You don't want to know nothin', whitey. An' I ain't about to tell you nothin'. This ain't no place for honkies to be. Come around here askin' questions. Don't put me on you're not the fuzz. Man, I can smell chicken shit like you a mile away. Now, get your ass out of here if you don't want to get hurt . . ."

Someone was pounding on the back window. He heard the clank of a rock as it hit the car. The crowd began to press in on the car. He was a stranger on their turf, and a white one, too.

He started the car and drove off. He knew he was close now.

He found the real estate office three blocks farther down, on Bridge Avenue.

It was a one-woman office. She was about sixty, fat and wheezy.

"No. 28 Almont? Yes, I know the house. We've bought and sold it once or twice over the years. We've done the same with almost every house along Almont, Bryant, and Baldwin. Happens when you've been in business in the neighborhood for—well, a good forty years." She shrugged. "Of course the neighborhood's changed. You can see that for yourself. We don't do much in that area anymore . . ."

"I wonder if you could give me some information about the place?"

She stared at him incredulously. "You're interested in *buying* it?"

"No. It's something else. Would you happen to know who lived there back in the thirties, or maybe in the early forties?"

"Not offhand. That's going pretty far back."

"I know."

"We do have a sales record of a lot of houses in the neighborhood, going way back. Owners, mortgage arrangements, and so on. If we had any transaction on 28 Almont, and I think we did, it'd be there." She peered at him suspiciously. "You the FBI? A private investigator or something?"

"No. It's just a personal matter. I'm trying to find out who lived there about that time. If you'd look it up, I'd appreciate it."

She hesitated a moment. Then: "It might take a minute or two."

"I'll wait."

She went into a room in the rear of the office area. He heard a file drawer opening. He sat down and waited. It was close in the office, and very warm. He felt the perspiration ooze through the shirt under his jacket. He sat there staring through the window at the traffic moving along Bridge Avenue. It seemed to him that he waited in that red leatherette chair forever. Actually, it was only two minutes.

She came out carrying a file. She seated herself at the desk, shuffled through the file, and took out a paper. Her eyesight was poor, and she brought the paper close to her eyes.

"Let's see. 1952 to 1955. An Italian family lived there then. Rovelli. All this was before that neighborhood went black, of course. And before them, a family named O'Malley. 1948 to 1952. Right. We bought it for the O'Malleys. I remember it now. Bought it from a man named Chapin."

"Chapin?"

"Ralph R. Chapin, it says here. Seller. Owner of record. Occupied the house for a long time. Lived in it all through the thirties, early forties. That's the area you're interested in, I guess."

"Would you happen to know anything else about the Chapin family?" She stared at him. "Such as what?"

"I don't know. Who the other members of the family were . . ."

"I'm sorry. I wouldn't have the faintest idea . . ." Then, suddenly, she snapped her fingers. Her eyes widened. "Wait a minute. Wait a minute. I *do* remember now. There was a son . . ."

"You remember his name?"

"Jeff. That was it. Jeff Chapin. It's short for Jeffrey, I guess."

"Jeffrey Chapin."

"Yes. Only reason I'd remember it in a million years was because he came from this neighborhood and got his name in all the papers. But if he's the one you're looking for, you'd better forget it."

"Yes?"

"He's long dead. He was drowned swimming in Lake Nipmuck."

After a long time Peter heard himself say, "Do you remember the year this happened?"

"No. I couldn't even come close. But as I said, it was in all the papers."

The *Riverside Daily News* was housed in a modernistic building, all glass and stainless steel. It was only five blocks from his hotel.

The sign in the lobby read: Morgue and Library. Third Floor.

The morgue was a large windowless room. Shelf after shelf carried bound volumes of the *News*, labeled by the volume, month, and year. The librarian was an elderly man, thin and anemic looking. He sat at an old beat-up desk, its edges scarred with the burns of a thousand cigarette butts. The desk was covered with newspapers and clippings. Both the man and the desk fit the place.

"What did you say the name was?"

"Jeff Chapin. Jeffrey, probably."

"And the date?"

"I don't know."

"The year?"

"I don't know that, either. He died sometime back in the forties. Drowned at Lake Nipmuck. I know the story was carried in the *News* at that time."

"You said the forties?"

"That's right, the forties." He paused. "Is there any way you might be able to find it?"

"Well, sir, you don't give me much to go on. We might and we might not. Depends whether he was well known around town. You know, a prominent person. A lot depends on the space and coverage he got. If the deceased was a nobody, I'd say you'd have no chance. You *could* go through ten years of daily newspapers, but you wouldn't like that very much. On the other hand, if the deceased had some kind of public name, we might have him in our obit file."

"Obit file?"

"Obituary file. We keep a list of people who died, year by year. Issue and date. Just in case any of our reporters need it for research or back reference. If you've got a little time, I could check that out."

"I'd appreciate that."

The librarian turned to a shelf on the wall just behind the desk. It was lined with a series of battered reference notebooks. He picked out one marked "1940–1950." The pages were tabbed, year by year. He opened the notebook. Peter could see the names of the deceased listed in alphabetical order.

"Jeffrey Chapin. Jeffrey Chapin . . ."

The librarian ran his finger quickly down the page. Nothing for 1940. He turned the page again. Nothing for 1941. Nor 1942. 1943. 1944. 1945 . . .

1946.

"Got it," said the librarian suddenly. "You're in luck."

"Yes?"

The librarian pointed to the notation. "See? Jeffrey Chapin. Issue, September 27, 1946. Page one."

"How do I get the issue?"

"Follow me."

He led Peter through row after row of stacks, each crammed with the tall clothbound volumes. Finally he stopped.

"Here we are. September 1946."

He took down the volume. It was heavy. He wheezed as he carried it to a battered table around which were a number of chairs. He dropped the volume onto the table.

"You'll find his obit in here. Put it back when you're through with it. Okay?"

Peter nodded. The librarian shuffled off. It was dark in the room. He turned on the desk lamp on the table.

He sat there staring at the big clothbound volume crammed with newspapers. For a while he could not bring himself to open it. He was afraid to open it. Finally, with trembling fingers, he opened the cover and turned to the issue of September 27. Page one.

The paper was yellowed with time, the print a little faded. Then he saw the story. And there was a picture to go with it.

BODY OF JEFFREY CHAPIN RECOVERED FROM LAKE NIPMUCK
Wife Reported Accidental Drowning on Night of September 25.

The body of Jeffrey (Jeff) Chapin, 32, was recovered from Lake Nipmuck early this morning. Police had been dragging the lake for two days.

According to Marcia Chapin, wife of the deceased, her husband had set out to swim the lake at night. She admitted that he had been intoxicated, and she tried to dissuade him but without success. Later, she attempted to follow him in a boat but was unable to find him. Alarmed, she called the police.

According to Mrs. Chapin, he was a very strong swimmer and had swum the lake many times. It is probable that Mr. Chapin caught a cramp in the chilly water. Late this afternoon, the Medical Examiner issued a verdict of "accidental drowning."

Mr. Chapin was a lifelong resident of Riverside. He was the son of R. C. Chapin and for most of his earlier life lived in the Bridge Avenue district, at 28 Almont Street. He was proud of the fact that he was one-sixteenth Pequot Indian. In his earlier years, he was an outstanding high school athlete, especially in tennis, and later he qualified for a number of tennis tournaments in New England and the eastern seaboard. For some years he was tennis professional at the Green Hills Country Club. He served in the Marines, suffered a hip wound in the Pacific, and was honorably discharged in 1943. Later he married Marcia Curtis, daughter of Mr. and Mrs. William E. Curtis of Mulberry Street. Mr. Curtis is the president of the Puritan Bank and Trust. Subsequently, Mr. Chapin took a position at the bank as a teller, and at the time of his death was assistant cashier.

Mr. Chapin leaves one child, a three-month-old infant daughter, Ann. Funeral services will be held Tuesday morning at the First Church of Christ, and burial will be at the Hillside Cemetery.

Peter studied the photograph. The face smiled up at him. It was faded and a little blurred, but even so it seemed alive.

It was a handsome face, virile, rugged. Dark eyes, black hair cut in the short haircut popular in the forties. The nose a little hawklike. The hint of high cheekbones. Good jaw. He wore a tennis sweater. But it was the half-smile playing around the rather thin mouth that fascinated Peter. There was something mocking about it. Amused. Even a little cruel. It seemed to be saying: *Once, I was you. And now, you are me.*

For a long time he studied the face of the man he had been. Then he took a nail file from his wallet and carefully cut out the article. He folded the clipping and stuffed it into his wallet. He felt a little guilty at this small vandalism. But then, he thought, they'll never miss it.

He closed the heavy volume and put it back on the shelf. He walked down the narrow alleys between the shelves until he emerged near the door. As he started to go out he heard the voice.

"One moment, sir."

He turned. Through a blur he saw the librarian sitting at the desk.

Peter hadn't even noticed him. The man looked a little annoyed. Of course—at the very least, he had expected some kind of thanks. The old man pointed to a register on his desk.

"You'll have to sign here."

"Sign?"

"Your name. All visitors who use the morgue have to sign in."

Peter went back to the desk. The librarian handed him a pen. He signed his name and started to walk out again.

"Hey, mister!" He turned. The old man was staring at him. "This some kind of joke or something?"

"What?"

"You better come back and sign again."

The name he had just signed was: *Jeffrey Chapin.*

He crossed it out and wrote "Peter Proud" over it. Then he mumbled his thanks to the librarian and went out.

Taking the elevator down, he walked through the busy lobby and onto the street. He got into the car. He checked his city map, and then headed up Main Street.

He knew exactly where he had to go.

PART THREE

I have been here before,
But when or how I cannot tell;
I know the grass beyond the door,
The sweet keen smell,
The sighing sound, the lights around the shore.
You have been mine before—
How long ago I may not know;
But just when at that swallow's soar
Your neck turned so,
Some veil did fall—I knew it all of yore.

DANTE GABRIEL ROSSETTI

Chapter 22

Hillside Cemetery was located about a mile beyond the city limits.

The approach to it was up a long hill. When he reached the crest, Peter could see the entire spread of the cemetery below him. It was big, much bigger than he had expected, and surrounded by a high stone fence. He could see the rows upon rows of headstones, the statues, the small marble tombs, the angels with outstretched arms and wings. Now they seemed like a silent white army, standing at attention on a lush green parade ground.

It seemed strange that his other body should be buried somewhere down there.

The sky had darkened, and now and then there was the ominous roll of thunder. Lean black clouds raced along under a backdrop of gray, bending low and running hard, like stealthy guerrillas. The wind had freshened; it whispered a wet word—rain. Peter looked at his wristwatch. It was a few minutes after six. Soon it would be getting dark. He had to hurry.

He drove to the main entrance. Two iron gates, now locked, blocked the entry road into the graveyard. The door to the cemetery office next to the gates was locked. He began to pound on the door. Nobody answered. The office was closed for the day.

He came around to the side and looked into the window. He could see, through the Venetian blinds, a couple of desks, and a big map of the cemetery on the wall. Somewhere inside, he knew, there would be some record of each grave, and who was lying in it.

For a moment he contemplated breaking the window and crawling in. But the traffic moving up and down this road caused him to think better of it. He went to the gates; they were barred from the inside. The rear half of the cemetery office protruded into the graveyard, and there was a back door there. Someone from the office must open the gates from the inside each morning.

A peal of thunder startled him. He stood there indecisively. He could come back tomorrow, of course. But he knew he could not wait. His grave was somewhere inside. He wanted to see it *now*.

He studied the wall. He could see that it was too high for him to climb over. He got into the car and drove it across the grass, parking it parallel to the wall. Then he got out and clambered up on top of the hood. It was easy for him now to grasp the top ot the wall, swing over, and drop to the other side.

He stopped and stared at the gravestones ahead of him. There seemed to be a thousand of them stretching over the horizon to infinity. Square stones, rectangular stones, some massive, some slender, and some small, for little children.

He began to walk past one row of stones and then another, looking for his grave. He had absolutely no idea where it was. All he could do was keep looking through this maze, looking at every stone in this damned graveyard till he found it.

The thunder continued to rumble, but the rain held off. The wind whipped up higher, spinning dead leaves in front of him in little vortices. He walked up one row, and down another. Then up the next row, and down the one after that. . . .

Where the hell was it, anyway?

He became angry, frustrated. He must have looked at hundreds of gravestones. His eyes ached from peering at the inscriptions as he walked by. He had to check every one; otherwise, he might miss it. After a while he estimated that he had covered perhaps a quarter of the cemetery.

He thought he felt a drop of rain. It was getting late now. The lead-gray sky and the oncoming night conspired to wreathe the graveyard in an eerie twilight. It was getting very hard to see. In fifteen minutes it would be too dark . . .

Then he saw it. It was a square stone. Massive. Made of polished granite. The inscription was simple:

Jeffrey Chapin
Loving Husband and Father
1914–1946

He walked over and caressed the stone with his hand. He ran his fingers over the graven letters.

Jeffrey Chapin. Loving husband and father.

His head seemed to explode. He had to bite his tongue to keep from screaming. Nearby, he saw an open grave. It had been newly dug, prepared for the next day. The grave diggers had left their shovels sticking in the fresh mound of sand.

For a moment he had a crazy impulse. He wanted to grab one of the shovels and, like some ghoul, dig down deep, into his own grave. He wanted to reach the casket and open the cover.

And look at himself.

He did not know how long he had been standing there.

It was dark now. A raindrop hit him in the face, then another. His pores oozed sweat. He could barely make out some of the gravestones around him. He thought of all the rotting bodies below them. Bodies like his, whose souls had left long ago to find some other house. All these stones, he thought, suitably inscribed. They seemed such a waste. They marked nothing but the organic or chemical remains of the dear departed.

Reason came to him again. He was an idiot, standing around the cemetery like this in the darkness. He stumbled back to the narrow cemetery drive, walked to the gates, opened them, and got into the car. His next move now was very clear.

As he drove, he thought of himself and Jeffrey Chapin. Their karmic resemblance was remarkable. Bits and pieces of the puzzle became clear now. There was the matter of the strange and painful attacks he would sometimes get in his hip. He knew the answer to that now. And the Prison Dream. Of course it hadn't been a prison at all. It had been a teller's cage at the Puritan Bank. Now the cage was separated from the public area by a glass partition. But at one time it must have been protected by bars or some kind of iron grill. The fact that he dreamed he was counting money spoke for itself.

He knew now that, as Jeffrey Chapin, he had died on September 25, 1946. As Peter Proud, he had been born on October 10 of that same year. It had been a quick reincarnation. And, of course, there was the Baby Dream. In his previous incarnation he had been the father of a three-month-old baby daughter, Ann. He and his daughter would be about the same age now. Or, to be accurate, his daughter, if alive, would be three months older than he was.

He came down the long slope, and at the foot of it he saw a gas station. It was drizzling now. He got out and went into the telephone booth in the station parking lot. A Riverside directory hung from a chain. He fumbled through the pages, his fingers trembling. He turned to the names beginning with "C."

Then he found it, as he had known he would.

Chapin Ann—16 Vista Drive—341-2262
Chapin Marcia—16 Vista Drive—341-2262

Without thinking, he dropped a coin into the slot and dialed the number. A woman's voice answered, soft, melodious, a little blurred. "Hello?"

He did not answer. He couldn't. *Say it to yourself and see how foolish it sounds.* "My name is Peter Proud. I'm the reincarnation of your dead husband. The man you murdered at Lake Nipmuck . . ."

"Hello? Hello? Who is this?"

He hung up.

Vista Drive. Lush and quiet and exclusive. Streets lined with maples and elms. Post lanterns at the gates, huge manicured lawns fronting columned Georgian homes, Colonials, and here and there a contemporary. Streets named not as streets but rather Lanes, Drives, Ways, and Roads. Masses of hollyhock and forsythia in the corners of the gardens, and spruces to green the winter. Classic street lamps with fat globes throwing off yellow light. Each house with an attached garage and big patio. A place of garden clubs, black maids, low speed limits. Big watchdogs and watchful police.

It had stopped drizzling when he arrived. No. 16 Vista Drive was a Colonial, and typical—white with yellow shutters, brick and stone and wood in the upper stories, post lantern in the driveway, a sweep of manicured lawn.

He parked the car across the street. Through the open garage door he could see the rear ends of a Cadillac and what appeared to be a Jaguar XKE. My love lives well, he thought. Very appropriate for a banker's daughter.

The lights were on in the house, although the drapes were drawn. In one window on the ground floor, light came through an aperture between the drapes. Curiosity overwhelmed him. He was tempted to get out of the car, run across the lawn, crouch under the window, and look in. Maybe she would be in there now. Maybe he could get a look at her.

It took all his willpower not to try. Reason kept his car door closed. A certain amount of light spilled out onto the lawn. There might be a dog in there. They might pick him up as a voyeur. He'd have a hell of a time explaining what he was doing there. He *couldn't* explain it. Even sitting here in the car and staring at the house made him conspicuous.

He started the car and began to move down the street. Tomorrow, he decided, was another day. He had just turned the corner when he passed a cruising police car turning into Vista Drive. The men in the car glanced at him curiously as they passed.

When he got back to the hotel a message was waiting for him: Hall Bentley had called and wanted him to call back.

He dialed Bentley's private number.

"Pete. Haven't heard from you." Then eagerly: "What's happened?"

Peter hesitated a moment. "Nothing."

"Nothing at all?"

"Not even a clue. At least not yet."

"Damn," said Bentley.

He had been on the verge of telling Bentley what had happened. But he pulled back at the last minute. He didn't want the parapsychologist in this just now. Bentley would only complicate things. Bentley was too eager; he'd want to blow this thing sky-high immediately. But Peter wanted to wait. He wanted to know more about himself. About Marcia. About everything.

"Pete, you're keeping that diary?"

"Yes."

"Don't leave out a thing. Not a single detail. It'll be important later, part of the general mass of evidence. I've already started to block out a report of my own."

"What kind of report?"

"A blow-by-blow description of what took place, from my point of view. How you came to me, why you came to me. No speculation, no projection. Simply telling it the way it is. Later, when you find out who Marcia is—and I say when, not if—then I'll get statements from Sam Goodman and Nora and the psychiatrist. Factual testimony as to their consultations and discussions with you . . ."

"Hall."

"Yes?"

"What if I *do* find who Marcia is? What happens then?"

"I've given that a lot of thought. Once you definitely identify her, I'll fly east. Take some special recording equipment with me, the kind I can hide somewhere on my person. Then we'll both confront her."

"Confront her?"

"That's right. Hit her between the eyes. Tell her who you really are. Come right out and tell her you're the incarnation of her dead husband.

Prove it by what you know. Meanwhile, I'll be recording the whole thing. Of course she'll go into some kind of shock. She won't have time to think about it at all. The surprise element of this setup will take care of that. Hopefully, the first thing she says will be an affirmation of what you know, and that'll be an enormous plus in terms of proof."

"Hall, you've forgotten something."

"Yes?"

"Won't this be—well, a kind of entrapment? If this idea works, we may force her into admitting she committed the murder."

"All right. Suppose she does. She *is* a murderess, isn't she?"

"Yes. I suppose so. Only . . ."

"Only what?"

"Only it seems—well, pretty dirty."

Bentley sounded impatient. "Look, Pete, it was pretty dirty of her to catch you in the middle of the lake, brain you with a paddle, and then let you drown. Whoever she is, she's concealed this crime for years. If all this works out—if we *do* find out who she is—and if we do manage to work out this trap as planned—then it's her problem, not ours. We can't be concerned about what happens to just one person here, for obvious reasons. I'm sure you see my point."

"Yes," said Peter. "Of course."

"Keep me posted. Give me a progress report every couple of days, even if there isn't anything to report. I have to tell you I'm going crazy here, waiting. I've bitten my nails way down. Maybe I ought to come east and join you."

"No," said Peter. "Let me look into this alone, Hall."

"It wouldn't be any trouble. I could close the office for a while."

"No. I want to do this myself. You'd only be in the way here. If anything breaks, I'll let you know."

He could hear Bentley's long and wistful sigh over the phone. "Okay, you're the doctor. All I can tell you is that I haven't slept more than two hours a night since you've been away."

Chapter 23

The next morning he drove to Vista Drive.

Later, he knew, he would contrive some way to meet Marcia. But right now he wanted simply to see her, face to face, and find out what she looked like now, what the years had done. His curiosity was excruciating. He kept visualizing her as he had seen her in the dreams—young and beautiful. Stubbornly, he preserved this image in his mind, even though he knew she would look much older now. Had she grown fat? Ugly? Was she a bridge-playing dowager now?

And the daughter. *His* daughter—Ann. What was she like? She would be twenty-seven now. It was odd that a woman of this age would still be living with her mother. He thought of her dispassionately. She was just a name to him. In the Baby Dream, he had seen her only as an infant. *And now,* he thought, *I have a daughter three months older than I am.* By his earlier incarnation, of course, but more and more he was thinking of Jeffrey Chapin and himself as the same man. As, of course, they were, if you thought of the soul as the real identity, and the body as nothing—mortal, dispensable, and destructible.

This time, he parked the car some distance down the street from the house. He knew that he could sit there for only a limited amount of time. Anybody parked in a car and watching a house in an exclusive area like this would be open to suspicion. After a time, somebody might even call the police. He contemplated the idea of driving slowly up and down the street in the hope that she would come out of the house. But that would be conspicuous, too.

He considered another possibility. He could simply walk up to the house and boldly ring the bell. But then what? How would he identify himself? A door-to-door salesman? Census taker? A man from the light and power company to examine the meter? No, it was ridiculous. He could never carry it off. He wasn't the type. Anyway, any subterfuge was impossible. Sooner or later, he would find some way to meet Marcia legitimately. It would be embarrassing to be seen now under some other guise.

Suddenly he noticed that there was only one car in the garage—the Jaguar. The Cadillac was missing. It was a good guess that the Jag belonged to Ann. That meant Marcia Chapin wasn't at home, anyway.

He decided to move on, stay away for an hour, then come back again. Maybe he could catch Marcia when she came home from wherever she had gone. Meanwhile, he would try to figure out some way to meet the Chapins. That was going to be very tough, since he didn't know anyone in town.

He had just started the car when he saw a woman come out of 16 Vista. She was young and slender, dressed in a plaid skirt and blue sweater. She was carrying a couple of tennis rackets. From this distance he could see that her hair was blonde and that she wore sunglasses. He was too far away to see the details of her face.

It must be his daughter. It couldn't be anyone else.

He watched her as she backed the car out of the driveway. Then she accelerated suddenly, the tires of the Jaguar screaming a little on the shiny blacktop of Vista Drive. She seemed to be in a hurry. He stepped on the gas and followed her.

He was hard put to keep up with her. She seemed an expert driver as she whipped in and out of traffic. He hoped for a red light somewhere ahead so that he could pull up and get a good look at her.

She took the parkway and he followed. She was moving very fast, and for a while he was afraid he might lose her. Then he saw her turn off at an exit marked: Green Hills. Another right turn, and then he saw it. He recognized it instantly as the same country club he had seen in the Tennis Dream. Everything looked the same, the big, rambling shingled clubhouse, the rolling fairways, the same small lake, which he now identified as a water hazard for one of the holes. There were four tennis courts now. In the hallucination, he remembered only one. They must have built three more in the years since.

She drove through the entrance, parked, and went inside. He followed. When he entered the clubhouse, there was no sign of her. She'd probably gone into the ladies' locker room. He stood there for a few moments uncertainly. A few of the club members were having coffee before beginning their rounds of golf. They stared at him curiously. This was a place where everybody knew everybody. A stranger was conspicuous here.

He walked over and studied the bulletin board on the wall. On it were pinned the usual routine club announcements, the various tournaments, and a list of those scheduled to take golf or tennis lessons each day. On the tennis list he saw the name Ann Chapin. She was scheduled for the next hour, from eleven to twelve.

He sought out the club steward, took out his wallet, and showed the steward a card. It was a courtesy card issued by private golf clubs to their members. If one's home club was reasonably prestigious, other private golf clubs throughout the country would extend privileges and offer their facilities. His father was still a member of the Los Angeles Country Club, one of the most exclusive in Southern California, and Peter had a joint membership. The steward glanced at the card, smiled, and held out his hand.

"Welcome to Green Hills, sir. What can we do for you?"

"I'd like to play some tennis."

"Fine. But you may have a little trouble finding a partner. I could look around . . ."

"Thanks. But that won't be necessary. Maybe I could work out with the tennis pro."

"Oh, yes. Ken Walker. He's an excellent teacher." The steward went to a phone near the bar and dialed a single number. "Ken? John Wicker. We have a guest from California. A Mr. Proud. He'd like to talk to you about a workout." He hung up and turned to Peter. "You'll find him in the pro shop. Just go out the main entrance and walk down the hill and to the right. It's near the first tee. Meanwhile, I'll arrange a locker for you."

The tennis pro was a tall, bronzed man in his middle thirties. He smiled warmly as they shook hands.

"Proud. Peter Proud. It's an unusual name, and it rings bells. You played in the Southwestern Tournament at San Diego, right?"

"Yes. But I didn't get very far."

"If you qualified for that one at all, you don't have to apologize. Anyway, welcome to Green Hills. What can I do for you?"

"I'll be here for a while on business. Haven't had a racket in my hand for almost a month and I'd like to sharpen up my game while I'm here. I thought if you had some time today . . ."

"I'm booked for the next hour. How about right after lunch?"

"That'll be fine. I have some time to kill. Mind if I come down and watch?"

"Be my guest."

The pro went out. The shop carried a complete line of tennis equipment as well as golf. He bought two Wilson T–2000 steel rackets, and sneakers, socks, shorts, jersey and sweater. He went into the locker room, changed, and then walked down to the courts.

She was in tennis whites now and volleying with the pro. There was a row of benches just outside the court and he sat down. Then he took his first long look at his daughter.

He was stunned by her beauty. He saw that her eyes were violet, so dark he could see them from where he sat. Her hair was blonde and finely spun. It was tied back in a high and tight ponytail, and when she ran and had to lean over to make a drop or placement shot, it fell over her right shoulder. Then she would fling it back with a tilt of her head. Her mouth was full and ripe and mobile, pink against the slightly tanned face. There was just the hint of high cheekbones, which seemed to give an Oriental slant to her eyes. She moved about the court with exquisite grace. Her legs were long and superb—perfectly fashioned, sensuously curved, the skin smooth and flawless, the kind you never saw on ordinary women. Her beauty was not surface. It was something she wore naturally. It was ripe and mature, the beauty of a full-blown woman of twenty-seven.

He remembered the Baby Dream, the brief, hallucinatory flash when, as Jeffrey Chapin, he had paced the floor with her in his arms. It was incredible to think that here he was now, on a warm spring day nearly twenty-seven years later, in some other life, watching her now, fully grown, about his own age.

He saw that her tennis was good—superb, in fact. Her stroke had plenty of power, and her shots were accurate. She had a good, strong forehand and an adequate backhand. She knew how to smash a lob, her drop and placement shots were shrewd, and once or twice she caught Walker flatfooted with a hard crosscourt shot. The pro was not toying with her. She made him play. Now and then they stopped while Walker made suggestions. Peter judged her as just a cut under professional tournament level. Well, he reflected, she comes by it naturally.

He was the only one there watching from the sidelines. He knew she was aware of his presence, and curious about him. Now and then she would steal a glance at him. When he caught her eye, she would quickly turn her head away.

Finally the hour was up. They walked off the court. Peter entered the gate and went directly to her.

"Like to play a little longer?"

She had bent over to put her racket into its cover. He saw the lush swell of her breast under her blouse. She looked up at him, surprised, and confused.

"I don't know."

"Of course, if you're tired . . ."

"No," she said. "I'm not tired at all." Then: "You're new here, aren't you?"

"He's a guest," said Walker. "From Los Angeles." He introduced them. They shook hands. The touch of her flesh was warm, exciting. The violet eyes studied him. They seemed bottomless. Suddenly they smiled. They were frank, totally without guile, very direct. They said: *I like you, Peter Proud, whoever you are. I like you very much. And I don't even know you.* He heard Walker saying: "I happen to know he plays damned good tennis, Ann. He'll make you run. And it's a chance to work on that backhand."

"Okay?" said Peter.

"Yes," she said. "I'd love to."

They volleyed for almost an hour. Watching her face as she ran, he lost the ball a few times. He found the experience exhilarating. He heard himself shouting, "Hit it back, hit it back!" just as he had done in the Tennis Dream. The young girl opposite him was not Ann Chapin; it was her mother, Marcia. He was Jeffrey Chapin, and this was many, many years ago . . .

Finally she raised her racket high in surrender and came to the net.

"Whew!" she said. "I'm pooped. Enough, enough."

"Thanks for the game."

"Thank *you.* How many chances do I get to play with *two* professionals in the same day?"

He grinned. "I'm not a professional."

"No? Then you're missing your calling. What *do* you do for a living?"

"Later. How about a drink first?"

"My God," she said. "I thought you'd never ask."

They walked up toward the clubhouse. He thought about the Tennis Dream again. He was sure he would never be tormented by it again. Now that he had re-created it, even in a vague way, it would vanish.

They took a table in the lounge area near the bar. He ordered a gin and tonic, she a vodka and tonic. They clinked glasses and smiled at each other. Suddenly she laughed.

"What's so funny?"

"I won't tell you."

"Why not?"

"You might be offended."

He grinned. "Try me and see."

"It's your name. Peter Proud. It's a funny name, strange. But marvelous. I love it."

"I hate it," he said. "But I'm stuck with it. So I grit my teeth and bear it."

"Where did you learn your tennis?"

"Southern California. Everybody plays at a very early age. They put a tennis racket in your little baby hand long before a rattle. In Los Angeles, if you don't play tennis, they think you're queer. They put you in corners at parties. And you? Where did you learn *your* tennis?"

"I don't know. I've always loved the game. My mother's been a member here for years, so it was always available. The courts, I mean; instruction. Of course, if you believe in chromosomes, I might have inherited it from my father."

"Your father?"

"He was the tennis pro at this club a long time ago."

"Oh? Then he met your mother here?"

"Yes. I suppose this is pretty corny. But they probably fell in love playing singles."

"Nothing like a good tennis romance," he said.

"Oh? Then you know all about them?"

"They're the best kind."

"Well," she said. "It's nice hearing that from an expert."

"Those who volley together, stay together. And so your father and mother lived happily ever after."

"No. My father's dead."

"I'm sorry."

"You don't have to be. He's been dead for almost thirty years. I never knew him. I was only three months old at the time. He drowned in some lake. It broke my mother up. She was madly in love with him—" Then she stopped. The violet eyes were astonished. "Why am I telling you all this?"

"I don't know."

"I know you about an hour, you're a perfect stranger, and here I am babbling along as though this is a confessional." She wrinkled her forehead, studying him. "You wouldn't be a priest in white shorts, would you?"

"No."

"Or a psychiatrist?"

"No."

"Then satisfy my very natural and lively curiosity—about lots of things. Like who are you? What are you doing here in Riverside? How long will you be here? Will the *real* Peter Proud please stand up?"

He told her, briefly, about his teaching, the book, his research project. He found he talked easily to her. The violet eyes watched him steadily. He sensed they were more than just interested; they were almost possessive. She seemed to have already marked him as an important entry in her life, even on this first and casual meeting. She was saying to him, *You have not seen the last of me, and I have not seen the last of you. Something is happening here, and we both know it.*

When he had finished, she stared at him.

"You said you have Indian blood?"

"That's right. No high cheekbones. But I'm one-sixteenth Seneca. Or maybe one thirty-second. I'm not sure, at this point."

"Talk about coincidence. I've got Indian blood in me, too, from way back. On my father's side. Mother tells me he was very proud of it."

"What tribe?"

"Pequot."

"Not too far apart geographically," he said. "Maybe it isn't coincidence at all. Maybe we met in some previous incarnation."

"What?"

"Maybe I was a Seneca warrior, and I wandered south by east, and I ran into the Pequots, and there you were. Daughter of a chief, and the most beautiful squaw east of the Hudson. So I talked to your father, and he tested my skill in hunting and fishing and found it good. After that, I paid him six belts of wampum, two horses, the pelts of twenty beavers, and took you back to my tribe. After that, we had five beautiful papooses and lived happily ever after. . . ."

"You're mad," she said, laughing. "You're absolutely mad."

They talked for another half hour. She told him she'd lived most of her life in Riverside. She'd never had to worry about money; her grandfather, now dead, had been president of the Puritan Bank and Trust. She had gone to Wellesley, had met a boy from Harvard, and after they had both graduated, they had married and gone to New York to live. He had worked in his uncle's law firm, and she had gotten a job in the advertising department of Lord and Taylor. She had been good at the creative end of it, writing copy and so forth, and eventually had made rather a large salary. But the marriage hadn't worked and they'd been divorced, and she didn't want to talk about *that*. It was fortunate they didn't have children, and the parting was reasonably amicable. Two years ago she'd come back to Riverside to stay. As a free-lancer, she wrote advertising copy at Stanley's, the largest department store in town, and also did some book editing for two New York publishers. Otherwise, she passed the time playing a lot of tennis and a little golf. She went out now and then with this man and that, but nobody excited her enough to change her life. It was all rather dull, but it was reasonably comfortable. Time passed, and she was getting older, and wasn't that true with everybody?

"Something I don't understand," he said. "You seemed to be all set in New York. And with all due respect to your hometown, it's a lot more exciting than Riverside. Yet you left it and came back here. Why?"

Her face clouded at that. Suddenly the violet eyes became veiled. He knew she did not like the question, and he regretted asking it.

"Look," he said hastily. "I seem to have touched a nerve somewhere. I'm sorry I asked you. Let's just say I was desperately making conversation, just to keep you here. Just so you won't go away."

She smiled at that. "Did it show that much?"

"Yes."

"I don't know why it should. The reason's very simple. My mother's been—well, sick for the last few years. She needed me."

"I see. You live with her then?"

"Most of the time. But I have a secret little place of my own. An apartment. Even Mother doesn't know about it. Just so I can go there once in a while and do a little private screaming."

"Then you *do* have something to scream about?"

"Doesn't everybody?"

"I would imagine that this apartment of yours has a telephone."

"It does. A private number."

"I could ask you to give it to me."

"You could."

"Only you're not about to give it to me."

"Not yet. Do you mind?"

"No, of course not." Then he grinned. "One thing you'll learn about me. I try. I'm very persistent."

She smiled. "I like that in a man."

"Okay," he said. "I'll try again sometime."

"I hope you do. I want you to."

"Another drink?"

She looked shocked. "In the middle of the day like this? Before God and everybody and the staid members of the Green Hills Country Club? God, no. Besides, I'm driving, and anyway, I've got to go. I've got an appointment."

"Is it important?"

"Very. It's with my hairdresser."

He looked at her hair and grinned. "Don't let her change anything." Then: "Will you be taking another tennis lesson tomorrow?"

"It so happens that I will. Why?"

"I thought maybe we'd play again." He smiled. "You know, work on your backhand a little more."

"You worked on it very well this morning. I thought you'd never hit one to my forehand. But yes. I'd love to play." She smiled at him. "But don't you have work to do?"

"It can wait."

She laughed, said goodbye, and walked away in the direction of the locker rooms. Now, as before, he was struck by her walk. There was something special about it. The tilt of the hips, the slight sway of the buttocks slightly controlled, the graceful rhythm of the long legs as they moved were superbly feminine. He tried to imagine that body stripped of its tennis clothes, totally naked. He thought of it hungrily. He imagined how she would feel in his arms, how that body would feel pressed against his, the smell of her hair, the taste of her pink mouth on his, her odor, and what she would do when those carefully banked fires he knew were there suddenly blazed . . .

Suddenly he hated himself. He felt a little queasy. Not just like a lecher, but *incestuous*. This girl had been his daughter once. And here he was, at the age of twenty-seven, thinking like a dirty old man.

The next day, they played tennis again. And on the following day he called the house at 16 Vista Drive.

"Hello?"

"Is Ann there?"

"Yes. May I ask who's calling?"

"Peter Proud."

"Just a moment . . ."

The voice was velvety, with a little slur. Older than he remembered it at the lake, but still identifiable as Marcia's.

The goose pimples popped out on his skin. Ann came on the phone. He asked her out for dinner that night, and she agreed.

They arranged for him to pick her up at the house at seven, have a drink, and then go on.

Chapter 24

He took a deep breath and rang the bell. It seemed a long time before anyone came. Finally the door opened, and she was standing there.

"I'm Peter Proud," he said.

"Oh. I'm Marcia Chapin. Ann's mother. Please come in." She closed the door and turned to him. "Ann's upstairs. She'll be down in a minute."

The blue eyes he remembered so well studied him. Then, puzzled:

"Have we met before?"

"No."

"You're sure?"

"I'm positive."

She continued to watch him, baffled. "That's strange. I have the funniest feeling that we—but no, I guess you're right. Peter Proud, if you'll forgive me, is such an odd name, I'd have remembered it if we had met." Then: "Ann tells me you're from Los Angeles, and this is your first time in Riverside."

"Yes. Or in New England, for that matter."

He was aware that she was still puzzled, that something about him nagged her.

"I don't know why we're standing out here. Why don't we have a drink while you're waiting?"

"Thanks. I'd like that."

He tried hard not to stare at her, lest she think him rude. This was the same woman he had seen in his dreams, no doubt about that. Yet even though he'd known she would have changed, part of him had expected her to look like the young Marcia he had seen so many times. Meeting her now was a shock. He judged her to be fifty, perhaps a year or two older. Here and there, the ghost of her once exciting beauty was still present—in the eyes, in the faint Oriental cast of her face, in the sway of her body under the red housecoat she wore. There were streaks of gray in once coal-black hair. She had thickened out somewhat, although she was not heavy enough to be called matronly. Her face had a faint pasty quality, an indoor pallor which seemed almost unhealthy.

Somehow, he felt a little let down. He had expected some kind of high drama in this first meeting. After all, he had lived with this woman a long time, both in his last incarnation and in his present life. In one, she had struck him down in the prime of his life, in cold blood; and in the other, she had tormented him endlessly. He had come a long way to find her, and it had taken him some time. Yet he felt no anger, no resentment, no desire for revenge. Only curiosity. He wanted to know *why* she had done what she had done, why she had been able to kill him with such savagery.

She led him through a large living room and into a combination recreation room and den with deep leather chairs and a small bar.

"Please sit down. What can I give you to drink?"

"If it isn't any trouble, a martini."

"No trouble at all."

She mixed the drink quickly and expertly, as though she had done it many times before. He noticed that all she took was club soda. But it was the room that fascinated him, and the photographs that filled the panel walls. It was definitely a man's room, from the furniture to each small decorative touch. There wasn't a feminine frill in it. Yet, as far as he knew, no man lived in this house.

The photographs particularly interested him. There must have been twenty of them lining the walls, and each was a photograph of Jeff Chapin. Sometimes Marcia was in the picture with him, the young Marcia of his dreams, looking exactly the way he had seen her.

Now Peter Proud had a good chance to see himself as he had really looked in his previous incarnation. The newspaper photo had been vague, a little blurred. These were clear. There was a photo of Jeff Chapin standing at the backline of a tennis court, poised to serve. A photo of him, smiling, in Marine uniform. Another in the same genre, Chapin again in uniform, sitting at the edge of a road somewhere with two or three of his buddies, smiling and relaxed, a cigarette dangling from his lips. And on each, the legend: *To Marcia. With all my love. Jeff.* There were shots of Jeff and Marcia in the big Packard Clipper, he grinning at the photographer, she smiling. Then the two of them lying on a beach somewhere. And another with Jeff laughing and carrying a protesting Marcia in his arms as he walked into the sea. Still another, a wedding picture, Jeff Chapin looking very young and self-conscious and ill at ease, Marcia, young and beautiful and radiant, and other members of the wedding party, people he did not know. There was a photo of Jeff standing behind a huge sailfish he had caught and which hung by a hook at the weighing platform on a dock. He was holding a fishing pole and mugging at the camera. And still others: Jeff Chapin, again in tennis clothes, face shining with perspiration, smiling and accepting a loving cup from a tournament chairman; Jeff Chapin in a business suit, sitting behind a desk, probably, guessed Peter, in the Puritan Bank and Trust. And finally, a framed military citation from the Marine Corps to Corporal Jeff Chapin for conspicuous bravery in action; and, below that, a medal and a ribbon.

It was eerie sitting here in a deep leather chair and sipping a martini and watching a panorama of his previous life up there on those walls, a kind of retrospective of who he was and what he was doing then, and those highlights of his life considered important enough to photograph and frame and hang here on these walls. He studied the pictures critically, thinking, *I wasn't a bad looking guy, not bad at all, a hell of a lot better looking than I am now* . . .

"That was my husband," said Marcia.

"Yes. Ann told me about him."

"He was a wonderful man. This used to be his favorite room. His own personal hideaway."

He stared at her. "Then you've lived here ever since . . ."

She nodded. "Ever since 1945. The year before he died. He loved this house so. After—after he'd gone, I couldn't bear to leave it. There was too much of him still here, you see."

She had finished her club soda and poured another. With the tongs, she reached into a silver ice bucket and picked out a cube of ice. He could see that her hand was trembling a little. She put enormous concentration into this small task. When she sat down, she held her own glass limply. She seemed far more fascinated in the martini he was holding. He was suddenly aware that he was tapping the rim of the glass with his fingernail, listening to the ring of the glass. He felt that it upset her, and he stopped abruptly, acutely conscious of her stare.

"Sorry," he said. "Just an old and annoying habit of mine."

"That's all right," she said. "Only it's so strange."

"Yes?"

"*He* had that same habit, too. My husband. He used to tap the edge of his glass the same way you do."

She seemed to have gone suddenly pale. A shiver ran up his spine. If he had carried one of Jeffrey Chapin's little eccentricities beyond the grave, how many more did he have that Marcia Chapin would recognize and identify in the same way?

He changed the subject, nodding at the photographs on the wall. "It seems a terrible thing. To die so young."

"He was only twenty-seven. Did Ann tell you how it happened?"

"Well, she said he drowned."

"But she didn't tell you *how?*"

"No."

"You know, it's so idiotic, the way tragedy happens. The thing is, you never expect it. I keep thinking back, and I keep thinking back, and I tell myself it couldn't have happened that way. It just *couldn't* . . ."

"Look, Mrs. Chapin, maybe I shouldn't have brought this up. I'm sure it's upsetting . . ."

"No," she said. "No. It happened such a long time ago. I'm over it now. I've been over it for a long time. I know it can't possibly interest you, but I don't mind talking about it now. I really don't. You see, we had this cottage at a lake outside of Riverside. Lake Nipmuck. It was late September, you know, when all the summer people had gone home. Jeff and I used to love to go out to the cottage then. It was so quiet and peaceful, so beautiful, a time when all the leaves were just changing into autumn colors." The blue eyes were vacant now, far away. Her voice was a monotone, as though she were reciting a much repeated and much rehearsed speech. Did she talk about this with every stranger she met? How often did she have this kind of discussion, this monologue about a husband who had been dead for twenty-eight years? Perhaps it was this room, with its photographs on the wall, that had set her off. And, of course, her own guilty memory.

"On this particular night, my husband had an urge to swim the lake. He loved to swim in the nude, and it was night, nobody could see him. It wasn't unusual for him to do this. He'd swum the lake many times, and he was a very strong swimmer. I begged him not to go—the water was too cold—but he insisted. He'd had, well, a drink or two, and he could be stubborn. When my husband got an idea into his head, nothing could stop him. When he had gone, I thought how foolish it all was. What would he do when he reached the opposite shore? He had no swimming trunks on. And he'd be cold. He'd catch his death of pneumonia. So I took out our boat and went after him, to pick him up and bring him back with me. But then—I couldn't find him. He had disappeared. He must have gone down somewhere. Something had happened, a cramp perhaps. I don't know. But he couldn't have made the other side; there wasn't time. I went around and around the lake, crying out his name. But he was gone. I went to the other side, to the hotel, and called the police. They brought him up from the bottom of the lake—

two days later. Have you ever seen a person who's been drowned and been under water for a while? They look so white, so bloated, so awful . . ."

He listened, and for the first time he felt a stab of anger. *Oh, you liar,* he thought. *You murdering bitch.*

"I'm sorry," she said suddenly. "I really don't know why I'm telling you all this."

"That's all right."

"Please forgive me. I know I've been boring you."

"Not at all."

She continued to apologize. "Really, I'm surprised at myself. I don't normally do this with anyone. I guess I wasn't thinking." She tried to smile. "It's like talking about your operation." She reached for his glass. "Another martini?"

"No, thanks."

She glanced at her wristwatch. "I'm sorry you have to wait. I don't know what's keeping Ann. She tells me you'll be here for a while."

"Yes. Several weeks, at least."

"I see." Vaguely he had the feeling that this news bothered her. But her voice was impassive. "I suppose you'll be busy researching your book —on the American Indian, isn't it?"

"Oh. Ann told you?"

She smiled. "She told me quite a lot about you. But it's interesting that you're doing a book on Indians. My husband was part Indian, you know. One-sixteenth Pequot, and very proud of it, too. People having any Indian blood at all around here are pretty rare. It's much more common in the western states, I understand."

He was about to tell her about his own Seneca heritage. But he decided against it. At that moment Ann came in. She was wearing a shirt-top jacket in a red and white print over white pants.

"Well, I see you two have met," she said.

"Yes."

"Sorry I made you wait."

"That's all right. I've been enjoying myself."

"We've been having a good talk," Marcia said, smiling. "He's very nice, Ann."

"I told you he was, Mother. Pete, we'd better go."

"But, dear," said Marcia. "You can sit down and have a drink."

"Sorry, we can't. We have a reservation, and we're late already. Ola's cooking dinner, and she'll be staying overnight, as usual." Then, a little anxiously: "You'll be all right?"

"Of course I will."

"In case you need me, we'll be at Mario's. The number's in the telephone index."

"I won't need you," said Marcia.

"You're sure?"

"Sure. Now you run along and have a good time."

As they drove away from the house, he wondered why Ann had been so solicitous. But he said nothing about it. He pointed the car up Vista Drive, and then Ann said, "Well, what do you think of her?"

"I like her."

She smiled. "The true gentleman and diplomat. Still, you wouldn't dare say anything else."

"Should I?"

"I don't know. I had an idea you two didn't really hit it off so well."

"Now, what gives you *that* idea?"

"Call it intuition. Certain vibrations tickling my very sensitive antennae. When I came in, you were both sitting there like a couple of stiff manikins watching each other. Sort of guarded. You know?"

"Well"—he grinned—"maybe. But we'd just met. How did I know I wasn't meeting my future mother-in-law, or something?"

She laughed. "I assume you're just being funny."

"Not really. Actually, the thought crossed my mind. Maybe it crossed your mother's, too. Don't mothers always see gentlemen callers as prospective sons-in-law for their daughters?"

"I guess they do, but only in Tennessee Williams' plays. Anyway, you're both a little premature, of course."

"Of course."

"But I love you for thinking about it at all. What did Mother and you talk about?"

"Some small talk. But mostly about your father."

She stared at him. "My father?"

"I don't quite know how she got on the subject. All those pictures on the wall, I guess. But she told me the whole story about what happened at the lake. How he died . . ."

"That's funny."

"Is it? Why?"

"She never talks about that particular incident to anybody. Not even to me." She stared at him. "Why you?"

"I don't know."

She shook her head, puzzled. "That's really funny. I don't understand it."

"I got the idea she's still in mourning over him."

"She is."

"But after all this time, isn't that a little—"

"Sick?"

"Look, I didn't say that . . ."

"I know you didn't. I did. The answer is yes. In that sense, she *is* a little sick. His death hit her hard. She never really got over it. I guess she must have loved him very much. Now and then she gets these vast depressions. It isn't normal, I know. I've never understood it . . ."

I do, he thought. *It's guilt, baby. Guilt is a monkey on your back. The biggest and heaviest monkey in the world. Guilt can drive you crazy.*

"You take that room you were in," Ann was saying. "It's a kind of sanctuary. I almost never go in it myself; it's too depressing. And all those photographs of my father. She'll go in alone and simply stare at them for hours, reliving memories. I'm used to it, I suppose. But it's still a little frightening when I see her do it. I wish she'd take them all down someday and put them away. She's reasonably attractive for her age, you know. She could still find another man. You'd be surprised how gay and charming and lovely Mother can be when she wants to be."

"Then she never remarried?"

"No."

"But there must have been other men. Afterward . . ."

"I don't know. When I was very young, I guess—at least I was told there were a few. They didn't last very long, and I don't blame them. I'd be turned off, too, if I had to compete with a ghost. The past few years, Mother's sort of withdrawn from everything, stays in the house most of the time. She used to go to the club now and then to mix with friends. Now she sees hardly anybody. Unless you count my grandmother."

"Her mother?"

"No. My father's mother."

"Oh? She's still alive, then?"

"If you want to call it that. Half alive would be a lot more accurate. She's old and completely senile. Lost her memory and doesn't recognize anybody. Just sits in a wheelchair and babbles. She's in an institution outside of town here. I haven't visited her for a year. I just can't stand it; it depresses me so, watching a human being wither away like that. But Mother's very devoted to her. She takes care of all the expenses there—housing, nursing, medical supplies—and it isn't cheap. Not only that, she visits Grandmother at least once a week, sometimes twice.

She'll sit around with the old lady half an afternoon, just to keep her company."

"But if the old lady doesn't even know who she is . . ."

"That's the funny part of it. Mother goes on visiting her anyway. She's made Grandmother her total responsibility. I suppose there's some emotional involvement with my father. . . ."

Suddenly she stopped. "Here we go again. Now you've got *me* doing it."

"What?"

"Talking about my father." She stared at him. "I don't know what's going on here. All of a sudden, he's become a prime topic of conversation. You come to town, and both my mother and I start to babble about him to a perfect stranger. After being dead for thirty years, he comes up stage front, as far as you're concerned. Why?"

"I don't know."

"Well, it doesn't make any sense. Now, if you don't mind, I'd like to drop the subject of my family. We've been hacking away at it long enough, and it's really a bore. Why don't we talk about ourselves?"

"Why not indeed? Where shall we start for openers?"

"Well, I know you're a bachelor, and I know what you do. You know I'm a maiden lady, and you know what I do."

"So?"

"I have a question for you."

"Proceed."

"How old are you?"

"Twenty-seven."

"When will you be twenty-eight?"

"On the tenth of October."

"My God," she said. "That makes me what they call an older woman." Then she laughed. "I feel like a character out of Colette. You know, the older woman with infinite experience who seduces the naïve young man."

"A three-months' edge isn't going to make you *that* good."

"How'd you know that?"

"How'd I know *what?*"

"That I was three months older than you."

She was staring at him in surprise. The violet eyes were puzzled. They wanted an answer. He cursed himself for not thinking.

"Just guessing," he said lamely.

"No," she said. "You *knew*. How? I never told you."

Suddenly he remembered something. He could have shouted with relief.

"One of those photographs on the wall."

"Yes?"

"It was a picture of your father and mother taken in the backyard, or somewhere. Your mother was holding what appeared to be a very new-born baby. Obviously, it was you. There was a date written across it, sometime in July, I think."

"Oh. Yes. July twentieth."

He'd have to be careful from now on, he thought. Think before he spoke. Know only what he was supposed to know.

"July twentieth," he said. "What's your sign?"

"Sign?"

"Horoscope sign."

"Oh. I'm a Cancer."

"Well, what do you know," he said, smiling. "I'm a Libra."

"Is that good?"

"It's perfect. Libras and Cancers mix well together. *Muy sympatico*. They often fall in love with each other and go through life together. They're particularly close right now, when Jupiter is in the solar seventh house and Mercury ends its retrograde period."

She stared at him a moment, then laughed.

Chapter 25

After they had gone, Marcia Chapin turned on the television set. A news program was on, but she found she could not concentrate. She turned off the set and opened another bottle of club soda.

She felt nervous, edgy. The club soda was worthless. It was supposed to help if you simply held a glass in your hand, but it did nothing for her. She watched her hand tremble as she held the glass. What I need now, she thought, is a drink.

She had felt fine an hour ago. But that was before he had walked into the house. Peter Proud.

When she had taken her first good look at him, something extraordinary had happened. She had suddenly felt tense. Somewhere a nerve had begun to jangle. She had taken an instant dislike to him. Something about him repelled her. What was it? His face? His voice? It made absolutely no sense. He was good-looking, well-dressed; his smile was warm; he had been very polite. Nothing he had said or done had in any way been out of line.

Then why?

She put it down as one of those mysterious things that sometimes happen between people. You meet a total stranger, and your reaction is automatically hostile. He has said nothing to you, he has done no harm to you, yet you cannot stand the sight of him. Sometimes you walked down a crowded street, and hundreds of people were swirling around you, and then you saw one face, a face that bothered you. Sometimes it even haunted you.

She had been so sure she had met him before, seen him somewhere. Yet she knew this couldn't be so; otherwise, she would have remembered.

She began to shake a little. She stared at the bottles lined up neatly on the glass shelf behind the bar. *Ten little Indians,* she thought. *Ten little Indians, all in a row, and if from them one should go. . . .*

And that little trick of his—tapping the edge of his martini glass with his fingernail. That had really given her a shock. Coincidence? Yes. What else could it be? But, my God, *what* a coincidence. Jeff had done it all the time. It was a habit he could never break, and after a while it had driven her crazy. "Jeff, darling, you're doing it again. Tap, tap. Will you stop it, please?" And then he would smile, saying, "I'm sorry, papoose, I wasn't thinking." Papoose. He'd call her that every once in a while. And then she would say, "It's very annoying, you know." And he would laugh and say, "Maybe I ought to learn to drink my booze from paper cups."

She thought of that night at the lake now, as she had thought of it a million times. They had been drinking martinis—Beefeaters, very dry, the way he liked them. She saw him now, so clearly, standing in front of her stark naked, laughing at her accusations, *laughing* at them, holding his glass and tapping it with his fingernail, and that big thing of his, the swollen red-tipped penis, standing straight out from his groin; she remembered his face, the eyes cold and evil over the smile, remembered his putting down the glass and beginning to walk toward her. . . .

Ohgod, ohgod, ohgod, I need a drink.

How long has it been? A month? How many Cokes and club sodas and ginger ales since she had had the last one? How many cases of Tab and Diet-Rite had she consumed? How many cups of coffee? And still that endless craving. Day upon day, letting her imagination go, thinking of the taste, the feel of it as it slid down her throat and warmed her insides and her soul itself with comfort and strength, and, above all, release. Numbing her memory, so that she could forget, even for a little while.

But I promised Ann. I promised Dr. Harvey. I promised Ola. I promised myself. And I don't want to go back to that place. I never want to see that damned room again, and walk in the gardens with some nurse, and drink all that fruit juice, and take all those pills, and sweat in that steam room. I don't want to go back there, ever. . . .

She thought of what lay in the bottom of her bureau drawer upstairs. The gun Jeff had brought back from the war long ago. He had loved guns. They had walked into the fields, and he had taught her how it worked. She hated the sight and feel of it, but she had gone along to please him. She had watched him shoot a small animal with it. She didn't remember what kind of animal it was now. She *did* remember the hole in the head, the mass of dripping blood and brains.

No, she thought with a shudder. *Oh, no, no.*

The bottle beckoned to her. Curiously, it was one particular bottle.

There were others on the shelf, but it was the bottle of Beefeater gin, the one she had just used to make Peter Proud's martini, that pulled her. The same gin she and Jeff had used that night in *their* martinis.

She held the bottle in her hand, caressed it. She loved the feel of it. It was sensuous, phallic, almost sexy. She unscrewed the cap. From this opening pours strength and power and calm and comfort and oblivion. Here in this bottle, if for only a little while, you can hide yourself. You can hide yourself where nobody can touch you, or even find you.

"Mrs. Chapin."

She turned. Ola, her colored maid, was standing in the doorway, staring accusingly. "You don't want to do that."

"I have to, Ola."

"But you promised Ann . . ."

"I know, I know. But I need one. Just one . . ."

"Mrs. Chapin, why don't you just put it away? Dinner's ready. Got a roast beef rare, just the way you like it. I'll make you some black coffee. After that, you can take your pill and watch some television and . . ."

"Goddamn it, Ola!" She almost wept. "I need it. Don't you understand? I *need* it!"

"You don't need it at all, Mrs. Chapin. It's just in the mind. You been off it for a long time now. Why start it all over again?"

"Get out of here, Ola. Will you get the hell out of here?"

"What about dinner?"

"I'll be in for dinner. I'm just going to have one. Only one. I swear it. Now, please. Get out of here!"

Ola shrugged and left. Marcia Chapin tilted the bottle and poured the gin into the glass. She did not even bother with the vermouth, or with the ice. She drank it down straight, her eyes closed in ecstasy.

When she opened them again, she saw Jeff. He was in every picture on the wall. Jeff laughing at her, Jeff with his arm around her waist, Jeff and she running into the sea. Suddenly she began to weep a little and filled her glass again.

Jeff, Jeff, you beautiful, sexy son of a bitch, why did you do what you did?

And, dear God, why did I do what I did?

They had dinner at an Italian restaurant in the center of town. Later, when he took her home, they stood in the doorway for a moment. She turned her face toward him, inviting him with her mouth.

He put his arm around her. He felt her body strain against him. For a moment he blended tightly with her. Her red, moist, half-open mouth was close to his. He knew that the touch of it, the taste of it, would make it impossible not to go further. Or at least not to try.

Then the same guilty, queasy feeling came to him suddenly. Thinking of who she was, and who he really was. Taboo.

He put his hand gently on her face, turned it, and kissed her on the cheek. When he released her, he could see that she was surprised. The violet eyes were puzzled. Not hurt, just confused.

"Thank you, darling," she said. "That was very sweet. Goodnight."

She closed the door. He stood there, hating himself, feeling like a fool.

When he got back to the hotel, there was a message from Hall Bentley. Please call back.

He knew he couldn't put Bentley off forever. Sooner or later he'd have to break it to the parapsychologist. He decided he might as well do it now.

When he'd finished, there was a long silence at the other end. Then:

"My God, you've done it. You've found out."

"Yes."

"How do you feel?"

"I don't know."

"Scared?"

"I guess so."

"I don't blame you. I'm just as scared as you are. I never believed it would come as far as this. I never really believed it. So X equals Jeff Chapin, and Jeff Chapin equals Peter Proud."

"Yes."

"You know that, and I know that. Now the job is to prove it to everyone else. So, let's get down to tactics and strategy. First things first. Suppose I fly to Riverside tomorrow. We'll set up an appointment with Marcia Chapin, get what she says on tape. I've already told you the procedure we'll use. I'll bring copies of the tapes I already have. They're duplicates, of course, of the originals in the vaults. I'm keeping those for the die-hard skeptics. We won't make the mistake Morey Bernstein made with Bridey Murphy. He released the story first to a single newspaper. We'll want a much wider impact from the beginning, a worldwide impact. Maybe we ought to hire a public relations firm. They'll know how to arrange everything—television, press interviews. . . ."

"Hold it, Hall."

"Yes?"

"I'm not ready for all this yet."

"What do you mean?"

"I want to wait awhile."

"What for?"

"Let's just say I have my reasons. Personal reasons."

There was a long silence. Then: "Pete, whatever they are, I have to respect them. But we can't afford to wait. We don't dare."

"Why not?"

"Well, being human and vulnerable, you could die. You could get hit by a car tonight, or by a heart attack tomorrow. I'll admit the chances are heavily against it, but there's always the possibility. If you do, the proof goes down the drain with you. I might add that Marcia Chapin is also mortal and she could die, too. Which also would play hell with this whole thing. You must see the urgency of all this . . ."

"All right. But I still want to wait. There are still a lot of things here I want to find out, in my own way, by myself . . ."

Bentley was suddenly irritated. "For God's sake, Pete, what are we talking about here? This is no time to play games. You've got something to tell the whole damned world. It's the most important thing the human race has heard since the beginning of time. Your personal reasons just aren't important . . ."

"They are to me."

"Look, why don't I just fly east . . ."

"No."

There was a long pause at the other end of the line. Then Bentley said, "All right. I guess I'm not the doctor here; you are. The question is—*when?* When do we take off the lid?"

"I'll let you know."

"Okay," said Bentley. He sounded grim. "But make it soon, Pete. *Very* soon."

He said goodbye and hung up.

He hadn't been lying to Bentley. The moment they broke the news to the public, all hell would break loose. Much of what he wanted to know would be buried under an avalanche of sensationalism, perhaps lost to him forever. He wanted to know who he really had been, that is, who Jeff Chapin really had been. And Marcia. He wanted to know what had happened between them. *Why* she had done what she did.

And then, of course, there was Ann.

The fact was, he was beginning to have second thoughts about this whole damned business. He had given no hint of this to Bentley, of course. But the parapsychologist already knew he was dragging his feet. But he had to have time. He had to think.

So far he knew very little about Jeff Chapin. All he had were the sketchy facts outlined in Chapin's obituary. He had pumped Ann about her father, but there was a point beyond which he did not dare to go. She would want to know why he was so interested, and obviously he could not tell her. Also, it was clear that she really didn't know too much about her father, beyond what Marcia had told her. And all he had gotten from Marcia was an impression that Jeff Chapin was a loving husband, and that she mourned him still. The photographs on the wall of the den attested to that. He would have to inquire elsewhere. It would take time as well as luck. Jeff Chapin had been dead for years. Probably he'd have to put together the portrait of the man he once was from bits and pieces. Try to find a contemporary of Chapin's somewhere. Someone who really knew him.

An idea came to him. He phoned the club and scheduled another game with Walker. He and the pro volleyed awhile, then played two hard sets. A small crowd gathered, attracted by this expert duel, and applauded frequently. The sun was warm, and when they finished, both men were sweating profusely. He won the first set, Walker the second.

Afterward, he invited Walker onto the patio for a drink. Obliquely drawing Walker out, he learned that a man named Dennis Reeves had been the assistant pro under Chapin. After Chapin had gone to war, Reeves had succeeded him. He was now retired and, with his wife, ran a small sports shop downtown called Tennis, Anyone?

He knew he had to have some kind of approach to Reeves. Otherwise, the man would want to know why he was so interested in Jeff Chapin. He decided on a subterfuge. It was pretty thin, but it was the best he could come up with.

The ex-pro was a man in his early sixties, with a red face and snow-white hair. He had a red-veined, bulbous nose and watery blue eyes. An athlete once, but now gone to unhealthy fat. Everything about him said he liked to drink.

"You see, Mr. Reeves, my father lived here in Riverside a long time ago. Moved to California and never returned. Jeff Chapin was a boyhood friend of his. They were very close as kids. I'm here on business, and my father asked me to look up Chapin and say hello, find out what became of him . . ."

"You'd be wasting your time, Mr. Proud. Jeff's been dead for years."

"Yes, I know that now. But I know my father would be curious. As to the kind of man he was, what happened to him. I wonder if you could give me some idea."

"Who told you about me?"

"Ken Walker at Green Hills. He said you were an assistant pro under Chapin. Said you probably knew him pretty well . . ."

"As well as anybody. And better than most."

"Could you tell me something about him?"

Reeves's face tightened. "I could. But I hate to speak ill of the dead."

"If you've got a few minutes, I'd appreciate it if you'd fill me in. Maybe we could talk over a drink."

Reeves responded immediately to this suggestion. He instructed his wife to take care of the shop, that he would be back shortly. They went to a bar and cocktail lounge two doors down the street.

Reeves looked at him over a bourbon on the rocks. "Since you ask, let me give it to you straight. The Jeff Chapin I knew was a no-good son of a bitch."

"Yes?"

"Now that I got *that* off my chest, do you still want me to go on?"

"Please."

"Maybe he was a good kid when he was a friend of your father's. But he didn't grow up that way. I didn't know too much about him before he came to the club. But he was a kind of local celebrity around here as a jock. He played some baseball and football, I understand, but tennis was his game. He was a natural with a racket. Plenty of power, and a big serve. He came from a poor family, lived in the Bridge Avenue district somewhere. Your father would probably know where."

"Yes. It was Almont Street."

"Right. Anyway, as I said, he came from a poor family. Or call it lower middle class. Blue collar. His father was a welder at the Standard Valve Company. Now, a kid like this doesn't learn tennis at a private club. He learns it at the public courts, like Pancho Gonzalez. Anyway, he got very good at it. Won a few big tournaments in and around New England, qualified for the National Public Parks Championship, and so forth. He was supposed to be an amateur. But the truth was, he was always hustling."

"Hustling?"

"Making bets on the side. For money. Suckering his opponents, giving them a game or even two, making believe his game was off. Then he would beat them into the ground."

"When did all this happen?"

"As I remember, this went on a few years after he got out of high school."

"He never went to college?"

"No. Either he didn't want to, or he couldn't afford to. I think he had an offer of an athletic scholarship or two, but when the schools found out he was hustling, the offers were withdrawn. Anyway, Green Hills, which then had only a golf course, put in some tennis courts. They began looking around for a pro. They couldn't find anybody they really wanted. The first-class pros all were established elsewhere and didn't want to change. Jeff was young for the job, but he put up a big, cocky front, and he'd developed quite a name. So they took him on . . ."

Reeves finished his bourbon and ordered another.

"I'd known Jeff around the tennis circuit, and he took me on as his assistant. The son of a bitch squeezed me, though. I had to give him ten percent of all revenue I made giving lessons on my own. All under the table. He was a man who had his eye on a buck at all times. I can't fault anybody for that. I suppose it's our Great American Ethic. But there are limits to everything . . .

"Anyway, Jeff caught on as a pro at Green Hills. He had a hell of a lot of charm when he wanted to turn it on. Especially with women. They really went for him. He was a damned good-looking man, virile and sexual. He knew how to smile at them and flatter them. I don't know, he had this quality that women found irresistible. Some of them, and I'm talking about some of the club women, couldn't wait to get in bed with him when their husbands were gone. For his part, he was an animal when it came to sex. He couldn't get enough. But, along with this, he had one hell of a cruel streak in him, too."

"Yes? In what way?"

"With women. Especially after he'd been drinking. He was a sadistic bastard when he was drinking. Sometimes he would actually beat up a girl just for kicks. I know. I was about his age, and two or three times we went out on double dates, until I couldn't take him anymore. And once, a girl, a waitress, took him to court. She showed the marks of her beating, but she couldn't convince the judge that Jeff had done it, and he got off.

"His friends, and he didn't have many, called him the drunken Indian. He had a little Indian blood in him from way back, and he never let you forget it. He loved to put on this superpatriot act, claiming he was the only real hundred percent American in town. He'd run off at the mouth after he'd had a few, calling other people wops, spiks, niggers, Jewboys, what have you, insulting them to their faces. All this got him into trouble in this bar or that, and he had his face pushed in a couple of times." Then he looked at Peter and said a little thickly, "Hell, I don't know why I'm talking so much. Your old man isn't going to give a damn about all this, Mr. Proud. Why don't I just shut up . . ."

"No. Go on. *I'm* interested now. And forget the Mr. Proud thing. My name is Pete."

"Pete. Yeah. Let's see, where was I? Did I tell you about Marcia Curtis?"

"No."

"Well, she was a member of the club at the time. The daughter of William Curtis, president of the Puritan Bank and Trust. This was around 1940. She was just a kid then, about nineteen, and just about the loveliest and sweetest young girl you'd ever met. Everybody around the club, and I'm talking about the people who worked there as well as the members, was crazy about her. She had more dates than she could handle, and I'm talking about the richest boys in town from the best families. Unfortunately, she was crazy about tennis. And when she met Jeff Chapin, boom. She went for him, head over heels. After that, she wouldn't look at anybody else . . .

"Like I said, Jeff was no fool when it came to the buck, and he saw his main chance. He played her for all she was worth. And she must have loved his performance in bed. She simply couldn't get enough of him. They both knew if her old man found out about it, Jeff'd be fired from the club. So they met at out-of-the-way places, motels, places like that. Then one day they just ran away and got married, and came back and confronted the old man with it. What's that French expression they use . . ."

"*Fait accompli?*"

"Yeah. Anyway, it was too late for anyone to do anything about it. The club was a pretty stuffy place, and the board didn't like the idea of one of their hired hands running off and marrying one of the members, so they fired him and gave me his job. Even though he was the husband of Marcia Curtis, and technically was now a member of the club, they wouldn't even list him as such. Now her father threatened to disown her for a while. But Jeff was out of a job, and they had no visible means of support. He could go back to being a tennis bum again, but there wasn't enough money in hustling, especially since he now had a young wife to support.

"But then the war came along. As I said, Jeff was this big superpatriot kind of guy, and he immediately enlisted in the Marines. He was sent to the Pacific and was wounded in the side, shrapnel in the hip or something, and in the process got himself a few medals. I'll say this. Even if he was a bastard, he was gutsy when it came to courage. The Marines gave him a discharge and he came back a big hero, his name in the papers, big parties thrown for him, everything. Her father was pretty embarrassed. He gave Jeff a desk in the rear of the bank, and a big title, and I guess a big salary. The year after that, the old man died and Marcia came into a lot of money . . ."

"When was that?"

Reeves wrinkled his brow, then shook his head. His voice was even thicker now. "Can't remember, exactly. Around '44, I think, maybe '45. Anyway, they moved into this big house on Vista Drive, and both of them lived it up. Jeff bought this fucking big Packard Clipper, and he loved to drive around town and show it off. And it wasn't always Marcia who was with him. Once in a while he was seen riding around with some other broad. I told you from the beginning he was a womanizer, and being married to this lovely girl didn't change anything. Then they had a baby—a little girl, I think. Couple of months after that, Jeff and his wife went away for a weekend at this cottage they had on Lake Nipmuck. It was in the fall sometime, and this crazy damned fool had been drinking, and he decided to swim the lake. According to the newspapers, Marcia tried to stop him but couldn't. He caught a cramp somewhere out in the middle and drowned, and they dragged the lake for him and finally found him. That's about it. His wife still lives in the same house, up on Vista, as far as I know. . . ."

As he drove away, he thought of the kind of man he had been in his previous life.

If Reeves was to be believed, he had been a first-class bastard indeed. If you accepted the justification for reincarnation, he had much to atone for. The law of karma was that, given another chance, a man improved himself, made amends, refurbished the old soul into something a little better in this life. If he had hurt others before, he helped those like them in this life. Karmic rectification. A man gets another chance, and he redeems himself for sins done in his past life.

He thought again of the Lake Dream. Only two nights ago, he had again been haunted by it in his sleep. He remembered that he had been drunk when he had come out of the cottage. He remembered the red bruise marks on young Marcia Chapin's neck and shoulders. She had been angry enough, that night, to murder him in cold blood. Why? Was a physical beating enough to drive her this far? Or was this the last straw, so to speak? The dream seemed to indicate there had been other similar beatings. He remembered the way he had been treading water and looking up at her in the boat, and recalled what they had said.

"*I'm sorry. I mean it. I'm sorry.*"

"*I know. You've been sorry so many times before.*"

Now he began to see some light—enough, at least, to make an educated guess as to what had happened.

Chapter 26

In the next two weeks he saw Ann frequently. They played more tennis. He took her to dinner several times, and once to a play at the Riverside Civic Center. Twice he had dinner at the Chapin home. Marcia Chapin was polite to him, but distant. Now and then he caught her studying him curiously. She inquired about his work—how it was going, and when he would be through with it. He told her blandly that it was taking longer than he had expected. He had to classify a large number of small subtribes, members of the larger Indian federations and confederacies in southern New England. They all had their distinct villages and sachemdoms.

She assumed that since he was on a short sabbatical, he would have to be back at UCLA in time to prepare and grade examinations for his students. When would that be? she inquired. The first week in June, he told her. He explained that he could set up the examinations so that he need only go back for a week, or perhaps not at all.

He had the definite impression that the sooner he left Riverside, the better she would like it.

One Sunday morning, Ann called him.

"Pete, how would you like to take a ride?"

"Where?"

"It's a place called Peaceful Valley. About forty-five miles from here."

"Sounds positively bucolic. Do we take a picnic lunch?"

"No," she said. "This isn't going to be any picnic. Just the opposite. If I had my way, I'd rather not go. It's something I just got roped into."

"What do you mean?"

"My grandmother's there. Grandma Chapin. She stays at a rest home there. I told you about it. Mother usually goes out there every Saturday, but she isn't feeling too well this morning, and she asked me to go in her place. I haven't been there in over a year, and I hate to go alone."

"Okay. When shall I pick you up?"

"I'll pick you up. And Pete?"

"Yes?"

"You're a darling for doing this."

The truth was, he was glad of the chance. He had planned to visit the old lady sooner or later, but that would have been tricky. He'd have to explain why he, a stranger, would have any conceivable interest in visiting her. Going with Ann solved that problem.

He was curious about Ellen Chapin. As far as he knew, she was the only flesh-and-blood relative of Jeff Chapin himself. And of course, in a crazy kind of way, she was *his* mother. Still, he felt no particular excitement at the prospect of seeing the old lady. He saw her as just another swatch in the patchwork quilt of Chapin's identity, part of the life and times of his earlier incarnation. And she had never appeared in any of his hallucinations.

The Valley Rest Home was set back a considerable distance from the main road. It was fronted by a series of terraced and manicured lawns spotted with small flower gardens and arbors through which cut meandering walks lined with metal benches painted white. It was a chill, blustery day, and none of the elderly residents was outside. The institution itself consisted of several dormitorylike buildings of mellow brick softened with creeping ivy.

They went into the administration building.

"We'd like to see Mrs. Ellen Chapin," Ann said to the girl at the reception desk.

"Are you relatives or friends?"

"I'm a granddaughter. He's a friend."

The girl checked a card file.

"You'll find her in Room 106."

They went down the deeply carpeted corridor, past a florist shop, a gift and book shop, a small drugstore, and a beauty parlor. The place had an expensive and opulent look. He reflected grimly that Marcia Chapin had taken care of her mother-in-law very well. She probably figured, *the bastard is dead, and I killed him, and I guess it's the least I can do.*

There were a number of elderly residents sitting in the recreation room. Their faces were wizened and desiccated, their bodies arthritic, their eyes blank. They sat in beach chairs or at glass-topped tables, and a number of them were staring at a television set, watching a late afternoon soap opera. The old people watched it with glazed eyes, and Peter felt they really didn't know what was going on, they weren't really following the story at all but were simply staring at the screen because it was there. As he walked past, none of them even had the curiosity to turn their heads and look at him.

He felt sorry for them all. He wanted to light up their vacant and hopeless faces. He wanted to tell them they would all get another chance.

"I hate this," Ann whispered to him. "I always feel like crying when I come here. If I ever get that old, they'll never put me away in a place like this. I'll kill myself first."

The door to Room 106 was open. They stood in the open doorway for a moment, watching.

Ellen Chapin was sitting on the edge of the bed. A plump, middle-aged nurse was spoon-feeding her some kind of cereal mush or baby food from a bowl. The nurse had a little difficulty aiming the spoon. The old lady was babbling something at the same time she was trying to eat. A little of the mush dribbled down her chin.

"There we are, Mrs. Chapin," said the nurse cheerfully. "That's it. That's very nice. Very good."

The old woman's babble was totally incoherent. She wore a flowered robe that seemed to engulf her slight figure. Her shoulders were narrow and huddled, the line of her back crooked as she sat on the bed. Her legs were sticklike and ribbed with huge varicose veins. Her face was seamed and chalk-white. Only her eyes, bright blue, seemed to be alive. Childlike, unblinking, they fixed themselves on the nurse, as though trying hard to perceive her instructions.

"That's it, sweetie. You're doing very well today."

The nurse's voice was gentle. Neither the nurse nor Mrs. Chapin saw them standing in the doorway. Ann rapped gently on the door. The nurse turned, but Ellen Chapin continued to stare straight ahead.

"I'm Ann Chapin, her granddaughter. This is Doctor Proud, a friend."

The nurse put down the bowl. "Please come in. I'm Miss Hagerson. I've met your mother many times."

Ann nodded toward the old lady. "How is she?"

"About the same. Still in a world of her own, poor dear. But of course she's been this way for a long time." The nurse smiled. "You know, your grandmother is really very sweet. Never gives us any trouble." She turned to Mrs. Chapin. "You never give us any trouble, do you, dear?"

The old woman was still unaware that they were in the room. Her vacant face was turned away from them, and her mouth continued to move. Peter watched her. Again he thought, this was my mother once. He felt nothing in particular, except pity.

The nurse patted Ellen Chapin on the cheek.

"Turn around, dear. You have visitors. Isn't that nice?" The old lady didn't respond. Gently the nurse took Ellen Chapin's face in her hands and turned her head in their direction, as though she were manipulating the head of a doll. "It's your granddaughter. And she's here with a friend."

The old lady's blue eyes took in Ann for just a moment, then moved to Peter.

"She doesn't know who you are, of course," said Miss Hagerson. "But she's aware that someone else is in the room, that she has visitors. And I'm sure it makes her feel good. Even people like this, people who have lost all touch with reality, can feel lonely . . ."

The nurse stopped suddenly, watching Ellen Chapin's face. Something extraordinary was happening. The old lady was staring intently at Peter. He began to squirm uncomfortably. She had stopped babbling, and the vacant face had suddenly become alive. Her eyes were straining at Peter now, as though trying to pierce a fog. Then, suddenly, she smiled.

"Jeff," she said. "Jeff."

He stood transfixed. His skin prickled. He glanced at Ann. She was staring at the old lady, open-mouthed.

"Isn't that interesting?" said Miss Hagerson. "She thinks you're her son, Dr. Proud. She's never done that before. Not with anyone . . ."

"Jeff, dear, where have you been?" The old woman's voice was perfectly clear and lucid now. The change was startling from the babbling of a few minutes ago. "Why have you been away so long? Why haven't you come to see me?"

She rose from her seat on the bed and came toward him. Her arms were outstretched, waiting for his embrace. Her mouth began to tremble. Tears filled the blue eyes.

My God, he thought, what is going on? Did this woman have some kind of mystic perception that normal people did not have? He didn't look like Jeff Chapin, and he didn't sound like him. Yet there was obviously no question in the old lady's mind that he was her son. It was weird and frightening.

She stood looking up at him, her eyes swimming with tears. She reached up and put her trembling hands on his shoulders. He looked helplessly at Ann and the nurse. Their faces were full of pity. They said to him, *humor her.*

He took her in his arms, feeling a slight revulsion and, more than that, fear. He wanted to thrust her away from him. Her thin body pressed against his as she sobbed on his shoulder.

"It's all right, Mother," he said. "It's all right . . ."

As they got into the car, Ann said, "You know, you were very sweet."

"Yes?"

"Putting on the act you did. It must have been quite a strain for you."

"It was."

"Anyway, you made her happy." Then: "I wonder why you, of all people, reminded her of her son."

"I'm damned if I know."

Suddenly she laughed. "You know who I am? I'm a female version of Hamlet. I've just seen the ghost of my father. Although you *are* a little young for that."

Chapter 27

The next night he was invited to dinner at the Chapin house. He and Ann planned to go on to a movie afterward.

Throughout dinner, Marcia Chapin said very little. She seemed taut, withdrawn. He was aware, again, that she was covertly watching him. And, again, he was sure she did not like him. The conversation was strained, desultory. Ann did most of the talking.

Suddenly Marcia broke her silence and turned to Peter.

"Ann told me what happened when you went to see my mother-in-law."

"Yes?"

"Strange that she mistook you for—Jeff. Why would she do that?"

"I don't know."

"It's really peculiar. I mean, you don't look anything like my husband. And you don't talk like him."

"Believe me, I'm as surprised as you are."

"Surprised?" said Ann. "He was stunned."

"But why *you?*" said Marcia. "Ellen Chapin's seen a lot of other men. Psychologists, doctors, porters—they're in and out of her room all the time. Why would she see *you* as Jeff?"

"For God's sake, Mother," said Ann, "I don't know why you're making such a thing of this. I think it's probably very simple. Grandma Chapin is way out there somewhere in another world. She must have been dreaming about Father when we came in. You know the way she babbles. Maybe she was even *talking* to him, at least in her imagination, when she saw Pete. She simply assumed he was Father, that's all. She doesn't recognize people, anyway. It was some kind of illusion—or delusion." She picked up the electric percolator. "More coffee, Pete?"

"Thanks."

"Mother?"

"No, dear." Marcia Chapin rose. "If you'll both excuse me, I'm going upstairs. I've got a terrible headache."

Marcia Chapin lay on the bed, still tense and very tired. She was also angry at herself for the way she had behaved at the table. She knew that her daughter had been upset with her. She'd apologize to Ann later. She could always use the old excuse—nerves.

Nerves. It was a good and useful word. It covered practically everything. It had been her standard excuse for hiding herself in all those bottles all those years. With it, you didn't have to explain all the real reasons why you sometimes thought you were going crazy.

Peter Proud. It was a funny name. It belonged in a book of nursery rhymes. But she saw nothing funny in the man himself. In fact she saw him as some kind of threat. She sensed in his presence here some vague danger.

He had said he was here to work on his book. It sounded plausible enough, but somehow she didn't quite believe it. Her intuition said he had come to Riverside for some other reason, and that he had deliberately sought out her and Ann. The way he had met Ann the first time, for instance, was suspicious. It was presumably by accident on the tennis courts at the club, but it seemed to her now that it was just a little too accidental. And the way he had ingratiated himself with Ann. She was very fond of him, probably in love with him. She felt that this was deliberate on his part, too. She felt that he would be here, in her house, often from now on.

She had sensed all along that he was watching her, that his interest in her was more than casual. But even more disturbing was that he seemed to show an inordinate interest in Jeff. He asked too many oblique questions about Jeff, and he was a little too interested in the answers. Why this fascination about a man who had been dead for almost thirty years?

Sometimes she wondered if he was who he said he was. Was that absurd name, Peter Proud, his *real* name? Who was he, anyway? Could he be a detective? Did he know something about what happened at the lake that night? But no, that was ridiculous. He probably hadn't even been born when Jeff died. And the case was long closed and forgotten, remembered only by her.

She decided she would call UCLA in the morning, just to check on whether he was who he said he was, to see if his name was on the faculty list.

And there was one thing more that bothered her. It wasn't just that he had Jeff's habit of tapping the edge of his glass with his fingernail. That was, of course, just coincidence. But about ten days ago she had arrived at the club to meet Ann for lunch. When she got there, Ann was playing tennis with him, and she had sat down on a bench to watch. The two of them had been so intent on their game that they hadn't noticed her. They were volleying when suddenly Peter had started to yell to Ann, "Hit it back, hit it back." He would serve and run up to the net and shout to her, "Hit it back." Exactly the way Jeff used to shout at her years ago on the court, in exactly the same words. *Hit it back.* She had sat there, stunned. Watching them then, she had seen two other people out there on the court. . . .

Of course it had probably all been her imagination. It was impossible that Peter Proud had used those exact words on the court. She recalled that she had had a drink or two before she had left for the club, and it had been a warm morning. She had felt a little dizzy sitting there in the hot sun. What had probably happened was that, watching them play, her mind had drifted back, and she had begun to imagine that Peter was Jeff and Ann was herself, and she was playing tennis again with Jeff long ago, before they were married, on that very court. And all of a sudden she was hearing Jeff yelling at her, "Hit it back, hit it back."

She had also made too much of the fact that Ellen Chapin had called him Jeff and embraced him as her son. Who knew what went on in the mind of a crazy old lady? Jeff's mother had been hit hard when he had died, and her mind had started to slip then. It had gone on for years, until the old lady had completely lost touch with reality. That was when they had had to commit her.

She would have to watch herself, watch what she said or did at all times. She was becoming somewhat irrational lately. Control, she thought. She had to stop drinking, for one thing. She had read somewhere that whenever you took a drink, you destroyed several thousand tiny brain cells. She had to quit, once and for all. She was seeing things where they did not exist.

I must relax. Relax.

She got out of bed and went into the bathroom. She ran hot water into the tub, sprinkled it with a generous amount of bath crystals, undressed, and stepped into the bath. Then, for an hour, she lay back, her head against the tub, her eyes closed, buried in the warm and billowy suds.

Finally she came back to the bedroom, still drying herself with a huge Turkish towel. She felt a little better now, a little more at peace. She stood naked before the mirror, looking at herself critically. Suddenly she hated what she saw. She was fifty-two, but at this moment she thought she looked much older, not so much in the body, but in the face. She stared at her pasty complexion, the puffiness under her eyes.

There were tiny red veins in her nose. The blue eyes seemed pale and watery. It was the damned drinking that did all this, she thought. I don't take care of myself. I should exercise, go on the wagon as long as I can . . .

Her breasts seemed to sag a little. She put a hand under each of them and lifted them up, pointing them at her reflection in the mirror. She remembered that Jeff loved this little gesture. Whenever she did it, it seemed to arouse him sexually. She would hold up her breasts and point them at him, teasing him, laughing at him. When she did that, he would usually take her right then and there. Of course she had been young then, young and beautiful, and the fire had burned just as hot in her as it had in him.

Suddenly she was aware that her husband was watching her. His face was framed in a picture that stood on the bureau. He was smiling at her in that special way of his—sly and very sexual. Jet black hair cut short. Dark eyes watching her appreciatively. In them now she saw the same lust she remembered so well. The same lust for her body he had shown all through their marriage.

She turned and, her hands still holding up her breasts, pointed the nipples at him. Then she said, "Remember this, darling?"

Her husband's face did not change. There was the same fixed smile, the same even teeth showing white against the handsome face.

Oh, Jeff, Jeff, you lying, loving, hateful, beautiful, treacherous son of a bitch. You damned skirt-chasing, womanizing, unfaithful slob. If you just hadn't slept with her that weekend, that particular weekend above all others, maybe you'd be here with me now.

She flung herself down on the bed, still naked, and buried her face in the pillow. For a while she half-dozed, thinking of the way it had been. . . .

She had married Jeff Chapin in 1941, when she was only nineteen. She had been enormously attracted to him physically, so much so that any other man paled by comparison. He was a beautiful and virile male, and he could never get enough of her. Neither could she get enough of him. She was passionately in love with him. They began to meet surreptitiously in motels along the highways outside of Riverside. Once or twice she stayed late at the club, and they met out on the golf course in the dark of night. His hunger for her seemed bottomless. His lovemaking was often savage; he would attack her like an animal—especially after he'd been drinking. Sometimes it frightened her. Sometimes there were bruises and scratches all over her body. At times like these, she thought him crude and insensitive, and toyed with the idea of breaking it off. But she knew she could not. She was hooked on him. And at times he could be very sweet and very gentle.

She knew he had an eye for other women. She knew that he had another life somewhere away from the club, in another part of the city. She knew that he frequented bars with old cronies, and that there was another women—a redhead named Molly Warren—he was often seen with. She had no idea who this Warren woman was, where she came from, or what she did, but she did not fear her competition. To her, Jeff's simple animal lust for her was a kind of security. She supposed she had been stupid, as young girls often are. Too much emphasis on sex, and not enough on other things. Yet she had loved him for what he was.

Finally, she and Jeff eloped. Her father was furious. He did not want even to see or talk to his new son-in-law. "You're on your own now, Marcia," he told her. "You've done a stupid thing and you've ruined yourself. This man Chapin is no damned good. All he wants is your money—or shall we say my money. But he isn't going to get it."

Her father tried to get the marriage annulled, but she was of age, and there was nothing he could do about it. Meanwhile, when the governing board at Green Hills learned what had happened, they fired Jeff instantly. That was her father's influence, too. Her mother had a nervous breakdown after she learned about it, and died a year later.

That year there was talk of war, and Jeff joined the Marines. She took a small apartment in the east end of town and lived on his allotment and waited for him. Two years later—or was it three?—he came back a hero. He had been wounded in the side and had won two or three medals for valor under combat, and the town couldn't get enough of him. He was the first real war hero they had, and the newspapers were full of pictures and stories about him, and parties were given for him everywhere. They even had a small parade for him up Main Street, and she sat next to him proudly in the tonneau of the open car.

In the face of all this, her father relented. Her mother had died and he was alone, and he needed her. Under the circumstances, it was hard not to accept Jeff Chapin now. He gave them both a big allowance and gave Jeff a job at the bank. The idea was to start Jeff in as a teller, so that he could learn what banking was all about, and then move him up to a desk behind the rail. About this time, she came into a lot of money left to her in trust by her mother.

After that, they bought this house on Vista Drive. And life with Jeff was marvelous. They went everywhere and did everything. Jeff bought a Packard Clipper, and they drove to New York or Boston for weekends, going to clubs, seeing the shows. They built a cottage at Nipmuck and spent marvelous weekends there. The club even relented, because they really couldn't keep a war hero out, and let Jeff use the premises because he was married to her and she was a member.

He could no longer play tennis, however, because of his disability. The wound in his side, above the hip, had healed, although he still had a big scar, but something had gone wrong with the surgery, and sometimes Jeff suffered big bouts of pain in his hip. It came on suddenly and went away just as suddenly. When it happened, Jeff drank to ease the pain. She hated it when he drank. He could become surly, even cruel.

He began to drink more and more, whether he had the pain or not. Once or twice, when she was so frightened of him she would not yield, he beat her and knocked her down. She threatened to leave him, and for a while she did. But he came to her, pleading for her to come back, promising never to lay a hand on her again. And she returned.

Meanwhile, she heard rumors that Jeff had been seeing the redhead, Molly Warren. She resolutely shut her ears to all of them. Seeing no change in his ardor for her, she took this as proof that the stories were false. Then she became pregnant with Ann. In the later stages of her pregnancy, of course, she had to deny herself to Jeff. He found this very inconvenient. He paced around the house, on edge, and drank more. He began to come home late at night. He had run into some friend, he said, and they had had a drink. He began to phone two or three times a week and tell her he would be home late and not to wait up for him. She endured it, tight-lipped, but she was sure the "friend" was female. Perhaps there was more than one. She didn't know; she tried not to think of it.

Finally, she went into labor with Ann. It was long and very difficult. There were complications, and for a time the doctor was worried, but she came through it all right. She was in the hospital for two weeks. Jeff visited her briefly each day, but he seemed uneasy, impatient, anxious to get away. And he showed very little interest in their daughter. But, she rationalized, men were not really interested in a child until it developed some kind of personality, until it could walk and talk. More than that, she suspected that he had wanted a boy rather than a girl and was disappointed.

She had just brought the baby home when she got the phone call. A woman who didn't give her name but whose voice dripped with delight and malice said, "Mrs. Chapin, I think you ought to know that your husband has been playing around with a lovely redhead. All the time you were in the hospital." She called the woman a liar, and the voice drawled on, "I'm sorry, dear. But if you're really interested in where the love nest was, try the Highview Motel." The woman hung up before she could say anything else. She had no idea who it was, though it occurred to her that perhaps it was some other woman Jeff knew, someone who was jealous, who wanted to do him harm. She could think of no one she herself knew who would want to hurt her this way. She was sure she had no enemies of this kind.

She said nothing to Jeff. If she had, he would only have denied it. And perhaps it was a vicious lie, after all. But the phone call festered in her, grew like a cancer. Finally, she felt that she *had* to know, or she would go out of her mind. She went to a private detective.

Two days later the detective came to her with his report. A man who answered to Jeff's description had rented Room 14 at the Highview Motel for two weeks—from the time she had gone into labor until the day she had come home with the baby. With the man was a woman, a redhead. The proprietor had positively identified Jeff and Molly Warren from photographs the detective showed him.

Sooner or later, she knew, she would have to confront Jeff with this. The outrage in her mounted every day. It was bad enough that he had been sleeping with this woman under ordinary circumstances, but to pick the time when she was in labor with his child, and then when she was lying helplessly in the hospital, was more than she could stand. How could he be so damned unfeeling, so cruel?

After that, she denied him her body. She made excuses: she wasn't ready yet; the doctor had told her to abstain for a while. Curiously, she still wanted him physically, although what he had done revolted her. She knew she could never forgive him, but she still wanted him. She thought she must be sick or insane to feel this way. In a twisted kind of way, she supposed she still loved him. What he had done was monstrous, unforgivable. Yet she delayed the time when she would tell him what she knew, then break off.

As for Jeff, he became mean, frustrated. He drank more and more. She ignored him and gave all her attention to the new baby. If he stayed out late or did not come home at all some nights, she did not complain. This almost total withdrawal on her part puzzled him. He knew something was wrong, but he didn't know what. He suggested that they spend a quiet weekend at the cottage at Lake Nipmuck. She agreed to go; both of them sensed that this would be the showdown.

She had thought of that night at the cottage every day of her life after that. She had dreamed of it a thousand times. She remembered every detail of what had happened, every word that was spoken. It haunted her still. . . .

He started to drink, and then he blurted out, "All right, Marcia, what is it? Why have you been giving me the treatment? What the hell is eating you?" Then she told him. He wasn't even contrite. Instead, he was furious. Not at what she knew but at the way she had found out. "You bitch," he yelled at her. "Spying on me. Hiring a detective!" Then she told him that she was leaving him. At first he didn't believe it. He apologized. "All right, I'm sorry, it was just an affair, and now it's over, and I'll never see her again. Does that satisfy you?" And she answered, "No. I just can't live with what you did. I just wouldn't want you to ever come near me again. Ever."

Suddenly he laughed. And he said, "You lying bitch. You can't get along without me. You've got hot pants for me right now." She slapped his face. He stared at her and laughed again. "All right, baby. If you're going to leave me, you're going to leave me. But before you do—how about one more for the road?"

He stood before her then, smiling at her, and began to take off his clothes, until he was stark naked. She watched him, horrified. He was standing there, huge and hairy and male smelling, his great red bloodswollen penis hard and erect. He shook his hips, so that it flapped from side to side, slapping against his legs. She found the whole thing sickening, obscene.

He had been drinking a martini. Finishing it, he said to her, smiling evilly, "You're really going to miss this, aren't you, papoose?"

She was sitting on the couch. He put down his glass and walked straight toward her. She got up and tried to run for the bedroom, but he caught her. She fought like an animal, tearing at him with her nails, but he was terribly strong. He ripped off her clothes, tearing them to shreds, until she was naked too. She continued to fight him savagely, and he became angry. Then he began to beat her, grabbing her by the neck, hitting her around the head and shoulders, shouting drunkenly, "You're going to be raped, baby. Might as well lean back and enjoy it."

He threw her on the couch and mounted her. Still she fought him off. He swore and pulled her legs apart. And then, suddenly, she could not fight him anymore. Not because she no longer had any strength, but because she *wanted* him. She hated herself—she thought of it to this day with shame—but she wanted him. She put her arms around his back and pulled him to her, and inside she became soft and wet, and she heard him begin to laugh, and then he penetrated her, and she started to moan with pleasure. Finally, at the climax, she screamed and cried his name, digging her nails into his shoulders and hating herself for being no less of an animal than he was.

After it was over, he rolled off and stood over her. He looked down at her smiling, and she began to cry softly, because she knew how helpless she was as far as he was concerned, and she knew that he knew it. And that no matter how much he humiliated or violated her, it would always be that way.

He was still drunk, and exhilarated with his victory. He poured himself a full glass of Scotch and drank it down, and then the idea came to him to swim the lake. It was a sudden idea, pointless, insane, but he was drunk. He had swum the lake many times, he said, but never without a suit, and he was just in the mood to do it.

Weakly, she tried to dissuade him, telling him the water would be cold, but he simply laughed at her and went outside.

She lay on the couch for a while, feeling a little sick, and then she began to worry about him out there in the lake. He was drunk, and this was late September. She knew the water was very cold, and although he was an excellent swimmer, he might be overconfident, and then who knew what could happen.

She put on her fur coat and went out, got into the boat, and took it far out on the lake. For a time she couldn't find him, but finally she picked him out.

She maneuvered the boat near him, and she could see that he was very tired. She remembered every word between them then. "Look, Marcia," he said, "I didn't mean what I said back there." She watched him coldly and told him to get into the boat. "I know," she said. "You've been sorry so many times before." Then he told her he had been drunk, and he didn't know what he was saying. He hated himself for what he had done to her back there, and he loved her and always had. And she answered that it was all right, they'd never talk about it again.

But, all the while, she knew it was a lie. He did not love her, he merely possessed her, and it *would* happen again. She knew that all she would ever be to him was a body, a kind of animal he would use for his convenience and pleasure, and that someday he would tire of her and simply throw her away. There would be more beatings, and more Molly Warrens, and more terrible humiliations. And she knew that, in spite of it all, she would never leave him, because she had this sick need of him, and she was a total slave to it.

She could not stand the thought of it. Out there on the dark lake, she saw her whole life stretching out before her, and she hated it. She knew, in that instant, that the only way she could be free of him and release herself was for him to die.

Truly, she didn't know what she was doing. There he was, in the water, looking up at her, his hair dripping water, his face shining wet in the moonlight, and suddenly she raised the paddle and hit him over and over. She could never forget the look in his eyes then. He cried, "No, Marcia, no, no!" and tried to grab the boat. She brought the paddle down again, slamming its edge against his fingers. He let go and looked at her for just a moment, his eyes amazed, and then he sank below the surface. She had seen those eyes staring up at her from a thousand martini and whiskey glasses ever since.

She reported him drowned, and they dragged the lake and brought up his limp, bloated body. She had to identify him at the morgue for the authorities, and when she saw the white, water-puffed face, she turned away and vomited. There was no way she could ever forget that, either.

There were no wounds on him, no signs of blood or marks of any kind, except some scraped skin on his fingers. They were puzzled about that for a time, but they decided that in hitting the bottom he had probably scraped his fingers on a rock. She was Marcia Chapin, daughter of William E. Curtis, president of the Puritan Bank and Trust, and she had reported her husband drowned. When she told them her story, it was good enough for them. They called it death by accidental drowning, and that was that.

And she had lived with it all for almost thirty years, had found only one way to forget, even for a little while.

My God, she thought, *I need a drink.*

For a while she fought it, knowing the aftermath. She got up off the bed, put on a robe, and wandered around the house. She stared at herself in the mirror again. She looked out the windows. She opened and closed drawers aimlessly, moved ashtrays from one place to another, straightened a picture on the wall.

Finally she went downstairs and into the den, took a bottle of vodka and poured herself half a tumbler. Then she drained it.

She felt the bite of the vodka, and its courage oozed through her body. She picked up the bottle of Smirnoff again and stared at it. She felt warm toward it, affectionate. My little, dear little, sweet little hiding place, she thought.

She poured herself another drink. The photographs of her dead husband stared at her from the wall. She held up her glass to him in a defiant toast.

Damn you, Jeff, you had it coming to you.

Then she started to cry.

Chapter 28

When they came out of the movie, the night had turned warm. A full moon was out. As they walked toward Ann's car, she said, "You know what?"

"What?"

"It'd be a shame to go right home. It's such a lovely night."

He slipped his arm around her waist. She drew close to him as they walked. The touch of her body excited him. A slight breeze came up, blowing her hair across his face. He could smell its subtle perfume.

"What do you have in mind?"

"A ride."

"Where?"

"To a favorite place of mine."

"What kind of place?"

"You drive," she said. "And don't ask so many questions. I'll tell you where to go."

They let down the top of the car. They drove through some neighborhood streets, and then, at her direction, they turned the car up a long hill lined with tall, stately trees. He stole a glance at Ann. She had her head back against the seat. Her eyes were closed, her hair was flying in the wind, and she was singing an aimless little tune.

It was all very familiar. The road, the tall trees. Only this time the car was not a 1941 Packard Clipper but a 1974 Jaguar. And the girl beside him was not a redhead but a blonde. He wondered who that redhead was of long ago.

But this was Ann Chapin, and he was still confused about her. Sometimes he saw her as his daughter, and sometimes as a stranger. Because he had been all mixed up about her, he had left her alone. He hadn't even touched her. He knew she was puzzled by this, but how in God's name could he explain? *Ann, I've never made a pass at you because once I was your father.*

Yet he wanted her so badly it hurt. He remembered something Freud had said or written. *A father always harbors incestuous feelings toward his daughter*. But again, he argued to himself, Ann Chapin was created by someone else, some other body—Jeff Chapin's. And that body is now rotting in the grave at Hillside Cemetery. This was *his* body, and it was very much alive at twenty-seven, in the year 1974. It was a whole new deal, a whole different life.

Or was it?

They had been riding uphill for a long time. Suddenly they burst out into a grassy slope dotted with trees. The slope ran to the edge of a high cliff, and far below was a panoramic view of the valley, with the lights of Riverside a great blazing carpet and the river a shining ribbon cutting through the middle of it.

He had been here before, too.

They got out of the car and walked to the edge of the cliff. They sat down on a slab of rock, and for a time they studied the view, saying nothing. Then she asked, "Like it?"

"It's beautiful."

"They call this Granite Mountain. I guess you'd say it's the lovers' lane of Riverside. You know, Mother told me that my father used to bring her here often before they were married. I'm not sure, but I think he proposed to her here."

They were sitting close together on the slab of rock, and suddenly she turned her face toward him. Her mouth was red and glistening and half-open. He kissed it, and then he kissed it again, hard, and then he pushed her back, and his hand was under her sweater, cupping the soft, curved mound of her breast. Her hand dropped to his groin, and at its first touch he grew stiff and hard, and he exulted in this because he had been afraid that, under the circumstances, he might not be able to perform.

He heard himself say, "Let's go back to my place."

"No," she said. "Here. *Now*."

Then she rose and took him by the hand, and they walked out of the moonlight and into the shadow of the trees nearby.

After it was over, they lay quietly for a while. Then she turned her head toward him.

"You know, I was beginning to wonder about you."

"Any further questions?"

"My God, no." She smiled. "Not anymore."

He took her home, and she invited him in for coffee. When they came into the living room, they saw Marcia Chapin.

She was sprawled in a grotesque position on the couch, dead drunk. Her head hung down over the edge of the couch so that her hair almost touched the floor. Her legs were flung wide, sprawled upward over the arm of the couch. The robe she was wearing had fallen apart, so that she was almost completely exposed. Peter saw the long white legs, the thick black patch of her pubic hair, and just above that, the diamond-shaped blue birthmark he remembered so well. On the rug, within arm's reach, were two vodka bottles and a glass. One of the bottles was empty. The other had been tipped over and lay on its side, spilling its contents on the rug.

He averted his eyes. It was obscene. Ann went to her mother and covered her nakedness with the robe. Then she turned to him, her face taut, a little pale.

"I'm sorry you had to see her like this. Still, you were bound to, sooner or later." Then quietly, bitterly: "My mother's an incurable alcoholic. And she has been for a long time."

"I'm sorry."

"No need to be. We're used to it."

She went to her mother and started to shake her. "Wake up. Wake up, Mother. It's Ann."

Marcia Chapin's eyes opened. She stared up at her daughter blearily. She mumbled something, tried to raise herself from the couch, but she couldn't make it, and fell back. Peter came over.

"I'll help you get her upstairs."

"No," said Ann. "Please. I'd rather you wouldn't. I'll get Ola. She's upstairs in her room."

She ran upstairs. He stood there looking down at the sleeping woman. His disgust had vanished; now he felt only pity and a certain emptiness. Again he reminded himself, this is the woman who killed me in my other incarnation, cut off my life before it had fairly begun. But now he no longer cared. He was happy with his new incarnation. Jeff Chapin was dead. In a curious kind of way, he and Marcia Chapin were even. She had taken his old life away, but she had given him something priceless in his new life—Ann. *Why* she had done what she had done no longer mattered. He could make a pretty good guess as it was, putting two and two together. He was willing to forget it, let it be. He was finished in Riverside now; his stay was over. He wanted to forget all about Jeff Chapin and resume his identity as Peter Proud.

Maybe it was better, he reflected, not to know who you had been in some previous life. The reincarnationists claimed that this knowledge would give you insights into how to conduct yourself in the present.

Yet it could be that you were better off not having any prenatal memory whatever. You might find that you had been a pretty sordid character. You might have been a thief or a murderer or a procurer. There would be a certain amount of shock or trauma in this, some damage to your present ego.

For example, his discovery that he had once been somebody named Jeff Chapin. He did not like himself as Chapin. Probably you were better off living your life as it came. It would be enough to know you would live a new life after you died, and forget about the details. Maybe the ancient Greeks had the right idea. The gods, they said, traditionally dip all souls who are about to be born into the River of Forgetfulness, in order to make them forget everything about their previous lives. When you thought of all the agonies of body and mind that most of us endure in one lifetime, why look for all the headaches and frustrations of other lifetimes?

Marcia Chapin stirred a little. She opened her eyes for a moment, staring straight up at him. They were glassy, vacant. She did not recognize him. She closed her eyes again.

Ann came down with Ola. Her black face was heavy with sleep. She did not seem surprised. Together, she and Ann got Marcia to her feet.

"Look," he said to Ann, "I'll say goodnight."

"No," she said. "Please stay. Please. I'll be down in a little while."

Later, after she came downstairs, she made coffee. She seemed tired and anxious to talk.

"I suppose Mother's drinking all began after my father drowned," she said. "I don't know for sure, of course; I was a baby then. But I remember that when I was just a child in school she was drinking then. Steadily. She'd drink all day long, and she'd be helpless at night. I'd call my Aunt Helen, and she'd come over and spend the night. When Mother was sober again, her remorse was awful. Sometimes it scared me. I was afraid she might kill herself.

"I stopped bringing my school friends to the house. All this went on for years, through high school and college. After a while, she simply let herself go. She stopped taking care of her face, her hair, her clothing, everything. She'd sit in that den for hours and stare at those photographs of my father, and drink. Finally, we had her institutionalized for a long time. The psychiatrists talked to her and gave us the usual story —stresses and strains, the problems of the female alcoholic in today's society. But I knew that her problem was a lot simpler. She just kept conjuring up this ghost, and the only way she could drown him was to put him in a bottle. I don't know why it happened this way. Other women lose their husbands, but they recover; they go on living. They re-marry. But somehow my mother couldn't. It was a pretty morbid situation. It still is . . ."

She went on to explain that when they brought Marcia back from the institution the first time, she seemed docile, quiet. She didn't seem to care. Ann or Ola cooked for her. For months she did not take a drink. Then, one day, she disappeared.

"I was in New York then," Ann continued. "I came right home. They found her in a cheap hotel in Boston. She was filthy, half starving, half out of her mind. And stone broke. She didn't remember where she'd been, or what she had done in all that time. After that, I left New York and came home for good. We put her in an institution again, a different one this time. They tried everything: psychiatry, drugs—nothing helped. When she came out again, she went into AA. For six months it worked. She didn't touch a drop. We began to hope that she was out of it. Then one night I came home and found her. She had fallen down the steps, dead drunk, and was bleeding from the head. They had to take I don't know how many stitches. Finally, we—Uncle Ralph, Aunt Helen, other relatives—decided it was no use. We figured we might as well make it available to her and stop playing games. In the past few years she's been pretty good, would actually go on the wagon for a few weeks at a time. But of course it's just going to go on. So you see why I have to be here to take care of her. She really doesn't have anyone else."

When he got back to his hotel, there were two telephone messages from Hall Bentley asking him to call back.

He crumpled the messages in his fist and threw them into the waste-basket. He still wasn't ready to talk to Bentley, not yet. Not until he was very clear in his mind as to what he had to say.

Chapter 29

The Civic Center was located near the center of the city. It was very new, a tribute to Riverside's cultural progress. It had been designed as a kind of minor league Lincoln Center. It had a theater, a forum, and a symphony hall, surrounded by plazas and fountains.

Peter parked the car deep in the layered labyrinth of garages under the complex. Then he, Ann, and Marcia Chapin rode up a series of small escalators to the esplanade.

Peter was startled by Marcia's appearance. She wore a long green satin dress and several strings of pearls. She seemed rested and relaxed, animated by the crowd and the occasion. Her eyes sparkled. She was really a striking woman for her age when she got dressed up, he thought. Regal. Now and then they ran into people they knew, who greeted Marcia effusively and seemed genuinely glad to see her.

"Good Lord," she said. "I haven't seen some of these people in years."

"Well, it's your fault, not theirs," said Ann. "You ought to get out more often."

"Yes. I suppose you're right."

He took them both by the arms and shepherded them through the dense crowd in the great chandeliered foyer. Tonight, he thought Ann particularly attractive. She was wearing a long black dress, sleek and tight fitting at the hips, and scoop-necked, so that the top of her white breasts swelled provocatively. It was set off by gold loop earrings set with sapphires, and two long antique gold chains around her neck, also set with sapphires. There was a special aura about her, sensuous and very feminine. He noticed that men turned to look at her. He appreciated their interest—and resented it a little.

They were ushered down the side of the hall. Every seat was taken. There was the usual anticipatory buzz. The musicians were already on stage, fiddling with their instruments. He checked his program and liked what he saw. Aaron Copland's *Short Symphony*, then Mozart's

Concerto No. 3 in G for Violin, and finally, Mahler's *Symphony No. 5 in C-Sharp Minor.*

The conductor raised his baton, and the orchestra began the *Short Symphony.* He was not a Copland buff, but he enjoyed this particular work. He was a man who took his concert-going seriously. He liked to concentrate from the beginning, unlike the usual audience pests who took this time to settle down. He identified them as the Fanners, people who created their own little climate by waving their programs in front of their faces. He noted the other species nearby: the Head-Nodders, the Foot-Tappers, the Seat-Shifters, the Coughers, and the Whisperers.

Then Sergei Pavlik came on for the Mozart, and the applause was tremendous.

Peter sat back and closed his eyes. He let the music wash over him like a warm sea. His mind began to drift effortlessly. He was tired. He had not slept well the night before. It was delicious to sit here and just relax. . . .

Images floated before him. Names, faces. Hall Bentley's, and Verna Bird's, and Elva Carlsen's. *"We have a soul here." "Yes, I see the soul." "And we have a body which houses the soul." "I see the body."* The face of Sam Goodman. The face of Dr. Ludwig Staub, thick glasses, heavy accent, blue polka-dotted bow tie. *"If it is of any comfort to you, they are not schizoid in character. The dreams of the schizophrenic are often flat. Unevocative."* Sam Goodman's Sleep Lab, and the obscene jangling of the arousal bell. *"I have a dream, Doctor."* The red candle is Evil, the white candle is Good. Good and Evil, Good and Evil. I am a man of many lives. Chalaf, and Makoto Asata, and Red Horse. Standing in the moonlight, looking at the cold, cold lake . . .

He saw the moon and felt the sharp cut of the wind, and he laughed aloud, thinking, Hey, hey, look at me, Big Chief Two Moons, with my war club flopping in the wind, and here I am in the forest primeval, by the shining waters, on the shores of Gitche Gumee. Nobody here but me. Chief Two Moons. The last of the Mohicans.

Far off, across the lake, the sign beckoned to him. Puritan, Puritan. Then he slid off the dock and into the water and started to swim. After that he got tired, and Marcia came along in the boat, and she hit him on the head with the paddle, and . . .

He heard someone calling a name from far off. A woman's voice calling a name, but not his name. It sounded something like *Pete, Pete.* It came nearer and nearer, across the lake, and he wondered who the hell this could be, and why *Pete?*

"*Pete, for God's sake. Wake up!*"

He opened his eyes. Ann Chapin, in the seat next to him, was tugging at his arm. Her face was pale, her eyes wide in horror.

"What is it?"

"You were talking in your sleep just now. *Yelling.*"

He looked around, bewildered. He caught a glimpse of Marcia, who had left her seat and was running up the aisle toward the exit. Her face was chalk white. The hall was in an uproar. People were on their feet all around him, their faces shocked, trying to get a glimpse of the shouter. On the stage, a few of the musicians bravely tried to carry on in a ragged fashion, but the result was pitiful. Most of them were standing blinking in the light, trying to see who owned the voice. Sergei Pavlik stood, still holding the violin under his chin, the hand holding the bow still held high, frozen into place. There was a look of amazement on his face.

"All right, you. Come out of there."

He turned to see two ushers, who motioned angrily for him to come out into the aisle. He rose and, with Ann, bumped past the knees in the row. He heard a man swear under his breath as he passed. When they finally got into the aisle, the two young ushers grabbed him roughly.

"Let's go, mister."

They pinioned his arms and hustled him up the aisle toward the nearest exit. Ann followed. Necks craned; a sea of heads turned to look at him. The conductor turned back to his musicians and tried to rally them back into the Mozart. They fumbled valiantly to find a new starting point in the middle of the concerto.

In the foyer, Ann inquired about her mother. An usher said a lady in green had come running out of the concert hall, hysterical. She had hailed a taxi and left. People surrounded Ann and him—an official of the Civic Center, a newspaper reporter, a uniformed policeman. Dazed, he heard them talking. Something about preferring charges. Disorderly conduct. Disturbing the peace in a public place. He heard Ann trying to argue with them. Something about having this problem, talking in his sleep. No, he was not drunk.

He began to emerge from his daze. He told them he was terribly sorry, that he had been having some kind of nightmare. He had simply dozed off, and he was completely unaware of what had happened. He apologized again, profusely. And suddenly he was outside with Ann. They sat on a rail near one of the fountains.

"I'm sorry," he said.

"Pete, what came over you?"

"I don't know. I can't explain it."

She shuddered. "It wasn't your voice at all. It was somebody else's, some other man's entirely. It was horrible. You started to mumble these words . . . something about being sorry for what you'd done or said . . . and then you suddenly called Mother's name."

"I did?"

"You said something about being sorry for what you'd said and done, and then you said something about loving her, and then all of a sudden you yelled out, 'Don't, Marcia, don't, don't . . .' Right in front of God and the Boston Symphony and everybody. In this crazy, wild voice . . ."

"I did that?"

"And that wasn't all. Mother was looking at you as though you were some kind of ghost. Then she started to scream, 'Jeff, Jeff!' " Ann stared at him. "Why would she do that?"

"I don't know," he lied. "I just don't know."

"I tell you, it made my blood curdle. The look on her face. Do you often talk in your sleep?"

He lied again. "No."

"Well, whatever you call it, it was sensational. It'll probably be in the newspapers tomorrow." Suddenly she smiled faintly. "Poor Sergei Pavlik. You should have seen the look on his face. And, of course, we missed the Mahler."

"I'm sorry about that too."

"We'd better go right home. I'm worried about Mother."

They went down into the garage and got into the car. He was still shaking. He raced the car out of the garage and into the street, forgetting the stop sign at the exit. There was the scream of brakes. A big Buick on the road stopped inches away from the side of his Pontiac.

"You'd better let me drive," Ann said quietly.

On the way home, he thought it through. He knew what he had to do next.

And it had to be done immediately.

The next morning he drove out to Lake Nipmuck. He found a real estate office dealing in lake-shore cottage rentals.

It was easy enough for the agent to identify the cottage, knowing that Jeffrey Chapin was the original builder. The agent said, "Some people named Swanson own it now. But it's never been on our master list for summer rentals. The Swansons always spend the summer there themselves." Then the man brightened. "The lake's pretty full up this year. This is the first of June, and practically everything's been rented. However, I *do* have one or two left you might be interested in . . ."

"No," insisted Peter. "I want this one. And I don't need it for the summer. What about the next two weeks?"

"I could try. But people here usually rent by the month."

"All right. Make it for a month."

The agent studied him. "The going rate's about a thousand a month."

"Okay. But I'd like to know right away."

The agent looked up a number, got on the phone. He talked briefly with the owner. Then he held his hand over the mouthpiece and said to Peter, "They're not interested. They expect to use the cottage in June themselves."

"Tell you what to do," said Peter. "Offer them two thousand."

The agent stared at him. His mouth dropped open a little. "Mr. Proud, you must be kidding! For that kind of money I could get you . . ."

"Go ahead. Tell them two thousand."

The agent quoted the new price. He put his hand over the mouthpiece again and grinned. "This time you've made them an offer they can't refuse. When do you want to move in?"

"Tonight," said Peter.

"*Tonight?*"

"Better than that. I'd like to go over and take a look at the place now."

The agent talked to Swanson again. The owner of the cottage relayed the information that there was a key hidden in a loose brick under the porch stairs. If Peter wanted immediate possession, he could use the key.

The agent located the cottage for him on a lakefront map.

In the dream, he had seen the cottage only at night. He had no idea how it would look in the daytime. Or what changes it might have undergone in over thirty years. Yet, when he got there, he recognized it immediately. Surprisingly, there was hardly any change at all. There was a bigger and more elaborate dock. Some of the trees he remembered had been cut down, and now there were cottages on each side of it that had not been there before. The cottage was freshly painted and trimmed in green. Across the lake he saw the same grove of pines, but now the tall sign above it read: Holiday Inn.

He found the key and went in. Here, everything was unfamiliar. The furniture was cheap maple. The place had a chintzy look, a musty smell. He threw open the curtains to air it out. The telephone was still connected. The Swansons must use the place on weekends.

He telephoned Ann and told her what he had done. It was his idea, he said, to finish the book there, away from all distractions. She was astonished to find he had rented the same cottage that her father had built years ago. He said he'd had no idea it used to be the Chapin's cottage. It was simply a remarkable coincidence; the agent he had spoken to had it listed, and he had taken it.

"Pete, sometimes I don't understand you. Why did you do a crazy thing like this, all of a sudden?"

"Just an impulse."

"But the same cottage my father used to own. The place where— well you know. Where it happened. Of all the cottages out there . . ."

"I told you, it was just a coincidence."

"I know. But just the thought makes me shiver."

"Look," he said. "I decided I'd like a place by the lake, and so I rented one. I thought we'd both enjoy it out there during the summer. But if it bothers you that much, I'll get rid of it."

"I'm sorry, darling," she said. "I guess I'm just being silly."

"I'm moving some things out there from town tonight. How about joining me? It looks as though it's going to be a beautiful weekend."

"All right," she said. "But I can't get there before eleven o'clock. I've got a board meeting at the store. After that, I want to stop in and look at Mother before I come out. She's been in a terrible state ever since the concert."

"Okay," he said. "Then I'll expect you late. You know where it is?"

She sounded surprised. "I ought to. Mother's pointed it out to me often enough." Then softly: "You know what, darling?"

"What?"

"I love you."

"I love you, too."

He hung up. So Ann would get there late. That was all right with him. He would have plenty of time to do what he had to do.

Chapter 30

He was packing a weekend bag to take to the lake when there was a knock on his door.

"Hello, Pete."

"Oh. Hall."

Bentley's huge bulk filled the doorway. He was smiling.

"Surprised?"

"No."

"Then you expected me."

"I suppose I did. Sooner or later. When did you get in?"

Bentley slumped in a chair. He lit a cigarette very deliberately. His gray eyes studied Peter. They were not accusing, merely curious. He grinned affably.

"About an hour ago. Checked in at a hotel and came right over. Normally I would have phoned, but you haven't been returning my phone calls lately. Naturally there had to be a reason, and I began to wonder what it was. It occurred to me that maybe you knew something I didn't know. And didn't want to tell me . . ."

"I'm sorry. I was planning to return to the Coast next week to tell you about it."

"All right. I'm here. Tell me about it now."

He knew there was no denying Bentley. There was no further point in it. He told him, leaving out nothing. When he had finished, Bentley was silent for a while. Then:

"You knew all this weeks ago, and you didn't tell me. Why not?"

"It took me some time to think it through."

"Why don't you just put it on the line?" said Bentley. "What you really mean is that you've decided not to go through with it."

"That's right."

"I see." Bentley's voice was flat, controlled. "Just like that. All you do is say 'no,' and this whole thing goes away."

"I'm sorry, Hall. I've made my decision."

"Suppose you tell me why?"

"I think you can guess. I've had certain misgivings all along. I dismissed them, because I never really believed all this would happen. But it has. I know my limitations, Hall. I don't want to become a world institution; I don't want to play Superfreak. I want to keep both my identity and my sanity. If people are looking for a prophet, let them look in the Bible. I'm not cut out for it."

"Just as simple as that."

"Not quite. It isn't just me. There are others to consider."

"A murderess, for instance."

"All right. It happened a long time ago. She's paid heavily for what she did. She's taken more punishment from herself than the Commonwealth of Massachusetts could ever give her. And she had some reason to do what she did. Jeff Chapin was a first-class bastard. You could say he got what he deserved. If all this is exposed, she'll go insane. She's almost on the edge now. Then, there's Ann . . ."

"Ah," said Bentley. He smiled frostily. "Now we're getting to it."

"All right," said Peter. He was angry at Bentley's remark, but he kept his temper. "I'm in love with her. I plan to marry her, and take her back to Los Angeles, and live quietly with her, and even have children. She doesn't ever have to know her mother was a murderess. Or who I was before I was born into this life. Once this thing broke, her life wouldn't be her own, either. She'd become just as big a freak as I would. She'd become just another clown in this big worldwide circus you're talking about hatching. It not only would ruin her, it would destroy any chance we'd have for a quiet and decent life."

"And that's it?"

"That's all of it. I like who I am and the future I intend to have, and I'm not going to blow all of it to play Christ the Second, or outdo Bridey Murphy, or get your name and mine engraved in stone."

Bentley stared at him. "Are you implying I can't wait till I ride to glory on your coattails? That I can't wait to bask in all this lovely publicity? I'll be goddamned. You really think I'm looking forward to all this?"

"Well, aren't you? Look, I'm not blaming you. I know you have a personal stake in this. You've been ridiculed by your peers for years, and you can't wait to go after the skeptics who have been laughing at you. You're a scientist, and this could mean not only vindication, but your name in all the journals . . ."

"Pete," Bentley interrupted quietly. "You're wrong."

"Oh?"

"You're so wrong. I happen to be a quiet man. I feel the way you do. I like my life just as it is. If I seem gung ho about this, it's for other reasons. This circus, as you call it, scares hell out of me too. Remember, what happens to you also happens to me. I become Superfreak Number Two. I agree that the notoriety, the controversy, the pressure may be too much for any man to bear. That applies to me too. Nobody can introduce a whole new religion without getting rocks thrown at him. And the rocks they throw at you will hit me as well. In the end, we may *both* be nailed up on crosses, side by side. You really think I want all that?"

Bentley was silent for a moment. Peter knew he was telling the truth. Then the parapsychologist went on. "You've lost your perspective, Pete. I feel for the three people who are going to be hurt by all this. But I'm talking about billions. The world itself. The whole damned human race. There's simply no comparison. I think I told you before, you don't even have the right of choice. You're in too deep; you're committed. And so am I. We may be a couple of reluctant martyrs, but we *owe* the world what we know. I can't think of any other way to put it. You think we have the right to bury a message like this? No!

"Now I suggest we both go see Marcia Chapin and tape what she says. She'll be off guard, and I'm sure we'll get some interesting corroboration . . ."

"Hall, you weren't listening."

"What?"

"I *told* you, I'm out."

"Pete, you can't do this."

"I'm sorry."

Bentley exploded. "You're not just a damned fool! You're a selfish bastard!"

"If that's all . . ."

"No. It isn't all." The gray eyes were blazing. "Maybe you're copping out, but I'*m* not."

"What does that mean?"

"Take it any way you like. Call it a warning."

The parapsychologist opened the door, then slammed it shut behind him.

A few minutes later, the phone rang. It was Marcia. Her voice came over the receiver in a hysterical shriek.

"Who are you?"

"What?"

She was drunk as well as hysterical. "Damn you, who are you? Why did you come here? What do you want from us?"

"Mrs. Chapin, I . . ."

"My daughter told me you rented our old cottage at Nipmuck, Jeff's and mine. And you're going out there tonight. Why? What are you trying to do? What are you trying to prove? In the name of God, why are you after me?"

"Mrs. Chapin, it's something I can't explain. But I'm not after you . . ."

"Don't lie to me. You've come here to torment me, I know that. To drive me crazy. To find out things. You're not Peter Proud. You're somebody else. You're someone evil. A devil, a ghost, someone. But, please." She started to cry. "Let us alone. Let Ann alone. Go back where you came from." Her voice rose suddenly in a scream. "Go away, you bastard. Do you hear? Go away and let us alone!"

Then she hung up.

When Hall Bentley got back to his hotel room, he gently unhooked the tiny buttonhole microphone from his jacket. Underneath his jacket, an almost invisible wire stretched from the microphone to a small and very sophisticated metal box attached to the inside of his wide belt. He opened the box and with careful fingers took out a tiny roll of tape.

In addition to his suitcase, he had brought a small tape recorder with him. Now he put the roll of tape into the machine and pressed a button. First, his voice came on, in a prerecorded introduction.

"This is Saturday, early evening. The date is June 1, 1974. I am Dr. Hall Bentley, parapsychologist. The place is the apartment of Peter Proud, in the city of Riverside, in the state of Massachusetts. I have flown from Los Angeles to interview him on the subject of his own reincarnation, and the proof thereof . . ."

There was a long pause. Then the sound of an elevator door opening and closing again. The sound of footsteps along a corridor. Then silence for a moment or two. After that, the sound of a door opening . . .

"Hello, Pete."

"Oh. Hall."

"Surprised?"

"No."

"Then you expected me."

He turned off the recorder, took out the tape, put it into a small box, and labeled it. He put it into a pocket compartment in the tape recorder, along with a number of tapes already stored there. On each was the legend: *REINC. PETER PROUD SERIES*, and the various recording dates.

He lay down on the bed and lit a cigarette. Sitting out there in Los Angeles and hearing nothing from Peter, he had suspected that something had gone wrong, that his subject, or client, or whatever you wanted to call him, had decided to go back on their agreement. This visit had confirmed that. But Hall Bentley had come prepared. He wanted every word he could get from Peter Proud preserved on tape. The interview on the hidden tape would help when Bentley broke the story. It was totally unrehearsed and would be hard to disbelieve. Even if Proud denied it later, the tape would be the truth, and his denial a lie. It would be infinitely better to have him there, in the flesh, to tell his story when they broke it to the press and television. But failing that, the tapes would be the next best thing—this particular tape, and the ones they had recorded in Los Angeles, and of course the final tape. The one he had yet to record.

The one with Marcia Chapin.

He imagined her reaction when he played the tapes for her, the ones detailing Proud's hallucinations, and the rest. He knew this would be a ghoulish and mind-blowing experience for her. She was sure to go into a state of hysteria, hearing the murder reenacted just as she had committed it. Probably it would unnerve her enough to make her confess that she had, indeed, murdered her husband in just this way. That would be the clincher. That would quiet a lot of skeptics.

He didn't know Marcia Chapin, not yet. But at this moment he felt sorry for her. It was possible that Proud was right. It was possible that she might go insane after this. He fervently hoped not. It would be much better that she stay rational, that she be able to answer the hundreds of questions they would throw at her. He considered himself a compassionate man. He certainly did not relish what he was planning to do. But he had to do it. As he had said to Proud, he couldn't let the private lives of a few individuals stand in the way. The stakes were too high. He, Hall Bentley, had the answer to the riddle of death in these electronic tapes. Maybe he was bugging people without their knowledge or consent. But this was for a sacred cause. In this case, the ends *did* justify the means.

Proud didn't know it yet, but he was still scheduled to be Superfreak. He might scream invasion of privacy, he might even want to kill him. Well, he was sorry about that. But that's the way it had to be.

He blew a cloud of smoke toward the ceiling and thought about it awhile. He saw the black headlines, the news exploding over television and Telstar, the crowds gathering in the streets and perhaps praying in the churches. He heard the roars of the skeptics too, the diehards crying fraud. He saw the pictures in the newspapers, the film clips on television, pictures of Peter Proud and Marcia and Ann Chapin. And of course himself, Hall Bentley. It was terrifying. He began to sweat, just thinking about it. For a moment he even contemplated backing out of it.

But he knew he could not. He knew he had to go on, stir up this massive witch's brew, and take the consequences. There was one small compensation. Some of his peers in the Establishment who had attacked him would have to apologize to him now.

Well, he thought, *why wait?* Might as well wrap up the whole thing right now. He looked at his watch. It was just after six. She would probably be home now.

He reached over and picked up the telephone book from the bedtable. He quickly found the number he wanted.

She lay sprawled on a chaise longue in her bedroom, staring at the bottle on the table next to the chaise. It was half full. She poured another drink.

Really, Marcia, you've got to stop this. Pull yourself together. You're seeing ghosts, ghouls, zombies.

Perhaps, she thought, I ought to go back to that place after all, just for a little while. Just to dry out. Whatever you said about the place, it was peaceful there. Nobody bothered you. You had time to think things through. Later on, of course, she could come home. After *he* had gone back to wherever he came from.

All right. Suppose he *was* at the cottage tonight looking for something. Whatever it was, he would never find it. After all, it had been almost thirty years ago. That was a long, long time. *Dear Peter Proud. Dear, mysterious Doctor Proud.* You can look till your eyes drop out, but you will find nothing.

She simply *had* to stop drinking. Because now she was beginning to hear things. Like that night at the concert. She had *thought* she had actually heard Jeff's voice. She had thought she heard the things she and Jeff had said that night coming from Peter Proud's mouth. But of course that was impossible. It was all her imagination. She would have to watch it from now on. She regretted she had called him a while ago. She had screamed at him hysterically. Surely by now he thought her unbalanced. But she was calm now. It was important to keep her wits about her . . .

The phone rang and she picked it up. The voice on the other end was strange to her.

"Mrs. Chapin? Marcia Chapin?"

"Yes?"

"You don't know me. My name is Hall Bentley. I have some information on Peter Proud that will interest you. It'll interest you very much. With your permission, suppose I come right over."

Chapter 31

It was nine o'clock when he finally arrived at the cottage.

Before he went inside, he stood on the doorstep and looked out over the lake. A half-moon was riding the sky. The lake reflected its dull sheen. It glinted on the aluminum boat pulled up on shore beside the dock. It was a cool night, but there was no wind whatever. Across the lake, he saw the illuminated Holiday Inn sign rising high over the grove of pines, the same grove which, years ago, had fronted a different sign. Faintly, he could hear the distant hum of traffic moving along the highway on the opposite shore. Other than this, the lake was almost unearthly in its stillness. It was still too early for the summer residents to come. Most of the cottages around the lake were still dark and shuttered, with an occasional light here and there.

He went inside and began to unpack. He hadn't taken much with him—just a few clothes and a couple of bottles of Scotch. He had taken the cottage for a month, but all he actually needed was one night. Tonight.

He had done all this so that he could reenact the Lake Dream. Recreate it, insofar as it was possible. Then, he was sure, it would disappear from his sleep forever, as had all the others. It was the last one, but it had hung on tenaciously. Only in this way was he sure he could exorcise it. Of course it would be only a very pallid reenactment. There would be no Marcia present to make it more authentic. But at least he could go through the motions. He had found that this had been enough in the case of the other dreams. He was still mystified by how all this worked. You relive the dream; you act it out, and thus relieve yourself of it. Like the *Ondinnonk* of the Iroquois. But how didn't matter; the point was, it worked. He didn't want any repetition of the experience he'd gone through at the concert.

But after tonight, the last hallucination would be gone. And he'd be free. The last of the Mohicans, he thought wryly.

He sat down and opened the Scotch. Plenty of time, he reflected, before Ann got here. He needed a drink. The place was oppressively quiet. It still had the damp and musty odor he had detected that afternoon. He stared at the cheap maple furniture, the ugly overstuffed couches and chairs with their shabby hair-stained fabric and soiled antimacassars. The Swansons, he thought, hadn't put much into this place. He wondered what the furniture had been like at the time of the dream. Probably the best. Certainly, Jeff and Marcia Chapin could have afforded it.

He had another drink. He began to feel good, very good. If he had had any doubts about this weird drama he was about to reenact, they were gone. Get it over with now, he thought. Soon, Ann would be here. They would be alone for the whole weekend. He smiled to himself. He wondered how much of the weekend they would spend in bed. Damned near all of it, he thought, if it were up to him. He had stopped at a supermarket, bought a lot of food. The refrigerator was full.

One more for the road. He poured himself another Scotch and drank it down. Then he took off his clothes. Naked, he went to the window and opened the curtains. The half-moon was still riding the sky, but it wasn't throwing much light on the lake. He had noticed that all the cottages near this one were dark. There was no one around. Nobody would see him.

He opened the door and stepped outside. There was still no wind, but it was cold, and he shivered. He stared down at the lake. It looked chilly and almost glassy. He could imagine how cold it was going to be. For a moment he thought of abandoning the whole thing. It was irrational, really; a weird charade. He was tempted to go back in, put on his clothes, and wait for Ann. He felt giddy, lightheaded. *Ondinnonk*. It had a weird sound. Crazy.

He walked down the short slope toward the dock. He recalled that it had been gravel the night Jeffrey Chapin, naked as a jay, had taken this same walk. Now it was flagstone. And the whitewashed stones that had lined it were gone.

He walked onto the dock. He stood indecisive, shivering. The lake spread before him, waiting. He heard it lap against the aluminum barrels that supported the dock. It looked cold, damned cold. He saw the Holiday Inn sign across the lake. It beckoned, warm and inviting. Maybe, he thought, when Ann came they wouldn't stay at the cottage at all. It was too drab, too chintzy. Maybe he'd take her to the Holiday Inn afterward. They could have a couple of drinks in the lounge, get themselves a big, comfortable room, spend the weekend there—as Mr. and Mrs. Peter Proud.

He sat down gingerly on the edge of the dock and looked down into the water. He could see the stones on the bottom amid the swaying weeds. He sat there for a while, still thinking about it. Then he decided. I've come this far; do it now and get it over with.

He took a long breath, dangled his toes in the water. It was cold, all right. He took a longer, deeper breath. *Well, here goes nothing.*

He slipped into the water. The first shock numbed him. But after that it didn't seem so bad. He set a course straight out toward the center of the lake, toward the big illuminated sign. Not that he was going to swim clear across to the other side. Far from it. Just a few hundred yards from shore would be enough. Then he would turn around and swim back, say, the moment when he began to feel the chill getting into his bones.

He swam easily, smoothly. He was used to the warmer waters of the pools and beaches of Southern California, and he found the cold of this water exhilarating. The whiskey in his stomach still warmed him. He felt his blood tingle pleasantly.

Tiring just a little, he turned on his back and floated. He saw the bald spot on the side of the mountain, the patch of smooth-faced stone. Just as Jeff Chapin had seen it out here almost thirty years ago. But now the trees around it, running thickly up the mountain, were not blazing with the colors of autumn but were dressed in leaves of fresh spring green. The water was probably just as cold as it had been when Jeff Chapin made his last swim.

He turned and swam a little farther. He was a good long-distance swimmer, and he did not tire easily. But he was almost to the center of the lake before he realized he was out that far. He decided to turn back.

Just as he did, he saw automobile headlights turn into the driveway of the cottage. For a moment their glare caught him directly in the face. Even from far off, they blinded him. Then they went off abruptly.

It's Ann, he thought. Her meeting must have broken up way ahead of time. She was some two hours early.

He started to swim back. A cloud drifted over the moon, obscuring it. It was dark now. He was just a little tired, and beginning to feel the cold. It would be nice to get back to the cottage, take a hot bath, have a drink or two with Ann, and then get under the blankets with her. He felt good just thinking about it. Of course, she had surprised him. He'd have some explaining to do when he got back. She'd want to know what the hell he was doing, swimming in Lake Nipmuck in the middle of the night. He'd have to think up some story.

The lights in the cottage were directly ahead. Ann was probably in-

R

side, wondering what had happened to him. She would find his car there, of course. He quickened his stroke just a little. The cloud completed its passage over the moon and swung clear of it.

Then he saw the boat.

It was moving straight toward him, and coming fast. He could hear the sound of the motor. He saw the yellow light glint off the metallic sides. It must be the boat that had been beached next to the dock. He strained his eyes. He could see now that the occupant of the boat was a woman.

He smiled. Ann had caught him in the headlights of the car and had come out to get him. She would give him hell for being such an idiot. But when the boat came closer, he saw that the woman in it wasn't Ann at all.

It was Marcia Chapin.

He stopped swimming and began to tread water. He watched her coming on. He couldn't believe it. He strained his eyes again. Maybe it was Ann, after all. Maybe his imagination was playing tricks. Maybe he was dreaming the dream all over again.

But it was Marcia, all right. No mistake about it. He could make out her face clearly now. Taut, pale. Looking strange. A weird mask in the moonlight.

My God, he thought. What is *she* doing here? But of course he knew.

Fear clutched him by the throat. He began to shiver violently. Fascinated, he watched her come on. He felt completely helpless. There was no way and nowhere he could run. The lake was his trap. He laughed suddenly at the absurdity of it. This is supposed to be a dream. This isn't for real.

This is where we came in, Marcia, baby. You and I.

But that was 1946, and this is 1974. And this *is* for real. This lake is real, and that boat is real, and the night is real, and the woman in that boat is real, and so am I, treading water here like a sitting duck, and the cold and the fear and the nausea are all too real.

She cut the motor. The boat drifted a few yards from him. She stared down at him. Her eyes were bright, feverish. Her pallor was heightened by the moonlight, which gave an obscene cast to her rigid face. He saw she was wearing a cloth coat. Long ago, it had been a fur coat. Stupidly, he wondered whether she had anything on underneath it.

"You shouldn't have come back, Jeff."

He had to think. *Think.*

"I'm not Jeff," he said. "I'm Peter Proud."

"Oh, no, darling. I know who you are. Your friend told me."

He could see her mouth trembling. Foam flecked her lips. He knew that she was completely mad.

"Marcia," he said desperately, "listen to me . . ."

"Why didn't you stay where you were?" Her voice was a wail, almost a shriek. "Why did you have to come back, Jeff? You had no right to do that."

"Listen to me. For God's sake, Marcia, listen to me. I'm not your husband at all. Jeff Chapin is dead. Do you understand? He's *dead*. I'm somebody else. Peter Proud . . ."

"I loved you, darling. I loved you so much, you'll never know. But you never believed that. You never let me alone. All these years, you never let me rest. Now you've come back to torment me. You're evil, Jeff. Far worse than you were before. You're a vile monster. It isn't just me. It's Ann. You've come back and seduced your own daughter. Our child. How could you have done that, Jeff? You're her father. How could you have done such a dirty thing? You've slept with her, you filthy bastard. And she doesn't know who you are, Jeff. But I know. You don't deserve to live again. And now, you're going to make me do it—all over again."

She sounded aggrieved, martyred. He calculated the distance between himself and the boat. She had drifted close now, only a few feet away. A couple of swift strokes, and he might catch her off guard. It was just possible. Grab the side of the boat and turn it over. But he was tired and cold. He didn't know whether he had the strength. But he knew he had to try. It was his only chance. He figured she would swing at him with the paddle, the same way she had the first time. He had to be very careful—move to one side, duck under water, anything.

He had no real idea of what she intended. She could see that he was tired. Maybe she planned on preventing him from swimming toward shore, maneuvering the boat so that it would always be in his way, forcing him to swim around it. Swinging the paddle at him, keeping him at a distance, and, finally, tiring him so much that he couldn't go on any longer and would drown.

"Damn you, Jeff, if you'd only just *stayed* dead . . ."

Now.

He went for the boat, arms flailing, legs kicking. He saw the startled look on her face, her mouth opening. She stood up and thrust her right hand into her coat. Just before he reached to grab the side of the boat, he saw it, staring him straight in the face. The muzzle of the gun. It was no more than three or four feet from his face. He had just managed to get his fingers on the edge of the boat when he saw the blinding flash, heard the roar, echoing and reechoing, across the lake.

In his last fragment of time, her face was fixed on the retina of his eyes. He transferred it to his mind for eternity. He had one more instant of consciousness before he sank. Then the lake closed over him. He went down slowly, very slowly, turning over once or twice, and at last the bottom reached up to take him, and he lay still, his mangled face buried in a deep cushion of muck.